BEAUTIFUL CARNAGE

SAVAGE SOCIETY OF EMERALD HILLS

HEATHER ASHLEY

Beautiful Carnage
Copyright © 2022 Heather Ashley

All rights reserved. No part of this book may be used or reproduced in any manner whatsoever without written permission except in the case of brief quotations embodied in critical articles or reviews.
The characters and events portrayed in this book are fictional. Any similarity to real persons, living or dead, is coincidental and not intended by the author.

ISBN: 9798352180778

Published by DCT Publishing
Developmental Editing: Cruel Ink Editing & Design
Copy & Line Editing: Outside Eyes Editing Services
Cover: Sarah Kil Creative Studio
Formatting: Black Widow Designs

Contact the author at www.heatherashleywrites.com

DEDICATION

To all the girls who spent their childhoods dreaming about that older guy...
The one you knew would ruin you if only he got the chance.

WARNING

This is a **dark** romance.
For a full list of trigger warnings, please visit: www.heatherashleywrites.com/triggerwarnings

PLAYLIST

"Or Nah" – Ty Dolla $ign feat. The Weeknd
"High for This" – The Weeknd
"Pillowtalk" – Zayn
"Touch Me There" – Emma Holzer
"Be Your Love" – Bishop Briggs
"Easier" – Mansionair
"Two Weeks" – FKA Twigs
"Dress" – Taylor Swift
"Nails" – Call me Karizma
"Do It For Me" – Rosenfeld
"Straight Shooter" – Skylar Grey
"Unholy" – Hey Violet

Listen along here.

PROLOGUE

COLE

Two years ago...

"Happy birthday, little lamb. Make a wish," I say, holding out the cupcake with a single candle shoved into the icing. My best friend's daughter hits me with her pretty smile and my breath catches. I cough to cover it up.

She leans forward, pursing her full lips—ones I most definitely shouldn't be staring at—and closes her eyes, gently blowing out the flame. Smoke rises in a single tendril between us.

"What'd you wish for?" We're standing outside while the birthday party Tristen threw for her rages on inside. It's a sixteen-year-old's dream—at least if she's anything like I was at sixteen—but she's standing out here in the cold... with me.

"If I tell you it won't come true." She grins up at me. A piece of her dark hair comes free of her ponytail and blows into her face. My fingers twitch at my side as I fight off the ridiculous urge to tuck it behind her ear.

"What if I can make it come true?" My voice has lowered on its own accord, and I'm suddenly very aware of how close together we're standing. Her eyes reflect the moonlight as she gazes up at me with unrestrained longing in them. Longing and a whole fucking mountain of hope.

I should take a step back, put some distance between us, but lately it's been getting harder and harder to stay away from her. Sometime over the last year, she's blossomed from the little girl who used to beg me for piggyback rides to a woman with curves in all the right places.

But she's Tristen's daughter and too fucking young.

Way, way too fucking young.

The man who's been like a brother to me almost my entire life would happily murder me if he knew the thoughts I've been having about his underage daughter. If I worried about things like morality, I'd wonder if there was something wrong with me, but I think it's become obvious by now I don't really give a fuck. Whether or not it's right, Fallon Ashwell has become the object of my obsession.

Only my loyalty to Tristen keeps me away, and lately I've been avoiding this place—his home—because I don't trust myself around his daughter.

She nibbles on that lower lip, the one I bet would be so fucking soft if I kissed her. The one I'd love to ruin if I ever get the chance, marking it with my teeth until she bleeds for me. Her blood would coat my tongue and stain my teeth and…

Fuck. I'm getting hard and it's only her inexperience that keeps her from recognizing the predatory look in my eye or what's happening behind my slacks. I shift my weight, trying to adjust myself without her realizing, but she doesn't pay attention to that.

No, she's still searching my gaze, for what I'm not sure. When she inhales as if she's working up her bravery, her tits rise and fall with the motion and it takes every ounce of willpower I've got not to let my gaze drop.

"I wished for my first kiss." She blurts it out, the words stringing together like she thought if she didn't get them all out at once, she'd chicken out.

She's never been kissed? Fuck.

My dick has never been harder. I could build myself a house using my cock as the hammer and I think I'm a little dizzy from how fast all the blood in my body has relocated straight to my hard on.

She leans forward, on a roll now. "I wished for it to be with you."

She utters the words that bring me back to reality, and fuck I hate that they do. Her eyes flutter closed, the long, dark lashes falling against the soft skin of her cheeks.

When she takes a step forward, I take one back. Everything in me is fighting back against my stupid fucking conscience. But she's sixteen. Six-fucking-teen. She has no idea what will happen if I kiss her. How I'll never be able to let her go, to walk away. She'll be mine, and she's not ready for what that means.

And if I touch his daughter, especially before she's eighteen, my relationship with Tristen will be ruined. This right here is a crossroads, and I'm not ready to handle the fallout, the carnage, from the wrong decision.

But what beautiful carnage it would be.

Her eyes open and the hurt that stares back at me almost changes my mind. But my resolve hardens when I think about how she was made to be mine, but the timing isn't right. I'm not a patient man, but for her, I'll make an exception. She may not be ready now, but the day she turns eighteen, I'm taking her, and I don't give a fuck what might stand in my way.

And until then... I need to keep my distance.

"I can't."

She raises an eyebrow even as her eyes turn glassy with unshed tears. "Can't or won't?"

"Both."

I hold out the cupcake for her. It's her favorite—strawberry with cream cheese icing. She takes it but the motion is automatic. Her fingers brush mine and a bolt of electricity shoots straight to my already aching dick.

Her lips part on a quiet gasp like she felt it, too, but I can't do this. She's still a sophomore in high school, for fuck's sake. I'm old enough to be her father. My stomach twists when I think about the years stretching out ahead of me, the ones where I'm waiting for her to be ready for what we're going to be.

"There are plenty of boys inside who'd be happy to make your wish come true," I tell her, softening my tone even as I force the words out through gritted teeth. Her first kiss belongs to *me*. Her first *everything* belong to me.

And because this one time I'm trying to be a better man than I am, I'm going to let her go. Let some pubescent asshole put his hands on her, his lips on her, because it's what she needs right now.

"I don't want them," she says, her eyes narrowing even as her lower lip wobbles just the tiniest bit. I know her better than she knows herself, and she's desperately trying to hold herself together. To not show me how devastated she is. "I want you."

If I had a heart, I might think this is what it feels like to have it ripped from my chest.

"You can't have me," I tell her as I reach up and swipe the

tear that's fallen down her cheek away with my thumb before bringing it to my mouth and tasting her sadness.

She straights her spine, tipping her chin up as fire ignites in her eyes. She is her father's daughter, after all. I smirk, building my walls back up, prepared to hurt her again and again if that's what it takes to get her to back off… for now. The damage can be repaired later.

Though… I don't need to worry about hurting her because it seems tonight she's going to be the one doing the hurting when she throws my truth right in my face with her next words

"You're going to regret this."

CHAPTER 1

FALLON

There's nothing quite like the sounds of your boyfriend fucking someone else.

Not that I'd ever let him fuck me—not after the promise I made my father.

Still, it's true.

The shrieks of, "Harder! Harder!" are a disgusting assault the second I open the door to his place. It's not like I thought this would last, but I figured he'd at least have the balls to end things with me before sticking his dick in someone else.

I should've known better.

Happy birthday to me, I guess.

I take my time walking deeper into his dorm room, not that the place is all that big. Emerald Hills Prep might be for the rich kids, but it's still a high school. I let my fingers trail along the marble counter, knocking a picture of Misha with his computer club buddies onto the floor and stepping over the broken glass.

Even the sound of it shattering doesn't stop the cries from the bedroom, so I doubt he heard. This chick deserves an Oscar for her over-the-top performance, whoever she is.

That little bit of chaos, leaving broken glass in my wake, is enough to tip my lips up into a hint of a smile.

I'm sort of detached, you know? Like when you know you're about to see something horrible, but you can't turn back so you go to that place in your mind where you're watching from above. Where you're not directly impacted by the emotions of the scene.

Or maybe I just don't care that much.

My heart's not even racing. I don't have tears tracking down my cheeks. I'm not about to go in there and ask him what I did wrong. Fuck that noise. Misha knew the score when we got together. There would be no sex, not ever, and he sure as hell wasn't my endgame.

Not unless it was him my dad agreed to marry me off to and considering his father is only a defense attorney, it's unlikely. Sure, he could be useful, but not chain-my-daughter-to-your-son-for-life useful. My dad would definitely hold out for a better arrangement. I'm not willingly signing away my freedom for some shitty attorney we could afford to hire for centuries at his hourly rate and still have millions left over.

I stand outside the door and let my palm skim along the hand-carved solid oak before taking a deep breath and pushing the door open. Even though I don't give a shit about Misha, it's not exactly fun to watch your boyfriend plowing into your arch nemesis.

Well, one of them.

My nose wrinkles as I watch Eden Matthews' fake tits—something she popped up with after Spring break last year—bouncing around while Misha fucks her from behind. His red face is sweaty, and his almost-orgasm face is not cute at all. I'm glad I've never personally experienced it.

Neither of them notices me right away, so I lean against the doorframe and watch the show. I pull out my phone and take a video to use against them at some point because I'm not about to let these idiots get one over on me. I don't know what I'll do with it yet, but I'm sure I'll think of something.

It's Misha's own fault. He left the door unlocked like he *wanted* me to walk in on this. Honestly, I wouldn't be surprised if he was too much of a pussy to end things with me, so he thought he'd let this do the job for him.

It's one of the reasons I agreed to go out with him when he asked. He didn't seem like the kind of guy who'd push me for things I'd never be able to give him, and I wanted a little bit of fun and to blow off some steam for a while, so we came to an agreement. He's been my boyfriend for three months, and while he's a surprisingly good kisser, he's still a teenage boy.

An immature teenage boy who obvious has no clue what to do with his mediocre dick.

Ugh. See? This is why the only guy I've ever truly wanted stands out. He's cocky and sure of himself, not the kind of man who'd be afraid to tell you exactly what he wants. High school boys are *so* not my type.

As always when I think about Cole, a shiver runs down my spine. God, watching these two fucking is like waiting for paint to dry. It's so... boring. Maybe it's the way Misha's face has turned red, and his eyes are clenched shut while he frantically pumps his dick in and out of his hookup. Or maybe it's the way it seems like Eden wishes she had her phone in her hand so she could be scrolling her socials.

Either way, I've seen enough.

With that in mind, I put my phone away and start up a slow clap. As I suspected, when Misha's striking blue eyes meet mine, there's not even a hint of shock or surprise at being caught. No remorse. There is a spark of relief in there that tempts me to kick him in the balls, but right now I'm not going anywhere near those disgusting things.

"Fallon—" he starts just as Eden's attention turns to me. A wicked smile slowly curves her over-inflated lips up. It's satisfied and smug and I roll my eyes.

That grin of hers falters at my obvious lack of jealousy or heartbreak. Misha was nothing but a way to pass the time, and the only thing I'm feeling about this is pissed off by his obvious lack of respect for me. I thought I'd trained him better than that.

I notice Misha doesn't bother pulling his dick out of her while he's talking to me, which I'm glad for. I don't want to see that.

I hold up my hand. "Save it. Now that you've no doubt picked up a full scope of venereal diseases, I'm not interested." That wipes the satisfaction off Eden's face as she glares at me.

"I think it's obvious we're over, Misha. If only you had the balls to tell me yourself, I could've been spared this disturbing display. As it is, I thought you had more self-respect than to climb in bed with the class whore, but here we are." I turn, tossing my hair over my shoulder in my best hair flip to date, and start to walk away, and then call out over my shoulder, "I hope you realize you've got the entire senior class's sloppy seconds!"

To be fair, Eden's probably fucked most of the juniors, too.

If they expected me to throw a tantrum, cry, beg, or whatever, I hope I leave them disappointed. Truly, the only thing I care about is the hit to the hard-won respect I've carved out for myself at school. This is a direct strike against my reputation, and I can't let it stand.

But I don't react in anger.

It's never gotten me anywhere before, and it won't now. I'll need to plan my revenge carefully for maximum pain and humiliation.

I am my father's daughter after all.

But all that can wait for later. As I get in my car and turn toward home, anticipation creeps into my blood and buzzes through my veins. It's not about the surprise birthday party that awaits me at home, the one I'm not supposed to know about.

It's not about meeting my future husband for the first time tonight, the one my father's picked for me. The same one he came to me a couple of months ago and asked if I'd be willing to make the sacrifice for him and our family's business.

It's not about the lavish gifts my father's no doubt got waiting.

The hopefulness that makes my head spin like I'm drunk has everything to do with the one man I can't have, the one I've been desperate for since before I turned sixteen. The one who only sees me as his best friend's little girl.

The one I crave so badly, I fear no one will ever measure up.

As I drive through the custom iron gates and make my way down the long driveway to my childhood home, I park behind his car, trapping him here, and a giddy thrill shoots all the way down to my toes.

He's here, and maybe this year I'll get my wish when I blow out the candles, because all I want for my birthday is Cole Callahan.

My dad's best friend.

CHAPTER 2

COLE

What the hell am I doing here?

I smile and nod at something Tristen says while I sip my drink, but truthfully, I'm not hearing shit. My gaze keeps flicking toward the door even though I refuse to admit I'm waiting for her. To catch even a glimpse of her.

Fuck, if Tristen knew the thoughts running through my head right now, he'd probably gut me right here on his polished Italian marble.

It's been hard enough pretending she doesn't exist for the past two years, but today she's eighteen—*finally*. Legal. Barely, but taking advantage of grey areas is my specialty.

I manage to tear my eyes away and focus back on my best friend when he asks, "Have you heard anything I've said in the last five minutes?"

"Sorry, I guess I'm preoccupied." I take another sip of my drink and force myself to keep my attention exactly where it's at and not stare at the door over his shoulder again.

I can't believe I'm this fucked up over an eighteen-year-old girl. My best friend's fucking *daughter* no less. There's a special place in hell for monsters like me, and long ago I resigned myself to spending eternity there. This little obsession I've got for Fallon Ashwell is only cementing my place once the Devil comes to claim me.

There are people everywhere and I hate almost all of them. If it weren't Fallon's birthday, no way in hell would I be here right now. But when Tristen practically begged me to come, something I doubt he'd have done if he knew the kinds of fucked up shit I imagine about his innocent daughter, my resolve to stay away shattered.

I immediately fixated on the way she'd look bent over and taking my cock.

Her sweet lips wrapped around it.

Her hair tangled in my fist while she screams my name.

Wondering if I can corner her somewhere dark and secret now that she's eighteen and show her she was meant to be mine, and there won't be an escape. That her wish over that cupcake when she turned sixteen bound us together, and now she'd never look at another man again.

Fuck. Now I'm hard and I have to try to hide it from the one man I'd usually confess my most depraved thoughts to. Tristen's like my own personal priest, the harbinger of my salvation. He knows everything, except this.

I loathe hiding it from him.

"You going out after this?" he asks before tipping back his drink. His way of asking if I'm going to find someone wet and warm to stick my cock in tonight.

"Nah, just business on my mind." *The business of shoving my cock so far inside your daughter she can taste it.*

He nods in understanding and maybe commiseration, but he

doesn't know the truth. If today wasn't Fallon's birthday, no doubt he'd be holed up in his office, working some new angle he's found to exploit his connections and build on the power of the Savage Society.

Tristen's eyes harden as he tracks someone across the room. I don't even have to turn to know it's Erika, his treacherous wife. That bitch is as fake as her tits, and I wish he'd divorce her.

Or let me kill her.

When his gaze meets mine again, I raise my eyebrow in silent offer. I've been asking him for years to let me dispose of her, but he never does. I don't understand why he continues letting this snake live in his home and be a part of his life, but it's his call to make, not mine. She's got to have something on him.

And, as predicted, he shakes his head but gives me an unhinged grin because he appreciates the lengths I'm willing to go to for his happiness. It wouldn't be the first time I've killed for him. Her blood on my hands would be nothing. We're closer than brothers, bonded by a lifetime of spilled blood and trauma.

It's why I didn't kiss Fallon when she wished for it on her sixteenth birthday, and why I haven't fucked her yet.

Yet.

"Just how drunk am I going to need to be for this?" Beckett asks as he sidles up to Tristen and me, eyeing the unfamiliar people lingering in the room with disgust. People Tristen invited for a reason he hasn't shared with the five of us, yet.

There's that word again—*yet.*

Rough-looking bikers and scum of the earth gangsters from Mulberry that have no place in Emerald Hills, or being this close to the Savage Six, mingle with the upper crust of our tiny town.

"A light buzz never hurts," Tristen says, clinking his glass to Beckett's as Romeo, Xander, and Lucas join us.

Xander's in his priest's robe and I almost choke on my drink when he winks at me, the bastard.

"It's still weird as fuck seeing you in that, *Father*," I say, and he nods like it's weird for him, too.

"Yeah, but look how fun it is to fuck with people," he says. He looks around before taking a flask out of his pocket, unscrewing the cap and stalking off to fling the holy water inside at unsuspecting party guests, most of whom would likely catch on fire if God actually existed. The five of us watch him as he makes his way around the room. People shriek and jump out of his way as he cackles like a madman.

"I still can't believe they ordained him," Romeo chuckles, swiping his shaggy curls off his forehead. The dude needs a haircut.

"I can't believe he doesn't burst into flames every time he walks into the church," Lucas adds.

I wait impatiently, while my four friends bullshit, for Xander to come back around so we can find out what the hell Tristen's keeping from us. We're all here, but where shit with Fallon is concerned, I'm on edge even without the secrets. My gaze flicks to the door again, and Lucas catches me.

He tilts his head but says nothing. Lucas misses nothing and no doubt, the second Fallon walks through that door, he'll put two and two together. My only hope is that someone hot and more age-appropriate comes in before she does, and I can play it off. These five may know everything about my business and life up to now, but Fallon's a secret I don't want to share.

It's how we operate. Total honesty within the Savage Society, and it's what makes us lethal and impossible to beat. But this is a secret that could tear us apart, and I'm not willing to risk it.

I'd like to think with enough patience and cleverness, I can figure out a way to have my cake and eat it, too.

Or keep my friends and make Fallon mine.

I'm distracted from my Fallon obsession by Xander moving back in to complete our circle. We stand on the edge of the room, in clear view of the door but away from most of the crowds. It's not by accident, and we can talk here without much risk of being overheard.

Even if someone wanted to get close, they wouldn't dare. Not with the six of us—the Savage Six as we're known in Emerald Hills—all keeping watchful eyes on the room around us even as we talk. Most men in our positions would hire bodyguards or have right-hand men that would watch our backs, but we don't. Our circle of trust only expands as far as the six of us.

"Now that everyone's here, can you tell us what the hell you're up to? I thought Fallon's party was going to be small and intimate," I say, cringing inside at that last word. Fuck, the last thing I need to do is get hung up on it and have Tristen suspecting I want to fuck his teenage daughter.

"Yeah, what gives, Tris? This," Xander swings his arm around, "Is a shitshow waiting to happen."

I looked over Tristen's shoulder again toward the door, but when *she* still isn't there, I let my gaze wander across the unfamiliar faces in the room. I pride myself on knowing any big players in my world, even if we've never crossed paths, and none of these people jump out at me as anyone significant. A bunch of petty criminals in leather vests with Fallen Angels patches on the back, some teenagers that look like they go to school with my little lamb, but no one worth a second glance.

I narrow my eyes and fill my glare with the promise of death as I focus on anyone with a dick that's not standing in my circle. Maybe I can preemptively keep them from looking at her.

"I don't like it any more than you guys do but trust me when I say it's necessary." He tugs his phone out of his pocket and looks down at the screen before giving us his attention again. "He's here."

"Who?" Beckett asks before draining the last dregs from his glass. He only looks mildly curious, like it doesn't matter to him either way. Beck's chill like that, but he also doesn't feel shit. He truly doesn't care. If he needs to jump in and handle shit, he's plenty capable but he doesn't get violent just for violence's sake. Well, not unless he's got someone in The Icebox.

"You'll see." Tristen turns towards the door, still standing beside me. I don't like that he's throwing us into this situation blind. It's not like him.

He claps me on the shoulder just as the door opens and Anton fucking Leven swaggers into the room like he fucking owns it. My fingers tighten around my glass until they're trembling from the force.

"What the fuck is this?" I hiss and out of the corner of my eye I notice my friends stiffening, too. What the hell has Tristen done? The Fallen Angels in the room suddenly make a whole lot more sense.

"You've got to be shitting me," Lucas scoffs from Tristen's other side. "What's he doing here?"

"Wasn't our kicking his ass back over to his side of town enough of a hint for him?" Romeo says, stepping up to my other side. Forget our huddle, now we've formed an impenetrable line of defense.

Anton's dark eyes sweep from one end of the row to the other before he makes eye contact with me, and his smirk widens into a full-on grin. One I'd like to punch straight off his face before stabbing him in the neck and letting his blood coat my skin.

"I need you guys to trust me on this," Tristen murmurs, low enough that Anton won't hear from across the room but all of us do.

I frown, not liking where this is going one fucking bit. "You know we trust you, but what the hell could you possibly need with that slimy piece of shit?"

"I'm with Cole. Getting in bed with Anton isn't smart, Tris," Romeo says, folding his arms across his chest while he glares at the asshole greeting all the people he knows in this room. *His* fucking people.

This shit's starting to paint a picture I really don't want to see.

"He's got motorcycle club connections I need if I'm going to grow further into Mulberry County, and expand outside of it," Tristen says. "Plus things have been going sideways with my shipments lately, and I think the little weasel might have something to do with it."

"It would make sense, considering we embarrassed him when he threw himself at our feet, begging to become one of us," Beckett says, sliding his flat gaze from Anton to Tris. "And your business is the easiest to sabotage."

"If he's the reason my shipments have been missing and two of my guys have been arrested at the train yard this month, I'm going to find out and then I'm going to tear his life to shreds." Tristen grins. "And if not, I'm going to use him for his connections so I can expand. You know bikers always need weapons."

"He's not giving you shit out of the goodness of his non-existent heart, so what's he getting in return?" I ask, and we all turn to Tristen.

At least he has the decency to look guilty when he meets my eyes.

"Fallon."

CHAPTER 3

FALLON

As I walk up to the front door, I practice my *surprised* face. I'm not a great actor, so I doubt I'll be very convincing, but for my dad, I'll try. I'm not even supposed to know this party's happening tonight, but my best friend Waverly has a big mouth.

She can't keep a secret to save her life.

It's a double-edged sword.

I settle my hand on the door handle and let my eyes flutter closed, breathing in deep before exhaling all the bullshit from Misha's treachery. My heart beats out a steady rhythm in my chest while I prepare myself. Everything seems quiet inside, and the only cars in the drive belong to my dad's friends, except for a couple of motorcycles, so maybe Waverly got things mixed up.

I hope she did.

All I want to do after the mess with my ex is curl up in bed with a bowl of ice cream and try and forget what I saw earlier. Too bad they don't make brain bleach, because short of that there's no getting it out of my head.

Tomorrow I'll start planning my revenge, but tonight I'll linger a bit in the anger of it all. Misha might not have meant much to me, but he *was* my first boyfriend and to have him betray me the way he did, well… it pisses me right the fuck off.

But there's no hope of my night playing out that way. Not with the not-quite-silence of shifting bodies and heavy breathing that greets me as I swing the door open and step inside. I let the door close behind me before turning around, and it's then that shouts of *surprise!* break out all around me.

I'm surrounded before I can even draw my next breath, people clapping me on the back and wishing me happy birthday. Waverly's here, and she flings an arm over my shoulders and pulls me into a hug, stealing me away from all the people I've never seen before in my life.

Maybe they're friends of my father's.

"How was Misha's?" she yells straight into my ear because it's so loud in here now that someone's turned on "Fairly Local" by Twenty One Pilots. The floor vibrates with every beat, and I feel the music rattling around in my chest.

"Tell you later," I say as the hairs on the back of my neck stand up like someone's watching me.

I turn, scanning the room before my gaze collides with a set of dark eyes that haunt my dreams. *Cole.* My pulse thrums erratically as my mouth goes dry. Shit, he's gorgeous.

He's in a black tailored suit with a black shirt underneath, the top two buttons undone so his ink peeks out. The stubble that runs along his jaw is perfectly groomed, as always, and I want to cry because I'd give almost anything to run my hand along it just once.

I'm falling into his eyes, hypnotized. Everything melts away, goes silent, ceases to exist. I don't even think I'm breathing. Seconds pass.

Minutes.

Hours.

It's hard to say. But then he blinks and tears his attention away, turning to talk to my dad and everything in the room slams back into deafening, overwhelming focus. It's too much and I suck in a breath, trying to slow my heart away from the edge of cardiac arrest. Right now, it feels like I'm teetering on the edge of death by infatuation, or maybe desperation.

Either way, I've got no hope of catching my breath.

Not with Cole here sucking all the oxygen out of the room.

Waverly gives me a knowing look. I might have, in a weak moment, confessed how devastatingly handsome I think Cole is and how I would absolutely *die* if he gave me even a hint that he was into me.

Ever since, I think she watches him and analyzes every little movement he makes or place he glances, going over it with the ferocity of a scientist about to make a groundbreaking discovery. The girl might be more obsessed with my little crush than I am, and that's saying something.

She's the romantic type, though. The kind of girl who'll get to pick who she marries and live the whole happily ever after thing. She can afford to be wistful, and I'm not *at all* jealous. Insert Rachel from Friends gif here.

"He totally checked you out," she yells in my ear, but I'm saved from having to respond by my father gesturing me over. Waverly chokes from where she stands beside me and I cut her a look that says *please, for the love of all things holy, stop*, before I tip my chin up and cross the room.

My dad taught me to never let anyone see your weaknesses, so I've gotten good at hiding behind a mask of confidence and easy gracefulness that doesn't come naturally. But I've learned to slip into the role whenever I need it. Most of those times are when he's hosting business dinners or has new associates hanging around. He's always included me in our family business, and I know the part he expects me to play.

Right now? With Cole staring at me like he wants to either kill me or eat me, plus Father Finnian, Beckett Fitzpatrick, Romeo Hudson, and Lucas Wolfe—or as my father and his friends are known, the Savage Six—standing in an imposing and impenetrable line all watching me, it's hard to keep my shaking knees in check and not wobble on my heels.

There's a reason all of the rich assholes of Emerald Hills are afraid of my dad and his friends. They're intimidating as hell.

"Fallon," Dad says, looking over the black cocktail dress I slipped into before I left school, knowing this party was waiting for me. "You look beautiful, sweetheart."

"Thanks, Dad," I say, smiling up at him while he puts his arm around my shoulders and tugs me into his side. Cole is standing so close, the heat from his body warms my skin and I fight the urge to shiver. I can't do anything about the delicious scent of his cologne. I'm inhaling it greedily, hoping that no one notices. Who knows when I'll be this close to him again?

I've been trying to figure out what scent he wears for months, but I've come to the conclusion it must be a custom blend because it smells dark and dangerous like it was made for him.

"Can you believe how grown up my little girl is, Cole?" Dad asks and I want to sink into the floor and die of humiliation. I mean, seriously? The *one* guy I want to see me as an adult, my dad has to go and rub right in his face how absolutely *not* grown up I really am. I shift my eyes out into the crowd to avoid looking directly at anyone while my cheeks burn.

If we're looking at maturity level, I'm more like thirty than eighteen. You don't grow up in a house like mine without seeing some shit, no matter how much my dad tried to protect me. The Savage Society is ruthless in everything they do, and from time to time that bleeds over. When your dad comes home covered in blood enough times, eventually you learn to look the other way.

"Happy birthday, Fallon," Cole murmurs, his dark eyes unreadable as he leans in and brushes his lips against my cheek. It's like a nuclear explosion goes through every cell of my body, and ground zero is the place where his lips touched my skin. Every atom inside of me rearranges itself into a new order, one that knows the touch of Cole's lips on her skin and doesn't know how to cope with the need for more.

I do my best not to react, other than to give him a small, polite smile when he pulls away, but his eyes are locked on mine again and I don't know what to make of the way he's suddenly decided it's okay to act like I exist. He's staring at me as if he can see right past the mask I'm clinging to so he doesn't see how affected by him I am.

Maybe turning eighteen really will change something between us. I held onto hope for two years—since the moment of my stupid confession on my sixteenth birthday—but eventually I gave up. It's why I told my father I'd marry for the business instead of for love.

I'm the one who looks away this time, not wanting my dad to get suspicious. I suck air into my lungs with a gasp and that doesn't escape Cole's notice either. His sinful lips tilt up into a smirk as he lifts his glass to sip his drink. I'm transfixed and can't stop staring at his throat as he swallows the expensive liquor down, and it's only my dad calling my name that snaps me out of my trance.

"We all know how important tonight is for you, sweetheart, and you know how proud I am of you," my dad says, and my attention is fully focused on him now while I sense the *but* coming and wait for the other shoe to drop. My shoulders tense and automatically my eyes dart around the room. Unease churns in my stomach when I notice how many people I don't recognize.

Maybe they're just friends of my dad's. No big deal. Right?

"But your birthday isn't the only occasion we're celebrating tonight." Dad says it with a huge grin on his face, but I see the truth in his eyes. He's unsure, hesitant to see what I'll say or do, and it hits me. I'm eighteen now. While I've been focused on school, Misha cheating on me, and my pathetic crush on my dad's best friend, my dad's been looking for a husband to marry me off to.

It shouldn't be a surprise at all. I knew this was coming.

I'd be pissed off at him if I hadn't agreed to this myself. My dad isn't the kind of parent who'd push me into doing something like this unless I agreed, and I did.

I *had*... a couple of months ago when I gave up all hope that Cole would ever want me like I wanted him. Back when I was sixteen and still heartbroken over Cole denying me the one wish I had on my birthday, I thought I'd wait forever.

All I asked for was a kiss. A *first* kiss. One I saved only for him, and he turned me down when I finally got up the nerve to ask. So Misha got my first kiss, and I've never regretted anything more.

Well, that's not true. Agreeing to marry a stranger to help the family business has rocketed to the top of the list, especially now that I see that something's shifted in Cole's eyes when he looks at me.

Then again... I haven't met my future husband yet. As my gaze shifts to lock with Cole's again, I know no matter who my father's chosen, he'll never compare to the man standing before me with eyes as black as his soul and a body made for sin.

But I've made my choice... and now it's time to face the consequences.

CHAPTER 4

FALLON

My eyes flick over to Cole; his jaw is flexed and his eyes are dark and violent. His fingers are turning white where he grips his glass, and while it's clear he's angry, what isn't is why.

"What else are we celebrating?" I ask hesitantly, ripping my eyes off of Cole and letting them sweep across the room again. There's a man who stands in a group of unfamiliar people, and all their attention is focused on him. He towers over them and looks like he's relishing the spotlight. I'm hoping I'm wrong about why he's here, that my dad somehow decided to put off this farce of an engagement for another night. Maybe he's forgotten?

The man's not bad looking with dark hair that's the sexy kind of messy, colorful tattoos creeping up his neck from out of his suit, and a straight, white smile that's currently charming every girl in a twenty-foot radius. But there's something about him that I don't like.

I tilt my head, trying to work out who he is, when he must

feel my eyes on him and turns his head, catching me staring. His grin widens and he winks before going back to his conversation. A low growl sounds from beside me and when I look, Cole's storming off.

I frown, but then my dad's talking again. "Your engagement, Fallon." He reaches down and squeezes my shoulder. "I'm so proud of you, and so grateful you're doing this. You have no idea how much it's going to expand our empire."

I nod, unable to form words. Any that bubble up die like ash on my tongue. It was easy to agree to a wedding with a stranger when it was an abstract thing that might or might not happen at some point in the far future. But now that it's really here, set in motion, an abyss of dread opens inside of me. My stomach twists uncomfortably, and all I want to do is swipe a bottle of champagne, sneak off somewhere private, and drink the entire thing until I pass out.

Yep, I'm definitely doing that as soon as I can escape.

Facing the reality of my choices makes the whole Misha thing seem like stupid childish drama in comparison.

"Who is he?" I whisper, hoping if I don't voice the question out loud maybe I can pretend like this isn't happening—even though I'm the one who agreed to do it. The concern mixed with excitement in my dad's eyes burns away any hope of backing out. I know he'd do it if I asked, but he needs this. He needs it like I needed him growing up, and he turned down countless business opportunities in order to be there for me.

I can do this for him.

"His name is Anton Leven, and he's the head of the Fallen Angels." Dad pauses like he's waiting for it to click for me, but the name's not familiar. I thought I was all studied up on the gangs and players in our little town—and the one next door—but apparently that's not the case.

I do know the Fallen Angels are a one percent motorcycle club that runs most of the criminal activity down in Mulberry. They've got a reputation for being shady as fuck even among criminals, but Anton must be new since I've never heard of him.

The man himself swaggers over and I don't miss the way women all over the room follow him with their eyes. His dirty smirk aimed in my direction shows he knows it, too. He's older than me but younger than my dad and Cole, and I wonder why he'd agree to an arranged marriage. It's obvious in the way he holds himself that he's confident, with no problem finding himself a wife if that's what he wanted.

He gives off total fuckboy vibes, though, and I instinctively know he'll in no way be faithful to me.

This is definitely all about the business perks for him.

Asshole.

I study him as he approaches, trying to picture my life standing at Anton's side. When I try, it's impossible. My traitorous brain keeps replacing his image with one of Cole—dark, wavy hair tousled like he just rolled out of bed, dark eyebrows framing darker eyes, and tattoos I've never had the pleasure of seeing for myself painting his skin.

The crushing weight of my decision settles onto my shoulders as Anton walks up, giving me another of his charming smiles. This guy's used to not having to work very hard for a woman, that much is obvious. His cocky swagger and the way he uses his smile like a weapon are things I might not have picked up on had I been anything other than obsessed with Cole Callahan for forever.

Cole's eyes are brimming with intensity while this guy's are cold and dead. I wonder if anyone else notices.

"Fallon, meet Anton Leven. Anton, my daughter, Fallon," Dad says, and Anton holds out his hand. I slip my fingers into his and he gives them a light squeeze before letting go. I feel nothing at his touch, not like with Cole.

I don't miss how his gaze drops down my body, and I don't know whether to straighten or shrink away. Do I want him to find me lacking or be impressed?

Before I can decide, his perusal is over, and his judgment made. The glint in his eye tells me he likes what he sees, at least enough to go forward with this.

"Why didn't you tell me your daughter was so beautiful, Tristen?" Anton says, turning that sharp smile on my dad.

"Because I might be a little bit biased where Fallon's concerned." Dad winks at me, but I don't miss the flash of irritation in his gaze. He doesn't like Anton, either. So why the hell is he marrying me off to the asshole?

"So, we're really doing this then?" I ask, realizing as it pops out of my mouth that I probably sound like a bitch, but I don't like beating around the bush.

This guy, Anton... He seems nice enough on the outside, but I know better. What I'm seeing right now is just the mask he wears. Like me, like my dad. All the powerful and wealthy people in this room do it, too. I won't know the true depths of his depravity until we're married, and maybe not even then. I imagine until then, he'll be on his best behavior.

At least in front of my dad.

"That's the plan, Princess," Anton says, all smooth with that deep, sultry voice of his. "Right after graduation."

I itch for a weapon, something to make him regret uttering that ridiculous nickname. Something to teach him I'm no princess.

But I've got nothing.

My hands start to sweat, and I blink rapidly to hide my

surprise. I want to ask what the rush is, but my dad must have his reasons, ones I plan to grill him about tomorrow, in private.

But graduation's only four months away. I thought I'd have more time.

I force a smile onto my face but inside I'm trembling. I... don't think I can do this.

My skin prickles and I feel a new set of eyes on me.

Cole.

I search him out, not caring if I'm being rude, and find him across the room, halfway in shadow with a new drink in his hands and a murderous expression on his face as he stares straight at me.

"So, what do you say, Princess? Will you be my bride?" Anton asks and I jerk my attention back to him before cutting a look at my dad. He's watching expectantly and my eyes drop to the massive rock Anton's holding out. He's not down on one knee or anything, but then I guess I wouldn't expect a man like him to kneel for anyone. That's not how my dad or any of his friends work, either.

Before I can think it through, I find myself nodding woodenly as his ring's slipped on my finger. It's weighing me down like a chain around my neck, one that's threatening to drag me to the blackest depths of the ocean where I'll be crushed under the weight of the water—if I don't drown first.

"Thank you," my dad whispers in my ear as he hugs me, and then he lets me go while I try to catch my breath and balance at the same time. He yells for champagne and a toast. Through it all, Anton watches me as a shark would watch his prey, studying, observing, patiently waiting to see what he can learn from my reactions. I keep my face a blank mask even as I'm frantic inside.

"Don't worry," Anton murmurs as he moves closer to me, so close his suit jacket brushes against my bare shoulder. The smell of gasoline and leather clings to him. "I'll take good care of you."

A shiver runs down my spine at his ominous words. They feel more like a threat than a promise of something to look forward to. I step back, taking the glass my father offers me with shaky fingers. Anton doesn't miss that either, and when his eyes gleam in the low light of the chandelier above our heads, I realize he gets off on my fear.

I force a smile, clink glasses, greet a million people I barely know—if I know them at all—and through it all, I'm spiraling. Lost. Twisting down into a despair I'm not sure how to climb out of. I've made a huge mistake, but there's no going back now.

When I've had enough, I swipe a bottle of champagne off the kitchen counter, not bothering to say goodbye to anyone on my way upstairs. I'm overwhelmed, and as I slowly walk up the stairs, tipping the bottle back and taking a swig straight from it, only one thing's on my mind—how desperately I want to be anyone but me.

CHAPTER 5

COLE

"What a dick," Romeo says as he moves to stand next to me, joining me in my violence-filled stare aimed in Anton's direction. I grunt out a half-response while I drain my glass, barely feeling the burn this time. I've lost count of how many I've had.

Romeo's eyes scorch into the side of my face, but I don't bother looking at him. I won't open my mouth, either, because if I do who knows what the fuck will spill out. Bourbon spikes through my veins and no doubt will loosen my tongue if I try to speak.

The only reason the man's still breathing is because Fallon made her escape already. If I had to watch him stare at her like he wants to devour her for one more second, things would've gotten bloody.

"We all hate Anton, but he seems to really be getting under your skin tonight. Any particular reason why?" he asks, reaching over and plucking my empty glass out of my hand and replacing it with his full one.

I slide my gaze over to him before flicking it back at the man I'm currently having murder fantasies about.

"You don't think it's bullshit that Tristen's marrying off his only daughter to a man who promised vengeance against us for not letting him into the Society?" My fingers tighten on my glass as Lucas stepped up on my right.

"We doing something about him?" He tilted his head towards Anton. Lucas is my partner for a reason. He can read me better than I can read myself sometimes. Of course he'd pick up on the prospect of violence rolling off of me.

"I think Tristen has a plan and we should trust him," Romeo finally says.

None of us speak for a few minutes while we watch Anton work his way around the room. Women follow his movements with their eyes, pushing their tits out as he passes by, giggling obnoxiously. He doesn't turn them down like I expect he should now that he's supposedly engaged to Fallon.

No, he turns up the charm with wider smiles flashing straight white teeth and friendly touches that are on the edge of indecent in public. Not even a half hour ago he was sliding a ring on Fallon's finger, and here he is, in her family home, not even trying to pretend he's not going to fuck someone else tonight.

Not that I want him to fuck her. Then I'd really have to kill him.

"We don't touch him... yet," I finally answer, and Lucas gives me a nod before melting back into the crowd.

Despite my restraint, fury ignites in my veins as I watch Anton's show of blatant disrespect. It leaves me wondering again what the fuck Tristen's thinking entering into any kind of agreement with this asshole, let alone giving him Fallon.

The girl who's meant to be *mine*.

This is what I get for trying to be a good guy when it goes

against my very nature. Waiting to make my move until she turned eighteen might've cost me my chance. But fuck that. I never lose, and I'm not about to start now.

My eyes cut over to Tristen who's busy toasting and laughing it up like my entire future isn't going up in flames thanks to this shitty decision of his. I have to believe he has a reason for not giving the Savage Six a heads up—or me at the very least. We should've discussed this, the six of us. Instead, he's getting into something that feels a whole fucking lot shady and like the worst idea I've ever seen in my life.

And I've seen some fucked up shit.

All I want to do is confront him, ask him what the hell he's doing. Tell him there are better ways to expand his business than marrying off his daughter to the scum of the earth. Better ways to hunt our foes than sacrificing the only person I was meant to love, outside of him.

But now isn't the time to cause a scene. Part of what makes people fear the six of us is our unflinching loyalty to each other and the knowledge that where one goes, the other five have his back no matter what. Public displays of disagreement will never be something we do.

But my fingers have a mind of their own, curling into fists as I fight to rein in the desire to take out my irritation on Tristen's face. I had a fucking *plan*. One he blew to smithereens here tonight, with no clue what he's done.

No doubt he knew if he told us ahead of time, we'd put a stop to this travesty, so he decided to surprise us with it instead.

I drain the rest of my drink and pass my empty glass to Rome before stalking out of the room. I can't look at any of these people a second longer or I'm going to explode. The alcohol and rage fight for dominance in my blood, and through my hazy thoughts, one need sticks out—find Fallon.

She disappeared shortly after Anton *Fuck Face* Leven slid his gaudy ring on her finger, so I can only imagine what must be going through her head right now. Fallon's a tough girl but finding out you're about to be chained to that asshole for life would have anyone questioning whether they'd rather chuck themselves off a cliff than go through with it.

Avoiding the ballroom where the party still rages on, I head to the library but it's empty. I check outside by the pool and even in the pool house, but there's no sign of her. She may have taken off with her friend, but I need to see her for myself. If she's crying over this, Anton won't survive the night.

First, I needed to change. If I'm going to trek out into the woods behind the house to see if she'd disappeared into one of her many secret trails back there—the ones she doesn't think I know about—I'm not going to do it in a suit.

I take the stairs two at a time, up to the guestroom that's practically mine for how often I stay here, and turn the handle. The lights are off, but enough moonlight pours in from the open curtains and the massive window to see Fallon asleep in my bed.

She's passed out in *my* fucking bed.

The rage burning through me quiets into a gentle simmer, one I can deal with later in the face of this new discovery. I knew my little lamb had a crush on me, but seeking me out like this when she needs comfort? That's the way it should be.

The way it was always meant to be.

I twist the door handle, shutting it silently before turning the lock. Fallon has no idea what she's begun by coming to me like this tonight, the wheels she's set in motion. I won't be stopped now. Nothing will get in my way because Fallon Ashwell belongs to *me*. She has since the moment she looked up at me with huge green eyes shining with innocence and offered me her first kiss.

She stood so close I could practically taste her lips, but for her I tried to be better. So, I stepped back, told her it was never going to happen, and tried to discourage her crush. But I'm not blind. I've seen the way she steals glances at me when she thinks no one's looking. The way she searches me out in a room. The way her smiles brighten just for me.

And it's a heady feeling, knowing how completely she'll give herself over to me when I tell her she's mine. Complete ownership over her mind, body, and soul so I can worship her the way she deserves.

But having her here in my bed, in my fucking t-shirt and her sweet cotton panties that I only get a tease of between her thighs, is too much. Too fucking much. How am I supposed to resist her?

When I move to stand above her, staring down at the perfection of the woman I shouldn't want, who's too fucking young and my best friend's *daughter* for fuck's sake, I know it's already too late. I'm hard as fuck and this need to possess her isn't going away. It's only getting stronger with every day that passes.

I bend to brush her hair off her face, letting the tips of my fingers skate across her soft skin and she shifts, turning her head into my touch like she's trying to press closer. Her movement makes the ring on her finger catch a tiny bit of light, enough to remind me it's there.

She wore that fucker's ring into my bed. That won't do.

I reach down and slip my fingers around it, tugging gently until it slides off. Then I tuck it into my pocket to deal with later. There are few things in this life that are certain, but one of them is that Fallon Ashwell only belongs to one man, and it's not Anton *motherfucking* Leven.

CHAPTER 6

COLE

It takes every ounce of self-control I possess not to rip Fallon's panties off and slide inside of her in one hard thrust. I don't give a shit that she's sleeping. She's made it more than obvious that she wants me.

The only thing that stops me is the desire to stare into her eyes and watch as I sink inside of her for the first time. To see the look in their emerald depths when I make her mine so completely, she'll forget there was ever a time she had to wait for me to take her.

So tonight, I'll sleep beside her for the first time, the first night of the rest of my life by her side.

She just doesn't know it yet.

The buzz in my body from the alcohol quiets the usual nagging thoughts that haunt me and keep me from sleeping. Or maybe it's her, here beside me where she belongs. Her scent lingers in the air, and I breathe it in greedily, filling my lungs with the sweet and decadent scent of honeyed figs and Fallon.

It's the scent of the trees that grow in the backyard mixed with something distinctly *her*.

I slip out of my jacket, hanging it on the back of the chair that sits in the corner, never taking my eyes off her. She's breathing steadily, so peaceful in her sleep that she hasn't moved at all since I walked into the room. She's so trusting, a coil of anger unfurls in my stomach.

Anyone could have walked into this room and found her like this, vulnerable and exposed in sleep. She's so careless of her surroundings, but now that she's mine, she'll never have to learn how dangerous the world around her really is. She's got no idea of the monsters that lurk just downstairs at her party. If she did, she wouldn't be sleeping at all right now.

I undo my cufflinks and toss them on the dresser, slowly unbuttoning my shirt and stripping it off. I'm unhurried, enjoying the view of Fallon sprawled in my bed, oblivious to the ways her world is changing second by second being here with me.

Toeing off my shoes, my slacks are next, but I keep my boxers on. Fallon is too tempting, and I don't trust myself to sleep naked beside her and not take advantage of the situation. I've been waiting a long time to slip inside her virginal cunt, and one more night might just kill me. I'm going to need the barrier between us, but tonight is the last time. After this there will be no holding back.

The half empty bottle of champagne on the nightstand is the only reason why I'm not waking her up right now and fucking her until her throat is raw from screaming my name. I don't even give a shit that we're in her dad's house.

But I want her to be fully aware of what's happening when we fuck for the first time.

I peel back the blanket and slide into bed, being careful not to jostle the mattress too much. The only thing I want to do is touch her soft skin, pull her against my body and sink inside of her before passing the fuck out, but if I brush even one finger against her body, my control will shatter.

At this point, it's only really an illusion of control anyway.

I lay stiffly beside her, only inches away but it might as well be miles. The space between us is electrified, crackling with the awareness that's always there, always pushing me closer, closer, closer.

Eventually, the anger at Tristen and Anton, and finding Fallon in my bed with another man's ring on her finger, starts to subside and my eyelids get heavy. It's not long after that I fall into a restless sleep, but it doesn't last.

My eyes snap open and I lay still trying to shake off my exhaustion and discover what woke me. Fallon's arm is slung across my chest, her leg over my hips, and she's using me as a pillow. Her hair tickles my chin and if I turn towards her, I could yank her panties to the side and be fucking her before my next breath because she's spread open for me like this.

Fuck.

There's only a thin shaft of moonlight drifting in through the open window now, barely enough to make out the outline of Fallon's perfect nose and her eyelashes, long and dark, lying across her cheeks. Her body heat soaks into my skin and her scent fills my lungs until my head spins.

No one has ever made me feel as out of control as she does.

My dick is so hard it aches, and all I can think about is how easy it would be to slip her panties to the side and push inside of her. To fill her up with my cum until it's dripping out of her cunt, sticking to her thighs.

I reach down and grip my cock, giving it a squeeze through my boxers and biting my cheek to keep the groan inside so I don't wake her up. She may want me, but I don't know how she'll react to this situation and if she starts screaming, Tristen will come running.

Explaining that Fallon is mine, and I plan to fuck her until she gives me an heir and takes my name and I've locked her down in every possible way, isn't exactly a conversation I want to have with him right now. Not when it would ruin this perfectly excruciating moment.

So I'm careful as I push my hand into my underwear and stroke my cock, imagining taking her now, rubbing my cock along her wet cunt until the tip catches just inside her pussy and pushing hard enough to force my way inside.

I have to reach around her thigh, and I'd rather be inside of her than fucking my own hand, but I'm too far gone to do nothing. I'm past the point of want and catapulting straight into *need*. It's either jack off or fuck her. That's it. Having Fallon this close when my control is so close to snapping is dangerous. I had a fucking *plan*, goddamnit, and everything's gone to shit.

My anger ratchets up with my need to fuck, and I'm on the verge of exploding when Fallon moans out my name in her sleep.

Moans out my fucking name.

Cole in this breathy tone that pulses across my skin. My cock jerks in my hand and I grit my teeth.

I don't do this. I *never* lose control. Ever.

But right now? I'm about to do something that wasn't part of the plan, and there's no way I can stop.

I shift myself so my dick is right up against the heat of her pussy and tug my boxers down so my cock pops out. There's nothing but a tiny layer of cotton keeping me from taking what's mine—what's always been meant for me.

Tonight I won't cross that line, but I've got no problem crossing others.

Fallon shifts and rocks her hips against me, right against my cock, rubbing her little pussy all over me as if she needs the friction as badly as I do. Even in sleep, her body knows who owns it.

"Cole," she moans again, her voice soft and husky from sleep.

I reach down and tug her panties to the side, slipping my finger lightly across her cunt, just enough to feel whether she's wet for me. She's fucking soaked, and I let my fingertips brush over her pussy again until they're slippery. My heart is jackhammering in my chest, and it's taking all my willpower not to fuck her now, but I don't.

I settle for using her arousal to lube up my dick, pushing the head right up against her opening and letting it slide against her while I jack myself off. Another centimeter and I'd be inside of her, but I hold back. Barely.

And as I come, swallowing down her name so I don't wake her up, I push the head of my cock just inside of her, so every drop of my cum shoots into that perfect pussy of hers. Knocking her up is something I'm going to have a lot of fun doing, and I didn't plan for it to start tonight, but there's no taking it back now.

I tuck myself back into my boxers and straighten her panties, sliding my finger along her pussy one last time and gently pushing any of my seed that escaped when I pulled away back inside of her.

Spent and satisfied, I lie back, letting my fingers play with Fallon's silky hair while I hold her. It doesn't take long before I drift into the best sleep I've ever had.

CHAPTER 7

FALLON

Ugh. I peel my eyes open and immediately slam them closed again. Why did I think drinking would be a good idea again?

My brain throbs in my skull and I try again to crack my eyes open. The bed beside me is empty but there's no mistaking this isn't my room. And the sheets smell like Cole. Was he here? Did he sleep next to me?

The sheets are wrinkled and messy, but other than that there's no sign he was ever here at all. How sad is it that my stomach sinks in disappointment?

I sit up, breathing through the wave of nausea that hits me. Despite how shitty I feel right now, I do remember a night full of sexy dreams starring none other than my dad's best friend. God, why can't I get over my crush on him?

I'm so fucking stupid.

When I slip out of bed, I take a second to wiggle my toes in the rug under the bed. It's something I've done every morning since forever, though I can't remember why I started. It's just a little ritual that grounds me to the day. It's like when I go outside and take off my shoes, burying my feet in the dirt or the grass. It reminds me to live in the present, and right now that reminder is exactly what I need.

Fantasies of what I want Cole to be to me aren't going to get me anywhere but in trouble and heartbroken. When I stand up to hit the shower, my thighs are sticky. *Jesus.* Those must have been some dreams last night. I only wish I could remember them.

By the time I'm done cleaning up and getting dressed, I'm feeling nearly human again. The nausea has shifted to hunger, and my brain is coming back online. It's then that the night before hits me. Yeah, I'm eighteen now.

Great.

Because that means I'm old enough to marry off. I still don't know anything about the guy my dad picked, but he's at least relatively close to my age and good looking. It could be a *lot* worse. Maybe.

Unless he's a monster, which I'm not ruling out.

I'm no stranger to the kinds of men my father does business with. Anton may have a pretty face, but it's probably masking something vicious and awful.

When I get downstairs, you'd never know a party happened here last night. The staff have already cleaned everything up to its usual sparkling shine, and breakfast is laid out on the kitchen counter. I head for the fridge first. Even a thorough toothbrushing didn't clear out the cottonmouth from my hangover.

A glass of fresh squeezed OJ does the trick, and when I polish it off, I pour another before grabbing a plate and loading up on everything carbs and grease I can find. No matter what I do today, I have a feeling I'm going to need the energy to handle it.

First thing on my agenda? Find my dad and talk to him about where his head's at with this match. He's always included me as much as he can in his business stuff because he taught me I'm capable of anything a son could've been for him. Eventually, I want to be the one to take over for my dad when he's ready to retire and as far as I know, he wants that, too.

I try to ignore the stab of hurt knowing he made this decision without even talking to me about it first. I always figured since I was doing this voluntarily, we'd figure out which way to go together. This is a stark reminder that he's fully in charge of the family business, and I really don't have a say at all, even in my own future.

I'm lost in my thoughts when my mom walks into the kitchen from the backyard, like she's coming from the pool house. Calling her my mom is generous considering she couldn't even be bothered giving birth to me. No, the only way she'd agree to have me is if she could hire a surrogate.

That's some next level vanity and narcissism, and when it comes to those two things, she's an absolute pro.

Erika Ashwell is perfectly put together with full makeup, blown out hair, and an outfit that cost more than my fancy private school tuition. Her heels clack on the floor and I try not to roll my eyes. Just for once, I'd love to see her with messy hair or in jeans. She would never.

Other kids' moms would take them to the playground and run around with them, play hide and seek, do arts and crafts, get messy and just forget about the need to look put together at all times. But not my mom. Where other kids had their moms, I had nannies and my dad when he could get away from work.

My mother had more important shit to do than be a parent, like fucking around behind my dad's back and shopping, brunches at the country club with her equally snobbish friends, and enough plastic surgery to fund her surgeon's beach house.

Her existence is nothing short of shallow and we've got nothing in common. Moments like these where I find myself alone with her, I have to resist the urge to get up and leave the room so we don't have to interact.

"Morning," I say because my dad raised me to be polite, even if it's the last thing I want to do.

She looks me up and down, from my wet hair to my boyfriend jeans with the rip in the knee and wrinkles her nose. "Yes, it's been a very good morning," she says before eyeing the food with the same amount of distaste she just did me and going to the fridge to no doubt pour herself a mimosa. It wouldn't be coffee—that might stain her teeth and she can't have that.

Of course, she wouldn't bother to act like she cares how my morning's been so far. She didn't even wish me a happy birthday yesterday. If it weren't for the party, I bet she would've forgotten.

Drink in hand, she spins and her gaze, green like mine, lasers in on my hand. "And where's your ring?"

I nearly choke on the bite of omelet I just took, staring down at my hand with my very empty ring finger.

Fuck, where'd that monster rock disappear to?

"I took it off to shower," I splutter through my coughs, taking a sip of my drink. Hopefully the wet hair convinces her. She looks mollified enough, though I don't think I like the gleam in her eye when she mentions my ring.

"Make sure you put it on as soon as you're done. We wouldn't want anyone to think you're not committed to your agreement," she says before her lips curl into what can only be described as a smug smile. For a second, I think she's glaring at me harder than usual despite the smile on her face. It's hard to tell with the emptiness in her eyes. I'd call them dead, but then I don't know if they were ever really alive. Sometimes she's got cunning behind her gaze, but mostly it's cold indifference or disgust.

Maybe the pool boy didn't fuck her hard enough last night.

But then movement catches my eye from behind her. Someone's sneaking out of the pool house, the one she just came from, and he's moving across the lawn towards the driveway. As he gets closer, I get a good look at his face.

And that's when it becomes abundantly clear that it wasn't the pool boy she was fucking last night. No, it was none other than my future husband who'd been between her thighs, and suddenly that smug and satisfied look in her eye makes a whole lot more sense.

CHAPTER 8

COLE

Sometimes being the boss fucking sucks.

Times like this morning where I had to leave Fallon in my bed before the sun had even risen because there was too much shit to do, plans to make, loose ends to tie up before she can truly become mine.

And I'm done waiting.

I smirk when I think about how my little lamb tried to block me in with her car, as if I couldn't get her spare set of keys from Tris. She wanted to make sure I couldn't leave, but as much as I wanted to, I couldn't stay.

I've already been to see my jeweler this morning, had the ring I took off Fallon checked for size, and talked to my guy about making something custom for her. Nothing made for someone else is good enough. She deserves only the very best, and custom is it. I've had the perfect ring in mind for months, and now he'll bring my vision to life. The ring I'll put on her finger will leave no doubt who she belongs to.

While he's working on that, I have other priorities today, the most pressing of which is talking to Tristen and figuring out what the fuck he's doing offering Fallon to Anton. There are other ways to grow his business, namely wiping out the head of the MC and putting in someone loyal to the Savage Society, which is what I'd do. If he's got a plan, I need to know what it is before I make my next move.

I press harder on the gas, flying my car more than driving it as I head towards The Lodge. There's a sense of urgency that claws through my veins pushing me on. I don't know what's causing it—maybe I'm just tired of waiting for Fallon.

Maybe something's about to happen that's going to fuck things up even more.

It's hard to say.

All I know is my gut instinct is never wrong, and I need answers before I decide how to handle the ring in my pocket. The damn thing needs to go back to Anton, and he needs to fuck off.

The Lodge is Savage Society headquarters. It's where the six of us conduct our business together. We meet here because it's the only place we can guarantee is one hundred percent secure from spying. No one has ever breached our fortress.

I climb out of the car and brush non-existent wrinkles out of my suit before buttoning the jacket and straightening my cufflinks. There's a reason they call us the Savage Six, why the entire town is envious of who we are. Why they all want to be one of us.

But we'll never let them in.

And the image of power and control, wealth and confidence we project is almost as important as the size of our bank accounts and the blood staining our hands where the citizens of Emerald Hills are concerned.

The Lodge towers up ahead—a deceptively peaceful looking building that would have you believe that it's for vacationing or relaxation. A modern log cabin that's more glass, warm wood, and metal than roughly cut logs stacked together.

Calling it a cabin is laughable, considering its sheer size and how impenetrable it is. The Lodge sits on the shores of Crescent Lake, overlooking both Emerald Hills and Mulberry further in the distance.

In short, it's the perfect spot for the six of us to look down on our pawns.

While I climb the steps, I think back to last night, the way Fallon's tight body pressed up against mine, the way my name sounded as she moaned it in her sleep, and how I got the barest tease of the way her cunt will feel wrapped around my dick when I came just inside of her. My steps falter and I have to adjust myself before I take the final step up to the front door. The blood pulsing through my veins is laced with a drug I don't think I'll ever get out of my system—Fallon.

Only the knowledge I'm meeting with her father keeps my hard on in check, deflating it just enough to be manageable. Tonight I've got important business to take care of, but tomorrow night I'll be fucking Tristen's daughter and there's nothing anyone can do to stop me.

With that in mind, I press my thumb to the scanner at the same time I lean forward and let my retina be scanned, speaking the password to enter. The sound of a heavy lock disengaging is the only warning I get before the door opens and I step inside, waiting just beyond the entrance until it's closed so no one can sneak in after me.

And believe me, people have tried.

Despite the intense security that keeps the peons out, the interior of The Lodge is mostly what you'd expect from six powerful men. Comfortable leather furniture, the faint smell of cigar smoke that always lingers in the air, and more than one bar with top shelf aged liquor scattered within the different rooms.

Each of us has an office here, and I move past mine and head straight for Tristen's. When I find the lights off and no one inside, I make my way to the lounge room—the one with billiards, darts, flat screens, and huge windows that overlook the cities below.

You'd think we'd want to look out at the lake, but the six of us prefer to stare down at our empire as we figure out how to expand it. How to control it. How to shape it to our whims.

Tristen's here, sitting in a wingback leather chair with a glass of something amber clutched in his hands, leaning forward with his elbows on his knees. His head hangs down and I can't see his face, but his shoulders stiffen, and I know he's aware I'm here.

You don't grow to be as powerful as we have without an almost supernatural awareness of your surroundings. It's too easy for some low-level gangster to sneak up and end you with a bullet to the skull, so hypervigilance is one of our favorite weapons.

Plus, Tristen and I have been inseparable since we were practically toddlers, so we've developed a sense for each other.

"Need a refill?" I ask as I pass him by on my way to the bar. Yeah, it's still early but I'm going to need a drink for this conversation. Tristen's already started, and judging by his body language, it looks like he's going to need a few.

"Not yet," he says, lifting his head and slumping back in his chair. He looks like he hasn't slept. There are dark shadows under his eyes, and he hasn't shaved.

I finish pouring my bourbon and move to sit beside him,

unbuttoning my jacket as I do. I take a sip, waiting him out. Tristen's not the type that responds well to an inquisition. He knows why I'm here and he'll fill me in when he's ready.

My drink is half gone by the time he speaks again.

"I needed to buy time," he finally says, tapping his fingers on his knee while he rests his drink on top of his other thigh. "I fucking hate that I have to use her to do it."

I face him, still saying nothing but giving him all my attention.

"He cut me off from Mulberry Bought the sheriff out from underneath me, somehow got the guys at the train yard to agree all shipments go through him first so I can't even get fresh supply in. I didn't see it coming," he admits, and I know it took a lot for him to divulge that to me. If I were anyone else, he wouldn't have.

His eyes meet mine. "Forget expansion. That fucker is trying to choke me out, and you know I can't let that slide."

My fingers tighten around my glass. "So you give him Fallon? For what?"

"It's only a ploy to hold him off. Make him think he's winning, that I'm desperate enough to let him have her in exchange for his cooperation. That I need him so badly I'd give her up for his help."

"And if he rushes the wedding because he suspects as much? He can't think you're just going to hand over your only daughter tied up in a pretty bow after he fucked you over."

"Anton doesn't know that I suspect him. His ego's out of fucking control and the prick thinks he's untouchable. I'm playing into that belief. I haven't questioned him or brought up my suspicions. But there are still a couple of guys loyal at the train yard who filled me in on what's been going down." He runs a hand through his messy hair. "I negotiated a deal with him. Told him he could marry Fallon if he helped free up my supply chains, helped me figure out who was behind my shipments disappearing. I also asked for him to use my stock exclusively for his club's weapons." He drains the rest of his drink. "Fuck, just saying that out loud makes my blood boil. Giving up *my* daughter. *My* supply chains. The ones I've spilled blood over, worked hard to gain over the years, and this little asshole thinks he can come in and hold them hostage and will still be breathing by the time I'm done?" He snorts. "He doesn't know shit about what's about to happen to him."

When we were kids, I once saw Tris break a classmate's arm because he stole his pencil. He's like me—won't tolerate people touching what's ours.

While I hate the idea that Fallon's promised to the new leader of the Fallen Angels, I understand Tristen's logic, why he needs to use her as his way to get closer. That doesn't mean I'm about to go along with his plan, not when I've got plans of my own for her.

"You know he's still salty about how we shunned him. He's gunning for you now, but I have a feeling he's not going to stop there. You're where he's starting, and once he's taken everything from you, he'll come for the rest of us," I say, tracing my finger around the rim of my glass and thinking about this new threat. My blood hums, the prospect of battle waking up instincts and bloodlust I resist most days in order to appear civilized.

"I know. That's why I needed to buy time, so we can figure out the best way to fuck him over."

"And in the meantime, you're going to toss Fallon into the middle of a brewing war?" My voice is harsher than I intend, and Tristen narrows his eyes as he watches me.

"I've raised her to handle herself. She'll be fine until I get her out," he says, and it takes every bit of my immense self-control not to launch myself across the room and pummel one of my best friends for his carelessness with the woman that's as good as mine.

He'd better hope she is, because if not... he'll have to deal with me.

CHAPTER 9

FALLON

After seeing my piece of shit fiancé sneaking out of the pool house after fucking my mother all night, let's just say I'm not in the mood for family bonding today. I need to get the hell out of this house before I go insane—or on a killing spree.

Honestly, I don't even know how I'm feeling. I guess disgusted is right there at the top of the list. I think about it while I pack up my camera bag, making sure my favorite lenses are inside and I've got spare batteries and memory cards.

I'm also disappointed. It's true I spent last night in another man's bed, so I don't have a lot of room to talk. But c'mon, this is my *mother*. How fucking twisted can you get?

Besides, it's not like Cole was there. And even if he was, nothing happened. I've been in love with him for what seems like forever, and in my drunken moment of weakness and despair, I sought him out.

Any hope I might have had of this engagement turning into

anything real, anything that would allow me to lead a happy life, has just gone straight out the window.

What am I supposed to do with a man who has no issues cheating on me with my own mother the very night we got engaged?

As I toss a couple of supplies in a backpack and then leave my room—without looking for the stupid ring—I picture slicing Anton's balls off and making him eat them. If he's lucky, I'll cook them up first and serve them to him for dinner. A dark smile touches my lips.

I was made in my father's image, after all, raised to be just as bloodthirsty as he is, and taught to hide it just as well. Appearing civilized, he likes to say, is as good as actually being civilized.

The smile slips as I round the corner into the kitchen, and I brace for my mother. The breath rushes out of me when I see the place is empty, and I hurry to the fridge and load up with bottles of water before I hit up the pantry for snacks.

Most weekends I spend at least part of one day out hiking the trails behind our house, the ones that disappear up into the foothills of the mountains. There's nothing between Emerald Hills and the top of the Cascade Mountains, so there are miles and miles of unexplored forest that no one around here ever bothers to step foot into.

But it's my happy place. The place that smells like pine and damp earth and fresh, misty rain that clings to your skin.

I don't waste time hanging around. I move my camera bag so the strap is across my body and adjust my camera strap around my neck. Slinging my backpack over my shoulder, I head out the back door and across the yard.

In only a few minutes, it's like I'm in a different world, transported away from my reality into this magical place of nature and wonder that I can never seem to get enough of. Here I can let all my worries slide away and pretend they're not mine anymore.

Here I can act like I'm someone else, some great explorer or maybe one of those crazy cat ladies who lives in a tiny cabin in the woods with a dozen felines who'd eat her dead body. I laugh at that last one, the mental picture of it, before I notice the clouds have parted—*sun breaks*, PNW natives call it—and these gorgeous shafts of light are shining through the thick branches of the evergreens.

Little bits of pollen and fauna catch in the sun, and I lift my camera, adjusting the shutter speed and aperture to capture this perfect image. Of course, no matter how much I adjust, the pictures never do the real thing justice. But every now and then they come close.

Out here, like this, I'm capturing these tiny moments of peace and the tension melts out of my body. I don't think about what my father's done, who my mother's done, or why I woke up in Cole's bed this morning.

I *especially* don't think about how disappointed I am that I woke up alone.

After hours navigating the trails, hundreds of tiny moments captured on my memory stick, and aching feet, I decide to call it a day. The sun sinks lower in the sky and it's getting harder to see with the thick spread of trees. A lot of photographers would refer to this time of the day as the *golden hour* where the light takes on a soft, almost ethereal quality that makes every picture you take look better.

But here? With the mass of gray clouds in the sky obscuring it, it's pretty much hopeless to get a hint of gold to go with the gloom.

Doesn't matter, though, because I needed today. The lack of perfect lighting to cap off a great day won't ruin it. The only thing that will is running into my mother before I have the chance to meet up with Waverly and get back to my room at school. The last thing I need is another run in with my egg donor.

My nature high doesn't last long because the second I step into the house, my mother's cackling laughter carries from somewhere deeper inside. All the tension I just worked so hard to get rid of piles right back onto my shoulders.

I sneak upstairs as fast as I can, doing a quick search of the guestroom and my bedroom for the ring, but I don't find it. Frowning, I wonder if I should tell my dad I lost it, but then I figure I'll come home next weekend and do a more thorough search. Until then, I can hide out in my dorm room and pretend I'm not engaged to a total dickface. See? Boarding school has its perks.

Between now and then I doubt I'm going to run into Anton or my dad, so it should be fine.

I grab my phone and send Waverly a message, asking if she's ready to head back to school. Everything I need is in my dorm, so it's not like I have any packing to do, but I do change out of my jeans and hiking clothes and take a fast shower.

By the time I get out, do my makeup and hair, and grab my camera's memory card so I can work on edits in between classes, homework, cheerleading, and social bullshit this week, it's been over an hour. I never got a chance to talk to my dad today, and I don't think I have a choice but to wait until next weekend. I grab my phone as it buzzes again. Waverly's blowing it up with messages wondering where I am.

When I'm home, in those woods, or shadowing my dad in his business, that's when I get to feel like me. The rest of the time, it's all just a show I put on for other people. There's a certain expectation of the kind of person I'll be, based on how wealthy and powerful my parents are, and I'm expected to live up to it.

So, in my expensive designer bullshit, I head out the door, back to my not-so-real life. At least I've got Waverly, and right now, faced with a fiancé I want to castrate, betrayal from not only my first ever boyfriend but also possibly my father, and a desperate sort of first love with a man who'll never see me as anything but a little girl, I need her more than ever.

That's why, when she throws open her front door and hugs me like she hasn't seen me in a year instead of just last night, I break down, smearing my makeup in a fit of tears while I let everything pour out of me.

Everything.

Like the *best* best friend, she stalks to her bedroom, straps on a thigh holster under her skirt, slips a knife into it, and asks me who we need to kill first.

And just like that, I know everything's going to be okay.

CHAPTER 10

COLE

I step out of the shadows a block away from the bar as my second approaches. I may not get my hands dirty as often as I used to, but I remember well how to be invisible when needed.

Lucas wears all black, guns strapped to every part of him they can be, and when he steps into the flickering light of the streetlamp, I give him a savage grin before opening my suit jacket and showing off my own hardware.

I don't expect tonight to end without some bloodshed, but it's not going to be ours.

Tristen may need to keep Anton thinking he's winning, but I'm not playing the same game. What I do tonight may fuck things up for Tristen's plan, but I'll make it up to him. Fallon's too important to me to see her used as a bargaining chip.

Lucas leans up against the wall in a casual move that I know for a fact is only to make him appear less threatening. It's a habit he's gotten used to because he's the most lethal man I've ever met, myself included—and I've built an entire business off killing people.

"Is there anyone in there you need alive at the end of this?" Lucas asks me, his eyes gleaming with the potential of violence.

I shake my head. "Unless Anton himself shows up, everyone else is fair game."

He nods like this is the answer he expected. We've been together a long time and he can usually anticipate my moods and what I'm thinking.

"Ready?" I ask him and he straightens from his spot against the wall.

We leave the shadows and walk towards Nine Circles—the bar the Fallen Angels use as their headquarters. The place is a shithole, but I don't expect anything better from some low level gangster who thinks he can play in the same league as us.

There are two men standing outside the door guarding it, or doing their best to look intimidating so people who don't belong will just pass on by, but unfortunately for them I've seen the true horrors of this world, and they aren't it.

With Lucas at my back, I step forward. They initially tense like they're going to stop me or tell me that I can't come in, and I fucking wish they would. My fingers itch to spill blood and I know Lucas is no different.

"You can't—" one of them starts to say, and I lift an eyebrow and wait him out.

He scans me from head to toe and when he gets to my face, his body visibly stiffens, and he steps back. I give him a smug smirk because who the fuck does this guy think he is to try and stop *me* from going somewhere I want?

It's obvious that he realizes his place and the deadly mistake he nearly just made when he grabs the handle of the door himself and pulls it open for me, avoiding eye contact. I step inside after confiscating the door guard's phone, Lucas never moving more than a few steps away from me, guarding my back like he always does.

It's one of the reasons that I have as much power as I do, because I can trust that no one will ever get through him to me.

When we step inside and the door closes behind us, the entire place goes silent. Every eye turns towards us. Good. At least they recognize the threat to their lives and give me the respect I deserve—the respect I've *earned*.

The bartender is the one who finally speaks, after several seconds of a standoff where Lucas rests one hand on the gun at his hip and the other clutches a throwing knife I know for a fact he never misses with.

The bartender slowly pulls his hands out from behind the bar and sets them on the top where we can see them. He's unarmed for the moment. No doubt he'll pull a weapon out from under the counter in less than a second, but he's willing to hear us out before blood is spilled.

I'm not sure whether to be disappointed or not.

"What do you need?" he asks, and while it's not the respectful greeting I deserve, he can be of use, so I'll let him keep breathing—for now.

"I've got a message for your boss," I say, opening my suit jacket and flinging it back so my weapons are on display. "He thinks he can steal something that belongs to me, but he should know by now," I continue, crossing the sticky floor towards the bar. Lucas stays by the door, his back to the entrance so no one can get behind him.

There are about a dozen men here now, all Fallen Angels, all halfway to drunk or high on the shit their gang peddles down here in Mulberry. All easy prey—almost too easy.

"That he shouldn't fuck with me," I finish, and come to a

stop in the middle of the room. I cross my arms over my body, grabbing a gun in each hand from the holsters inside my jacket and pulling them out.

Lucas fires the first shot, straight between the eyes of a guy sitting at a table to my right, and I'm not far behind him, taking out a couple of guys at the end of the bar. The bartender reaches for whatever weapon he's got stashed under the counter, but I center the gun in my right hand on his forehead and click my tongue at him.

"I wouldn't do that if I were you."

We lock eyes and neither of us blinks while Lucas finishes off the rest of the men in the bar. The scent of blood and gunpowder hangs heavy in the air, and I breathe deeply, enjoying the nostalgia of it. I don't get my hands dirty nearly enough anymore.

"I'll tell him whatever you want, just leave," the man says, looking less brave than he did a few minutes ago, when he thought he had an entire bar to back him up. Now he trembles where he stands, and I revel in the knowledge that I did this to him.

"How do I know you'll keep your word?" I ask, sauntering toward the bar with my gun still trained on his head. I tuck the one in my left hand away in my right holster and then dig in my pocket for the ring.

The ring Anton dared to put on my Fallon's finger.

A mistake he'll come to regret.

"I promise. I'll tell him whatever you want." The man's eyes are wide and the gun in his hand shakes as I walk around the bar, rounding the corner so we're standing close. The bartender turns to keep his attention on me, so he doesn't see Lucas moving around the other side to his back.

But I do. I watch as my second gets into position and then the man starts to cry as Lucas forces him to his knees. The bartender's gun clatters to the floor at his feet and the smell of piss hits me, ruining my buzz.

I wrinkle my nose and kick his weapon out of reach, bending down to grab his hand while Lucas holds him in place.

He struggles and screams and tries to fight, but he's no match for a professional assassin, especially with his hand in my grip.

"Your promise is worthless to me," I say, yanking his pinky finger back until it snaps, and he screams again. "Besides, I prefer to send a more visual message. It's less likely to get lost in translation."

I break the fingers on his right hand, and by then he's a piss-covered, blubbering mess. I start with the ones on his left and the fight has gone out of him. I look to Lucas who's watching with an almost bored look in his eyes.

"It's not as much fun when they give up," I say, and he nods.

"Pussy," he spits at the guy before elbowing him in the head to knock him out. Now that he's retreated to the place in his mind where he doesn't feel the pain, he's no use to us awake.

I break every finger except the ring finger on his left hand, which I force Anton's shitty, gaudy ring down on, breaking bones and taking off skin in the process. Lucas takes out his knife and helps me cut away the finger to make the ring fit and when we're done, we drop the guy to the floor still breathing... for now.

Once Anton gets my message, he might not be so lucky.

"Now what?" Lucas asks while we step over the bloodbath and out the front door. The two bouncers stare at us with wide eyes but wisely say nothing as we leave.

"The board's been set. Now we wait for Anton's next move."

CHAPTER II

FALLON

My skirt swishes against my thighs as I walk into school on three-inch heels. Dark hair cascades down my back, perfectly straight and glossy, just like my lips. I hold my chin up high, shoulders back with perfect posture as I strut down the hall like it's some high-end runway. As much as I hate the show I'm expected to put on, I still do it every damn day.

It's exhausting.

But even I have to admit it's good practice for what my life's going to be like married to the head of a gang. Make every man want what your husband has, and every woman envious of you.

I'd much rather be in jeans hiking through the woods with my camera strapped around my neck, hunting for my next perfect shot—the one I'll someday display in my own gallery.

But I've never been good at telling people no. When my dad sat me down and told me what my job would be as a gangster's wife, my first instinct was to put an end to the whole thing. But then I remembered all the times he missed out on business deals and opportunities because he stayed home with me so I wasn't raised by nannies, and the guilt nearly swallowed me whole.

So, here I am, in the green and gray plaid skirt that barely covers my ass, thigh high stockings, getting eye fucked by every guy I pass in the halls and trying to act like I don't notice or care.

My frigid ice bitch persona is in full effect.

At least this is normal. I'm used to it. After this weekend's craziness, I could use more regular right now.

Waverly walks beside me, and our lockers are side by side, so we stop to pick up our books before first period. She finishes before I do and spins, leaning back against her closed locker and surveying the crowd still lingering in the hall.

"Ugh, brace yourself," Waverly murmurs and I close my locker while I push my shoulders back and take a deep breath.

Then I spin and come face to face with my cheating ex Misha and the class skank, Eden. He's got his arm slung over her shoulder and he's watching me warily, like he's afraid I'm going to attack him. I'm not—at least not now when he's expecting it.

I haven't forgotten I need to plan some epic revenge, but the weekend kind of got away from me.

Eden's staring down at her phone and doesn't look interested in Misha at all until he stops at his locker, which just happens to be three down from mine, and she blinks as she looks up. When she spots me, suddenly she's curling into his side and grinning up at him with a sultry smile on her red painted lips.

"Hey, Fallon," Eden purrs. "Do anything fun this weekend? I know I did." She runs a stiletto tipped hot pink nail down the front of Misha's chest. Those things look like claws, and I bet if she was at all into him, his back would be totally shredded.

The idea nearly makes me snort, but I'm well-practiced and I don't let my mask break.

Beautiful Carnage

"Bitch," Waverly hisses from beside me in solidarity, and I appreciate her having my back.

Before I can come up with some witty clapback for Eden, and probably because my attention was focused elsewhere, Carter Van Buren sneaks up on me and throws his meaty arm over my shoulder.

I'm immediately drowning in way too much cologne, and I shove his big body off of me. "Don't touch me."

"Aw, c'mon, babe. That's not what you were saying at the kickoff bonfire."

Carter's the star linebacker on our football team and makes sure everyone knows he thinks he has a big dick.

I smile up at him sweetly. "You mean when you tried to drug my drink so you could date rape me? And I caught you and kicked you in the balls?"

That cocky look drops off his face and his eyes harden. In fact, his entire demeanor changes. Now he's looming over me and pinning me against the lockers with his body.

Eden laughs, tossing her blonde hair over her shoulder, and says, "See you at practice, Fallon." And then the bitch saunters away with my pathetic ex-boyfriend draped all over her.

"I thought we agreed you weren't going to bring that shit up," Carter says, leaning so close I can smell what he had for breakfast on his breath. Gross.

"I never agreed to that."

"Back the hell off, Carter," Waverly says, stepping up beside me and forcing him to move away.

"I need a date for the party Isaac's throwing this weekend and you're going to be it," he informs me, his self-assured swagger back in place.

I laugh. "Why the *fuck* would I ever do that?"

"Rumor has it you never say no," he says. He's not wrong…

except in this, I have zero issue telling him to fuck off. I'm a people pleaser, but this asshole's a straight up rapist and that's well past where I draw the line.

I mock gasp. "Is that the rumor? Well, how about this?" I lean into his broad chest and tilt my head up so he can clearly see my entire face. "No."

That's when he snaps, gripping my upper arms so hard he's definitely going to leave bruises. "You're going to be my date to the party, or I'm going to drag you into that bathroom and bend you over the sink and take what I want right now."

He reaches out and grips the back of my neck so hard it hurts but I don't even blink. With his other hand, he moves it up my skirt, making sure I know exactly who's in control here. I may be five ten, but he still towers over me. There's no way I could overpower him.

A shiver runs through my body because as much as I might fight and claw and knee him in the balls, he's got at least fifty pounds on me.

I can scream now, but it's his word against mine. Waverly's here, but one of his friends has pulled her away and a quick glance out of the corner of my eye tells me she's yelling at two of them, but they've basically formed a wall. Carter's the captain of the football team and basically untouchable.

This… is going to be a problem.

That gleam in his eye? I have no doubt he'll follow through on his threat. Finally, I nod, and he steps back, smoothing my skirt down and patting my ass. "Good girl," he says, and my teeth grind together. Condescending prick.

"I'll text you the details," he says, backing up. "And don't even think about standing me up. You know what'll happen if you do."

The start of class bell rang five minutes ago, but my heart is still racing when he whistles and his asshole friends take off after him like well-trained dogs, all high fives and bullshit.

Waverly hurries over and looks at me with concern. "Are you okay? What'd he say?"

How can I tell her that he just threatened to rape me to get me to go out with him? After the things she's been through, a reminder of her tragic past isn't what she needs this morning.

And who the hell *does* that?

Then again, I shouldn't be surprised. My dad's world is a whole lot darker than anything Carter's ever seen and that's where I grew up. I guess I always felt protected, though, between Dad and Cole.

Thinking about Cole helps steady me. If I told my Dad or him about Carter's threat, I don't think he'd still be breathing by the time Isaac's party rolled around. But I want to earn my way in their world. I want to prove I'm just as capable as they are, which means dealing with this situation on my own.

I've got a week to figure out what I'm going to do.

"Just his usual bullshit," I say, adjusting my books with trembling hands. I give her a smile that's as fake as Eden's tits. "Let's go. We're already late."

Waverly groans. "Professor Masters is going to give us detention. You know that old witch hates when we're even a second late." She looks over at me hopefully. "Want to skip?"

I shake my head. "I'm not risking my perfect GPA so Carter can take valedictorian. That just lets him win."

She deflates. "Yeah, I guess you're right. Fine, but you owe me lunch off campus."

"Deal."

We head to class, and I set my phone to record all my lectures so I can review them later. I'm too up in my head to concentrate on anything. Between my lost engagement ring, the engagement to Anton, especially now that I know he's fucking my *mom*—ew—and this Carter thing, I'm a mess.

When classes are done for the day, all I want to do is drag myself to my dorm and bury myself under the covers while I binge ice cream and get lost in a movie. But I've got cheer, so I suit up and jog out to the field.

Eden's on the team, and since I'm captain, step one of my revenge involves making her do everything twice. Laps? Sorry, didn't see you finish. Pushups? Whoops, I lost count. By the time practice is done, she's so mad she's practically spitting. She's covered in grass stains and sweat and I'm just a little lighter.

When the team's dismissed, I start the walk back to my dorm, but someone calls my name. That voice raises every hair on the back of my neck. I turn and see Cole fucking Callahan leaning against the passenger door of his insanely expensive sports car looking good enough to eat. The man is sex personified in his tailored black slacks and black button down rolled up to show off his deliciously inked forearms.

His hair is a little messy and windswept, but it only adds to the effect of him just rolling out of bed. I can't tell what he's looking at because he's got black sunglasses over his eyes. I'm still in my cheer practice skirt and a top, and I'm hyper aware of how little I'm actually wearing right now. Plus, I'm all sweaty.

Not exactly the way you want your crush to see you.

"Hey, Cole. What are you doing here?" I ask when I get close enough. His cologne is dark and dangerous, and I want to bury my face in his neck and breathe him in.

"I'm taking you home," he says with that deep, sinful voice of his that would rumble against my palm if I was brave enough to put it against his chest.

"Huh? I am home. My dorm is right over here," I say, pointing behind me.

"Not anymore. Get in the car," he says again and steps forward. My heart picks up speed as I try to figure out what he means. He knows I live in the dorms during the week, just like all the other kids that go to EHP. It's a private school where the rich parents who are too busy or don't want to deal with their offspring send us to become the next generation of entitled assholes. Kids come from all over for the opportunity to mingle with the ultra-privileged that walk its halls.

The vibes rolling off Cole are intense, though. I think if I resist, he might throw me over his shoulder and force me into his car.

"What are you doing?" I ask again.

"We're wasting time, Fallon. Get in the fucking car. I'm not going to tell you again." He leans back and pulls the passenger door open. Cole's my dad's best friend, and he wouldn't do anything to hurt me... right?

Even without knowing what he's up to, I want to obey. Inside I'm jumping up and down and throwing confetti like it's my birthday all over again because *he's here.*

For me.

This is the most attention he's shown me since the night I turned sixteen. So, I say fuck it. I've had the worst day and I just don't want to resist. I move past him, taking a breath of the deliciousness that's Cole before I lower myself into the seat of his low-slung car.

"Buckle up," he orders before slamming the door and rounding the car, and I look out the passenger window, spotting a very jealous and pissed off looking Eden glaring in my direction.

And when Cole slides behind the wheel, I decide I don't care where we're going. He could drive us off a cliff as long as my last moments are spent with him.

CHAPTER 12

COLE

Something's bothering my little lamb.

In the past, she'd be peppering me with questions about where we're going and why I picked her up. Why I'm bothering to pay attention to her at all.

But today she sits silently staring out the window, her shoulders tense like she's carrying the weight of the world on her delicate frame.

My fingers tighten on the steering wheel until the leather creaks underneath, and my jaw clenches. Someday soon she'll come to me with all her problems. She just doesn't know it yet.

I need to earn her trust. After the way I've acted towards her over the past two years, pushing her away at every opportunity, I'm not surprised she's putting distance between the two of us. That doesn't mean I have to like it. She should know she's mine, has been since the second she made that wish. The timing just wasn't right.

Now she's all grown up and I don't give a shit what people think, she's never belonged to anyone but me. Never *will* belong to anyone but me. She's the missing piece to the life I've been building all this time, and now she's exactly where she was born to be.

She's caught in my web, and there is no getting free. The harder she fights, the more tangled she'll become.

"Are you going to tell me what's bothering you?" I finally ask when I can't take the silence any longer. My thoughts are running rampant, my imagination going wild with every possibility of what could've happened between when I left her in my bed and this moment.

"Are you going to tell me where we're going?" she counters rather than answering and my lips twitch. She's got balls, my little lamb. I know grown men who wouldn't dare speak to me that way for fear I'd slice them open, and they'd have to watch their entrails decorate my floor before taking their last breath.

"Home."

She turns to look at me, blinking those huge green eyes that are so innocent and easy to get trapped in, and I take my eyes off the road for a second to stare at her. She's so expressive and easy to read, even though I know she thinks she hides her feelings so well.

If it wasn't for her distress, everything in my world would be perfect right now. I'm finally doing it—claiming Fallon as mine. Tristen's going to want to kill me, but who better to keep his daughter safe and happy than his best friend? In time, he'll come around.

And if he doesn't, well…

Things might get ugly.

But I'm not giving either of them up.

I'll worry about that if it happens. For now, Fallon's here and only I can touch her. The tension I've been carrying for *years* melts away as I realize it's done. Nothing and no one will take her from me, and now I don't have to spend sleepless nights counting the days until she turns eighteen and I can make my move. I don't have to worry about tiny dicked high school boys making a move on her while she doesn't suspect the games they like to play.

I might actually sleep tonight. Drift off with my dick inside of her after I make her mine in every way imaginable. I shift as I look back at the road, trying to get more comfortable with a hard cock between my legs.

"You're taking me to Dad's? Why?" she asks, sitting up straighter. There's an undertone of panic to her voice that I don't like.

"No, I said home. To my home. *Our* home."

She seems to deflate as she sinks back against the leather seat, her fingers playing with the hem of that goddamn cheerleading skirt she's wearing. The edge of it just brushes the top her thighs and it's enough to make me hard all over again, picturing bending her over in that. I'm wondering if she's got something lacy or cotton on under there, letting my mind drift to once forbidden territory when I should be paying attention to Fallon.

Her body language. Her reaction to what I've just told her.

She stiffens again when it hits her. "Wait. *Our* home? You and I don't have a home, Cole."

"Then what am I looking at?" I ask, gesturing toward the building still barely visible through the fence that sits on the other side of my windshield. "That looks like our house to me."

I don't miss the pretty pink flush on her cheeks, and I wonder whether her ass would turn that color under my palm, or whether that's the same shade as her pussy. I didn't get a good look the other night in the dark, but that's about to change.

Right on time, I pull into my driveway and nod to Brooks,

one of my guys who's currently manning the gate. He tips his head and opens it, and I don't miss the breath Fallon sucks in as my house comes into view.

It's huge—way too big for just me—but that's beside the point. I've got an image to uphold, and this helps project it. I'm close to the rest of the Savage Six and the Lodge. We all live on the East side of the lake in houses that tower over even our most wealthy neighbors.

I don't know why Fallon's surprised—she grew up in a house just as big as mine. I've never invited her here on purpose. The temptation to have her in my bed was too great, and I knew if she stepped foot inside of my home, I'd cross a line I wasn't prepared to just yet.

I had the house built about five years ago up on a hill overlooking Crescent Lake. The back side is mostly windows, and there's a path that goes down to a set of docks where my boats and jet skis are housed. The house itself has seven bedrooms—one for each of the other six should they choose to stay over, much like I have a room at Tristen's.

Soon, those rooms will be filled with our children. But I'm getting ahead of myself.

I pull up near the front door and turn off the car. Fallon looks at me and opens her mouth and then closes it again. I watch, fascinated just to look at her soft lips as they move, imagining them on every part of my body. I nearly groan but swallow it back just in time.

Control. I need to stay in control.

My little lamb is the only person who's ever tempted me to lose it.

"Something you want to say?" I ask, reaching over to tuck a piece of hair that's fallen into her face behind her ear, and she shivers at my touch.

"I..." She looks back out the window. "I want to say so many things, but I'm afraid if I do, I'll wake up and this will all be a dream... or a nightmare."

"Only one way to find out, little lamb. Open the door and step into your new life." She'll soon find out that life with me will be both, but for now, I like her off-balance like this.

She steels herself, lifting her chin and pulling her shoulders back. Tristen raised her well, and she's never been one to cower away from uncertainty. She doesn't know that I've spent an unhealthy amount of time watching her—these last two years in particular. Staring at her social media accounts for any new scrap of information. I like to think I know her better than she knows herself.

Always have, always will.

She wraps her fingers around the door handle and opens it, and when she steps out of the car, I get a flash of white under her skirt that tests the strength of my resolve to let her settle in before I fuck her against every surface of the house.

Something's buzzing and it distracts me from Fallon long enough for me to notice her phone wedged between the seat and the center console, so I grab it, entering her password on the first try.

One-one-one-one.

My birthday—November 11th.

The blackened thing in my chest, that might've once resembled a heart, thumps in the way only Fallon can make it. She's just as obsessed with me as I am with her, and a twisted grin settles on my face as I hurry to get what I need before she notices I've got her phone.

I snap a screenshot and text it to myself before wiping the evidence from her phone and sliding it into my pocket. She's made this too easy on me.

Fallon's one of those girls who keeps everything on her phone so she never forgets her upcoming projects, practices, games, responsibilities, and all the other meaningless bullshit that occupies her time. But she also tracks her cycles in a handy little app that'll make putting my baby in her a whole lot easier, now that I've got the information I need.

Before I can put my plan in place, though, I need to know what's bothering her—and whether or not blood needs to be spilled to fix it.

CHAPTER 13

FALLON

This isn't the Cole Callahan I know.

The cold, sometimes cruel, aloof man who likes to pretend I don't exist is long gone.

In his place is a stranger who wears his face. His dark, hauntingly beautiful face. And I don't know what to do or how to act around him.

As if today wasn't hard enough, now I think he might be playing with me the way a cat teases a mouse. I've wanted him for so long, I can't remember a time I really noticed anyone besides him. When he walks into a room, everyone else disappears.

I so desperately want this to be real, but I'm afraid.

What if this is some elaborate trick to show me he's not interested? That maybe if he crushes my heart so thoroughly, I'll give up my dream of the two of us ever being together?

I stop in my tracks when the reality of this hits me, and I spin back towards Cole. He's getting out of the car, but his eyes are locked on me. "You can't just kidnap me," I say. "I'm engaged. My dad made an agreement, and I have to stick to it."

Cole slams the car door closed and stalks towards me, all the warmth from the car ride gone from his expression. It's angry, almost feral in its intensity and instead of backing up a step, I lift my chin higher and brace myself. I don't know what kind of women Cole's used to, but I'm not about to cower away from him—especially since I know he won't hurt me. Not physically at least.

I have no doubt he could destroy me emotionally and turn my heart to ash if he wanted.

He steps right in front of me, so close our toes touch and his chest presses against mine. His fingers curl possessively around the back of my neck, and he pulls me even closer. Our noses are practically touching and it's like I'm falling into his navy eyes. They're so dark, they almost look black in his anger.

"Consider the engagement over. You'll wear no one's ring but mine." I know the words he says, but I'm not sure I understand them coming from his vicious lips.

I'm also trying very hard not to shiver at the possessive note in his voice and the way he's holding me. This is better than even my wildest fantasies when it comes to my crush on Cole, and now that something appears to be happening, I don't know how to act.

A little voice in the back of my mind tells me I should be angry—irate, even—that he's throwing away all the plans I've committed to for my father. That he's taking the decision out of my hands. I should fight harder, but the thing is…

I don't want to.

I only agreed to the marriage because I thought I'd never get to have Cole.

"What are you doing, Cole?"

"Something I should've done a long time ago." I shiver again as his nose brushes against mine. His breath is minty and warm against my lips as he speaks and if I tilted my chin up an inch, we'd be kissing.

The look in his eyes is… intense. The kind that steals the very breath from my lungs and makes it impossible to draw another. "You can't just tell me the engagement is off. I gave my word," I say, but the protest sounds weak even to my ears. It doesn't help that my words are a little bit breathless.

The cocky tilt of Cole's lips tells me he knows I don't really mean it, and it's then that I notice I'm trembling. It's like in the last minute my soul separated from my body and it's slowly coming back into me, and as it does, I'm becoming aware of so many overwhelming sensations.

Cole's fingers gripping the nape of my neck, holding me possessively yet gently at the same time. The way my palms have gone to his chest, pressing against the firm muscles there and how warm he feels even through the expensive fabric of his tailored button down.

The way goosebumps line every inch of my skin and how when Cole moves even closer, until there's no space at all between us, my knees go weak. And I hope he doesn't notice how my nipples are tight and probably visible through my uniform top.

All in all? This is better than all my Cole-related dreams, and I don't know how to handle it. I want to jump on him, to beg him to be my first, to own my body the way he's owned my soul since I decided he was the man for me. It's never belonged to anyone but him.

His body is made for sin and being pressed up against it is pure torture.

But I still don't know what game he's playing. Men like Cole don't just change overnight. He's rich, powerful, gorgeous, and dangerous. A combination that every woman wants, and he expects me to believe he wants *me?* After basically ignoring me for the last two years?

I don't lack confidence, but I'm also a realist. I'm an eighteen-year-old girl engaged to marry another man, and if that wasn't bad enough, my dad's his best friend.

It's with that in mind that I push against him, trying to put some space between us, but he doesn't let me. My heart is going crazy in my chest, pounding against my ribs like it's trying to break free from its cage.

"Stop fighting, Fallon. Stop. Fucking. Fighting," he growls, tightening his hold, and I do. I go completely limp and let him hold me up. I don't *want* to fight him. Even if he's just messing with me, having him this close is everything I've ever dared dream in that place in my mind where I knew no one would judge me.

"Here's how it's going to go, little lamb," Cole says, as his other hand goes around to splay across the middle of my back so he's holding me up. I'm completely lost in him, under his spell and I don't even want to break free. If this is a dream, I never want to wake up.

"You're mine in every sense of the word. No one looks at you the wrong way. No one touches you. And if Anton fucking Leven thinks he's going to marry you, he's going to learn quickly why Emerald Hills fears me and the Savage Six."

I gasp as the weight of his words sinks in, and the dark tone in his voice as he says them. But then he keeps talking.

"I'm not a patient man, yet I waited for you. I tried to do the right thing by giving you time. I went against my nature, and now another man thinks he has a claim on you. Fuck that. You'll sleep in my bed, you'll wear my ring on your finger, you'll take my last name, and you'll give me a house full of children."

My mouth falls open because I think I should probably say something, but no words come out. I'm having trouble processing what he's saying.

His words keep repeating over and over.

Sleep in his bed.

Wear his ring.

Take his name.

Have his children.

And because he's Cole…

Because he's the only man I've ever wanted…

All I can do is nod my head and give in when he kisses me.

CHAPTER 14

COLE

She tastes like temptation, ruin, and the sweetest torment as I kiss her. I think I've waited for this moment forever, and still the intensity of it is unexpected. I haven't touched a woman in years, too put off by their over eager attempts to lock me down.

And with Fallon occupying the entirety of my mind, there was never room for anyone else.

Now her body molds to mine, so pliant and warm, as she opens for me, letting me in, kissing me back with as much unrestrained desire as I'm kissing her. It's like a prelude to the way we'll fuck, how we're kissing now, and I never want it to end.

But there are so many things we need to discuss, and if I let us get carried away here in the driveway, I'll have bodies to bury when my men see parts of Fallon that belong only to me.

And that'll ruin Fallon's first night here in her new home.

So, I gather every bit of my strength and I pull away from the kiss, even as her lips follow mine, trying to keep it going. Even as my little lamb whimpers and presses closer, I take a step back and let the air clear the lusty haze between us.

"Let's get inside and then we can finish this conversation," I say, taking Fallon's hand and intertwining our fingers. I lead her into the house and give her a brief tour, but I don't really give a shit whether she knows her way around. Fallon's a smart girl, she'll figure it out in time.

Besides, I have staff to handle anything and everything she could possibly want or need. Case in point? Gordon has already brought her bags in from my car—the bags she has no idea I broke into her dorm and packed for her while she was in class today.

When we get to my bedroom, she stands, looking around with wide eyes. It's a large space that overlooks the lake, and in the center of it all is my bed. I've imagined her here so many times, stroking my cock to the image of her naked and spread out for me to devour on the cool black sheets. Having her here is everything I've been aching for, and I can't wait to make my fantasy a reality.

Tonight.

She walks over and stands at the wall of windows at the back of the room, staring out at the lake and saying nothing. I know she's trying to make sense of what's happening, that it all seems sudden to her, but this was always inevitable. Fallon just didn't know it.

I step up behind her, resting my hands on her hips and she sways back into my hold like it's the most natural thing in the world. Her head falls back onto my shoulder, and I take a second to just breathe her in before I ruin the moment.

"When I picked you up today, you were quiet. Tell me why," I demand, moving my hand off her hip and around to her bare flat stomach where I can keep her pinned against me should she get the idea to pull away. There will be no space between us, no distance. Not after waiting two fucking years for her.

And this goddamn cheerleader uniform has me hard as fuck. I keep picturing flipping up her tiny skirt and fucking her right on the sideline of a Friday night game just to show everyone she's mine.

She stiffens, breaking me out of the dirty scene playing in my head, and like I thought, tries to pull away. I don't let her.

"It was nothing, don't worry about it. I'm handling it."

I grip her chin tightly and force her to look at me so she knows how deadly serious I am about this. Her eyes widen when she sees the look on my face. "That's now how this works, little lamb. Your problems are now mine. Tell me. I'm not going to ask again."

Her wild green eyes get impossibly wider, but I know her. She's wondering whether she should test me on this. Whether she should fight back, demand to stand on her own to handle this. My little lamb is independent and strong. She doesn't think she needs my help because that's how Tristen raised her, but she's wrong.

So very wrong.

If she continues to deny me, I'll have no choice but to show her how fucking serious I am about this thing between us. In fact, I sort of hope she pushes back. Tying her to my bed and edging her until she's crying for me to end it, to give her the relief she's so desperate for, is my idea of the perfect evening.

Fallon's so innocent—she can't possibly begin to imagine all the ways I plan to acquaint myself with her body. All the ways I can bring her pleasure… and pain.

All the ways she'll crave me.

She searches my eyes, my face, for some clue as to what she should do. I raise an eyebrow, waiting for her decision, hoping she chooses correctly. While playing with her would be fun, I want her trust more. I want her to learn that I'm the only one she can depend on, the only person she truly needs in this life.

When she looks outside of herself, I want to be the only person she sees.

She looks away, back out the window to the last rays of scattered sunlight hitting the lake. "It's a few things," she starts, and I let my hand drop back to her hip while I wait her out.

She huffs and shakes her head. "You don't want to deal with my stupid high school problems, Cole."

I find myself spinning her so she has no choice but to face me and backing her up against the window, trapping her between my body and the glass. My fingers curl around her throat just tight enough to let her know who's in control here.

"What part of 'you're mine' are you not getting? If someone fucks with you, I want names. It'll be the last thing they do. I don't give a shit if it's some asshole tripping you in the hallway or fucking with your locker. High school or not, they fuck with you, they fuck with me, and they'll regret it. Now, I want names."

She blinks up at me all innocence and perfection and for a second, I can't breathe. I think my heart even stops beating. Everything just goes... quiet. Total silence while I tumble into her eyes.

I forget about pushing her on whatever happened today, and instead switch to the plan I've been working on all along. There will be time to hear about her day after.

My fingers tighten just a little around her delicate throat and she swallows hard, her sweet lips parting in a soft gasp.

"Tell me, little lamb. How did you imagine giving me your virginity? Pretty words whispered in your sweet little ear? Gentle hands and slow kisses?" I let my nose drift along the side of her face, breathing her in.

"Or would I push you up against this glass and bury myself so deeply you'd taste me on your tongue? Break the last barrier between us and have you screaming my name so loudly your throat bleeds?"

She shivers, and it's not the reaction I expect. Fallon's inexperienced. Innocent like no other I've ever met. Part of me wants to give her the soft, drawn out first time she deserves, but the darker part of me—the louder part of me—is winning this particular battle.

Her body's pressed against mine, and my dick is hard as fuck. Painfully hard. I've been waiting two long years for this moment, and now that it's here I don't want to take my time. I don't want to savor every second. I want her legs wrapped around my waist and my cock so far inside of her it hurts.

And when she whimpers and clutches my shirt in her fingers, drawing me closer, I decide that's exactly what I'm going to have.

CHAPTER 15

FALLON

I'm clinging onto Cole like he might disappear if I loosen my grip even a little. If I let him go, I might wake up from whatever dream I'm in. That's the only explanation for this—no way is it reality. I'm just not this lucky.

And if it's a dream, I need to take advantage.

I'm pressed up against the windows at the back of his bedroom. The glass is cold against my skin, the parts that aren't covered by my cheer uniform at least. Cole's running his nose along the side of my face and his hips are pinning me in place.

He's turned on, too. He's thick and long and so, so hard. I messed around with Misha some, but that was only fingers and mouths. And when it comes to Cole, there's no comparison. Misha's practically a little boy.

My mouth goes dry as my pulse skyrockets. Cole says he wants my virginity, but will I give it to him? It's promised to someone else, and if I do this, the deal is off for sure. There's no taking it back once it's gone, but I've never wanted anyone else to have it.

"Well, little lamb? Should I push up this tiny skirt, rip off your panties, and fuck you until my cum is dripping between your thighs?" I tremble as the fingers of one of his hands fall to my thigh and begin to drag up to the hem of my skirt.

I've never done anything like this, and if the things I've seen and read are to be believed, we should probably take this slow, right? That's why someone invented foreplay. Except…

I don't think I need it. I'm uncomfortably wet and every time Cole's skin touches mine, it's like electricity arcing through my veins. My pulse races and I'm practically panting. I think I might be rubbing myself on him, too, which would be embarrassing except for the way he's looking at me.

It's like he wants to devour me, and I am so here for it.

So instead of listing all the reasons why we should stop and think this through, or talk about it, or slow down, all I do is nod. One tiny nod and Cole growls and does exactly what he said he was going to.

He yanks my skirt up and rips my spankies and thong down my legs. They tangle around my knees for a moment, but he doesn't care—his fingers are already shoving inside of me. He's not gentle and I don't want him to be.

I've been waiting for this for so long, had given up hope of it ever happening, that I want to feel everything. I want to experience Cole while he's wild and savage and completely unhinged. I always imagined he had a side to him like this, but to get to see it for myself?

Pure. Fucking. Heaven.

My head falls against the glass and my eyes flutter closed while he pumps his fingers in and out of me. He's slowed down now so it's languid and unhurried, even as the fingers still wrapped around my neck tighten. It's obvious he's barely holding on, and I want that last bit of restraint to break.

To snap and see the true nightmare of Cole Callahan.

"Cole," I choke out his name and he stops fingering me. I want to cry at how depressingly empty I feel when he pulls his fingers out, but then I crack my eyes open and he's sucking one digit into his mouth, tasting me on his skin.

"You're so fucking tight, Fallon. I just might break you after all," Cole says, but he sounds like he likes that idea. He lets go of my neck and I suck in a breath of air, only to lose it a few seconds later when he starts to unbutton his shirt.

Slowly, as if he's taunting me, button by button more of him is revealed. More hard muscle, more raised scars covered in ink, more black swirling designs etched into smooth skin. He's a dark god, vengeful and full of wrath, but also so beautiful it hurts to look at him.

He's utter perfection.

He steps back, putting space between us for the first time in minutes or hours—time has lost all meaning—and I drag in a ragged breath. My head swims and whether it's from lack of oxygen or how fast my heart's beating is hard to tell.

But then my focus is lasered in on his hands going to his belt. The only sound in the room is my harsh breathing. If it weren't for the burning heat in Cole's eyes—well, that and the hard dick that was wedged between us—I'd wonder if he's even affected by me at all.

His belt buckle clinks as he undoes it, and he drags the leather out of the loops of his pants. Once it's free, he wraps it around his hand a few times and then snaps it, looking at me with a gleam in his eye I'm not sure how to interpret. He snaps the belt once, twice—and I jump at the loud crack.

"Someday, little lamb, I'm going to strap you to my bed with this and make you come until you pass out." He tosses the belt aside and then flicks open the top button of his black slacks. "But not today."

My skin is burning as I watch him strip down to nothing but a pair of tight, black boxer briefs that hide nothing. He's perfect, and while I'm confident, he's intimidating. I still don't understand why he wants me, why all the sudden he's interested when he could have anyone.

"Why—" He cuts off my question with a hard kiss as he presses his body into mine again, pinning me to the glass. I'm slippery between my thighs and every bit of my flesh tingles in anticipation. I feel like I'm buzzed on something stronger than champagne as Cole grips my thigh and hikes it up around his waist.

He rocks his hips, rubbing his cock against me and I tear my mouth from his to cry out when he hits exactly the right spot.

"I'm going to fuck you now, little lamb," he tells me, while he reaches between us and frees his massive cock from his boxers and then grips it, rubbing it across my pussy. I'm so wet he almost slips inside, but he teases me. He pulses in and out a few times, just the tip of his dick barely slipping inside of me.

"Wait," I say, needing to think this through or figure out what's happening. I don't know, this is just a lot and I need to process.

"No. I've waited long enough." His hand goes back around my throat and he groans as he slams inside of me. "Fuck," he bites out, holding still and giving me a second to adjust.

But he's inside me.

I'm fucking Cole Callahan.

"Oh, my God," I pant, and he grips my chin, forcing me to meet his dark eyes.

"From now on, I am your god," he says, and then he's pulling back and thrusting into me so hard my back slams against the glass.

I always heard your first time hurts, and it's true. It does. But it's also so good.

So, so, so good.

Because it's Cole. Because even as he's ripping me apart, he's putting me back together. I'm clawing at his back as he ruins me, desperate to get closer, to crawl inside of him, to leave my mark so I know this is real. So even if it ends, he'll remember me.

"You want to come, little lamb?" he asks, slowing his movements and turning his frantic thrusts into more of a slow grind… that rubs my clit with every roll of his hips. His dick is as deep inside of me as it can go, and it's like he knows my body better than I do, because it only takes a few seconds before his hand tightens around my throat again and my pussy clenches around him like I never want to let him go.

"That's right," he purrs as his nose touches mine and he watches me fall apart. "Your pussy is desperate for my cum, isn't it? It's trying to suck it right out of me."

His words are spoken through clenched teeth, and then he's biting me on the neck, leaving his own mark while he comes inside of me with a groan that's so sexy and obscene, it sets me off all over again.

When he's done, we're both breathing hard and I can't believe that just happened. I'm too dick drunk to worry about what we just did, and when Cole slips out of me, his cum slides down my thigh leaving a sticky mess behind.

Then it hits me and I look up at him in horror. "You didn't use protection!"

"And I never will," he says, totally unapologetic. He gets

down on his knees in front of me and stares between my legs before his fingers are there, pushing inside of me.

Pushing his cum back inside.

Shit, why is that so hot?

"I'm not on birth control," I tell him as he stands up and tucks his still glistening dick back into his boxers.

"Good," he says as he grabs my hand and pulls me towards the bed, stopping to strip off my disheveled clothes with a gentle touch so unlike what I just experienced from him. I open my mouth to protest, but then close it again. *Good?* What am I supposed to do with that? It's like he *wants* to get me pregnant. I shake my head.

He pulls back the blanket and gestures for me to crawl into his bed, and suddenly I'm so tired from today, I don't want to overthink or protest. All I want to do is climb into this bed that smells like Cole and pass the hell out. To let him take control. So, I do.

I get between the sheets and Cole follows, curling his body around mine. He pulls me against him, my back to his chest, and his hand slides up between my breasts so he can wrap a loose hand around my throat, but it's not a hard grip—just possessive.

And it's here, like this, that I fall asleep.

I just hope that when I wake up tomorrow, it hasn't all been a dream.

CHAPTER 16

COLE

When my phone buzzes for the third time in five minutes, I can't ignore it any longer. It's not like I'm sleeping, but the last thing I want to do is detach myself from Fallon and go deal with real world bullshit.

But in my business, when the phone rings you answer because it could be life or death, and the only people who have my number wouldn't call repeatedly unless shit was going down.

When I look back at Fallon, she hasn't moved. I can't help but smirk. Even now, she's full of my cum and so well fucked she passed out immediately after. We've got shit to discuss, but for tonight it can wait.

I pull my slacks on and step out into the hall, closing the door softly behind me before I look down at my phone, which has just started ringing for the fourth time.

Tristen.

Shit.

I accept the call before lifting the phone to my ear and stepping away from the bedroom door. "What's up?"

"I'm at the gate. Tell Brooks to let me in."

Normal people wouldn't stop by their friend's house at midnight, but then none of the Savage Six are normal. I don't even hesitate, texting Brooks to let him through. Tristen lives just down the road, and despite his house being as big as mine, sometimes he just needs space from his cunt of a wife.

My stomach twists knowing his daughter's currently up in my bed with her no-longer-virgin pussy full of my cum, but he's going to find out eventually. I'd rather it be once my ring's on her finger and my baby's in her belly so there's no doubt about my intentions, so I'm hoping she stays asleep and doesn't come looking for me.

I'm pouring us both a drink when he walks in, and I silently hand it off to him as he passes on his way to flop down on my couch. His hair's a mess like he's been running his hands through it.

He drains half the glass in one and then leans forward, elbows on his thighs, clasping his drink between his palms.

I don't speak, deciding instead to wait him out. It's not lost on me that my dick is still stained with blood from taking his daughter's virginity, and because I'm a sick fuck, it makes me half hard when I think about it.

Maybe there's something to this whole sneaking around thing that I like. I've always been unapologetic about the shit I do, but fucking Tristen's eighteen-year-old daughter right under his nose gets me hot.

I shift in my seat so he doesn't see my hardening cock, but then he looks up at me, really seeing me for the first time since he walked in and he smirks. "Fun night?"

I'm not wearing a shirt and Fallon left her mark all over my chest and back. Normally that shit pisses me off, but not with her.

I want to tattoo the bite marks and scratches onto my skin permanently.

"You could say that," I say, lifting my drink and taking a sip.

"Sorry for interrupting, but that little fuck Anton called me tonight making demands, and I need you to keep me from going down there and slaughtering him before burning down his entire operation."

I'm not sure that I'm the right guy for the job considering I've been contemplating how fucked we'd be if I did that myself, but the thing about being the most powerful men in Emerald Hills is that it's on us to keep Mulberry's gang bullshit from spreading into our town.

Some people think war's good for business, and maybe it is in some places, but not here. You know that saying *don't shit where you eat*? We don't want to fill the streets where we live with blood unless it's necessary, and I'm not sure Anton's worth it. He's nothing. A blip barely worth our time, and if it wasn't for us underestimating him and giving him an in to choke Tristen's business up, he wouldn't even be a consideration.

The fucker is ambitious—too ambitious—and that makes him dangerous, reckless, and unpredictable.

"Maybe we should've let him into the Society," Tristen muses, slowly spinning his glass between his fingers. "Expanded it to be the Savage Seven."

I scoff. "That piece of shit? No, we did the right thing. He's not one of us."

"Even if it costs me my daughter?"

Rage begins to burn in my veins, hotter than the alcohol, but I swallow it back. I'm not ready for Tristen to know yet that Fallon's mine and that I'll protect her with every bit of power, money, and violence I've got. "It won't."

"He's demanding a dinner with Fallon. Wednesday night."

He looks up at me with the most unsettled expression I've ever seen on his face. "Alone."

Is this Anton's next move? After the message I sent him, I figured he'd back the fuck off, but once again I was wrong. This will be the last time I underestimate that fucker.

He's got balls, I'll give him that.

"Why?" I manage to ask through the haze of homicidal rage currently sweeping over me.

Tristen shrugs. "Who knows why that little shit does what he does? You know as well as I do he has an ulterior motive for all of this, and isn't that why I agreed to this shitshow in the first place? To figure out what he's up to and how I can cut his legs out from underneath him without starting an all-out war?"

"Why haven't you filled Fallon in on your plan? She still thinks you're actually willing to sell her off to the highest bidder."

He rubs his eyes before blowing out a breath. "It has to look real. If she knows it's not, Anton isn't going to believe it either. For now, she has to stay in the dark."

"So let him have his dinner but do it on your turf. Invite him to your place, call it a family dinner." The words burn bitter like bile on my tongue as I say them. "I'll come and back you up, and if you want, I'll call in Beck and Lucas, too."

Romeo's too damn impulsive for this. If we invited him, the first time Anton said something he didn't like, he'd smash his face into the table. And Xander... well, he's too unhinged even for this. I still don't know how he convinced the church to make him a fucking *priest* of all things.

Tristen thinks it over, and while he's in his head, I see movement by the door just as Fallon, wearing nothing but my black button down over her deliciously naked body, stops in the doorway. She looks like she's just been fucked with messy hair and sleepy eyes. She's absolutely fuckable like this, and I grip the arm of the leather sofa to keep from stalking over there and taking her back to bed.

Her sleepy gaze locks on me—until she spots her dad. Then her eyes go comically wide and her panicked gaze darts back my way.

I give her a subtle shake of my head and she spins and disappears back upstairs. With the adrenaline flooding her system, at least I know she'll be awake and ready for round two once I get rid of Tristen.

"I think that'll work," he finally says, jerking me out of my Fallon fantasies. There's nothing I can do about how hard my dick is, at least not until we settle this and I can go back upstairs. "But I'll talk to Beck, and you bring Lucas."

I nod my agreement and he sets his glass down, standing and stretching. "I'll text you a time," he says, clapping me on the shoulder before heading for the door, and I stand, finishing my drink.

He turns back with a smirk. "Have a good night."

I almost choke on my bourbon. If only he knew *how* good my night's about to be, spent balls deep inside his daughter.

CHAPTER 17

COLE

This is how I'm going to start every day—with my head buried between Fallon's thighs and the taste of her on my tongue.

She's still sleeping, but when I suck on her inner thigh, marking her like she marked me, she whimpers in her sleep. I hope when she walks around school in her tiny school uniform, everyone will see that she belongs to me.

Her eyelashes flutter like she's close to waking up, so I move back to her pussy, swirling my tongue around her clit.

I know the exact moment she fully regains consciousness because she gasps, and her thighs tighten around my head. That's when I push a finger inside of her, wishing it was my cock. But last night I wasn't gentle with her, and there's a good chance she's sore this morning.

As much as I like the idea of her feeling me inside of her with every step she takes today, I don't want to hurt her. Not really.

So I suck on her clit and fuck her with my fingers until she's gripping my hair so tightly my eyes water and screaming out my name with her release. I crawl up her body and even though I'm hard as fuck and the only thing separating her pussy from me pushing inside of it are my boxers, I don't push things that far.

I'll give her a few hours to recover.

I kiss her and she throws her arms around me and kisses me back with every bit of the enthusiasm I just had eating her pussy.

"It wasn't a dream," she says, her voice still husky with sleep or maybe that's from her orgasm.

I look down at her dazed expression. The green in her eyes is mossy this morning, darker and glazed from the high of getting off. I don't think I've ever said this about a woman before, but she's so fucking cute.

I reach down and pinch her side and she squirms underneath me. "Fuck," I groan at the same time she smacks me.

"Hey!"

"Now you know you're not dreaming, little lamb." I can't help but rock my hips a couple of times, rubbing my length along her slick pussy. It'd be so easy to tug my boxers down and slip inside of her…

But it's like my words have put out whatever heat was between us only a few seconds ago, so I pull back. Fallon is an expert at overthinking shit, and she's starting to get in her head.

I move off her to give her room to breathe, but I'm not going far. She needs to learn that whatever's bothering her isn't going to get better by putting space between us. She's mine now, and I'm hers. Whatever shit needs to be handled, I'll do it. I'm not about to let her pull away because she's scared.

She's got a faraway look in her eyes, and she's pulled the sheet up to cover her perfect, fuckable body. I frown, hating that she's hiding herself from me.

"Do I need to fuck you to get you out of your head?" I ask,

completely serious. I'm already hard and I have no problems fucking her as many times as it takes for her to understand that this is happening. Neither one of us is going anywhere.

Plus, pleasure-tinged pain is a great distraction.

She scowls at me. "I'd dare you try if I didn't think you would," she says, and she's right. If she challenged me like that, she wouldn't leave this bed until next week.

I'm tempted to do it anyway, but right now I need her to talk to me. I knew once I touched her, our sexual chemistry would be off the fucking charts, but this is about more than sticking my dick in Fallon. She's *mine*. All of her, even the parts she doesn't want to share right now.

Eventually she'll learn better, but now she's going to need convincing.

"Tell me what you're thinking," I demand.

She gnaws on that soft lower lip of hers until it's bruised, and I reach up and pry it out from between her teeth with my thumb. "Tell me."

"I don't understand what changed. I was practically invisible to you, and then suddenly you show up at my school and decide that you have some sort of say in my life?" She shakes her head, her just fucked mess of hair brushing her shoulders. "Is this some sort of sick game you're playing?"

I should be offended by her question, but I'm not. Not when my little lamb doesn't really know the kind of man I am. I don't play games—that's more Romeo's style. I take whatever the fuck I want—no games needed.

In time, she'll learn.

"You're not a game to me, Fallon. Never have been. I thought you were a smart girl," I say, letting a hint of disappointment drip into my words. Her eyes narrow and her cheeks flush the most stunning shade of pink. "Your father's my best friend. Out of respect for him, I made a vow to myself I wouldn't touch you until you turned eighteen. It was fucking torture, but I wanted to do this right."

I rub my palm across the stubble on my face, choosing my next words carefully. I don't want her to think I only want her because she's been promised to another. My feelings for Fallon go so far beyond normal, healthy infatuation. I've been obsessed with her for years. It makes me a sick bastard, but I'm *her* sick bastard.

She occupies so much of my mental energy, there's room left for little else. If she runs, I will never stop hunting her.

But I'd rather she just submit.

"Then he took it upon himself to promise you to someone else," I say, spitting the words. I try to rein in my temper, but it's impossible where Fallon's concerned. "So, I'm done waiting. I don't want you because of a game or a contract or to prove I've got the biggest dick in this town—which I think you now know I do." I smirk at her.

"I want you because you were born to be mine. You were raised to stand by my side, the perfect queen to my king. The only woman who knows our world and doesn't shy away from it." I reach over and grip her chin, forcing her to hold eye contact. "You. Are. Mine. Don't question it again."

She swallows hard, searching my gaze for something before she finally nods, and I reluctantly let her go.

"When I ask you what's bothering you, I expect you to tell me. There will be no secrets between us. Do you understand?"

She looks like she wants to argue, that fire in her eyes reigniting, but in this I won't bend.

"Does that mean you're going to tell me every little thing going on in your life?" she snaps.

"The things you need to know."

She scoffs. "Fine. Then when something happens that you *need to know*, I'll tell you."

"Little lamb…" I warn.

She gives me an overly bright smile showing too many teeth, and her bravery hardens my cock. Normally someone challenging me like this would mean death, but Fallon? I want to sink inside of her and force her to give in, to break her spirit and build her back up so I'm the center of her world.

"What? You don't like that? Well, you're the one who set the terms." She slides out of bed, keeping just out my reach. That doesn't stop my gaze from dropping down her naked body, soaking in every inch. I'll need it to carry me through the day.

As much as I want to tie her to this bed and fuck her until she's got my baby in her belly, I've got plans to make for tomorrow night's dinner and she has school. If I keep her out of class, Tristen will start to question her.

Right now, Fallon needs to understand who's in control, and it's not her. I stalk around the bed and her eyes widen when she sees me coming. She backs up, but she's not fast enough and I pin her to the wall, my fingers wrapping around her slim throat.

I lean in and run my nose along the soft skin of her cheek and back towards her ear, breathing her in. "You don't want to provoke me, little lamb. Things can get much, much more difficult for you if you try to fight. There will be no secrets. No lies. And you'll tell me what happened yesterday," I murmur in her ear before nipping the sensitive lobe with my teeth.

She shivers, and I grin before pressing a kiss to her neck.

I feel it the moment she decides as her body tenses.

And when she speaks, she ignites a rage inside me like I've never known.

"Carter van Buren threatened to rape me."

Seven words that translate to death.

Fallon keeps speaking, but I don't hear any of it. Not over the plans already laying themselves out in my head on how to make this boy's suffering as brutal as possible.

He thinks he can get away with tormenting my little lamb?

He's about to meet the big, bad wolf.

CHAPTER 18

FALLON

Cole's gone silent.

That eerie kind of silence like a still lake, where you know there's so much going on under the surface and if you just threw a rock in and disturbed the glassy top, something would emerge and drag you under to a cold, watery grave.

That's what I think about when I look at Cole now.

All his heat and intensity from earlier has turned off and now he's just blank. Blank and cold, the same Cole I've known for the past two years. I wonder if it was always a mask worn to keep distance between us. If I can believe anything he's said to me this morning, I'd guess yes.

Footsteps sound in the hallway and Cole drops his hold on me, moving almost inhumanly fast to rip the sheet off the bed and wrap it around my naked body before whoever's out there walks in on us.

"No one gets to see you like this but me," he practically

growls, and I have to admit the possessiveness in his voice shoots straight between my legs.

His housekeeper—I'm assuming—who I've never seen before, clears his throat from the doorway. If he's affected at all by the state of Cole and I, he doesn't show it. In fact, he's pointedly avoiding looking in our direction.

"Breakfast is ready," he announces. "And you weren't answering your messages." He gives Cole a pointed look before spinning and walking away.

That seems to snap Cole out of his weird mood, and he settles that dark, intense gaze of his back on me. He eyes me for a second before walking over to his closet and bringing me one of his shirts to wear.

Once it's buttoned, he studies me again, but I must pass his inspection. "Come," he says, taking my hand and leading me out of the room. I'm all too aware of the fact I'm naked under his shirt. The floor's cold under my bare feet and the only heat comes from his strong hand gripping mine. My nipples are practically slicing through the soft fabric of his shirt, and my head's still spinning over the way this morning's gone.

Cole deciding that I belong to him is just plain insanity.

I follow him down the stairs and into what looks like a formal dining room. It's massive, and the table is big enough to seat a dozen people easily. There's a place setting at the far end waiting and another to the left of it.

I figure Cole wants me to sit beside him, so I move in that direction, but he clicks his tongue and shakes his head, tightening his grip on my hand. "No, you sit with me."

I laugh. "We're right next to each other."

He scowls up at me as he sits, and then tugs me into his lap. "From now on, you'll eat with me like this while we're in private. I'll feed you, and then you'll feed me." His eyes gleam at that last part, and I'm sure I'm missing something, but I have no idea what it is.

I may have been a virgin, but I'm not totally uninformed. I messed around with Misha and I have the internet. It's not exactly rocket science how sex works.

Plus, you know… last night with Cole.

But this is breakfast, and I still don't really understand what Cole wants from me. What he's doing with me. How can he go from totally cold and indifferent to saying that I'm his and I'm going to live here now? How am I going to explain any of this to my dad when I see him next?

Cole is so overpowering, it's hard to catch my breath let alone wrap my head around what's happening between us.

I'm about to start asking questions again when Cole's manservant or whatever steps out of the kitchen and drops a plate in front of Cole. One single plate. The food smells delicious, and my stomach growls, but the plate is on Cole's other side and out of my reach.

"Thank you, Gordon," Cole murmurs.

I look hopefully up at Gordon, but he's already retreating into the kitchen.

"He's not going to bring you anything else. If you want to eat this morning, you'll eat what I give you."

I hop out of his lap. "That's fine. I'll eat at school."

His dark eyes glitter. "No, you won't. Did you know, with a big enough donation you can make even the oddest requests, and they'll practically drop to their knees to accommodate you?"

I narrow my eyes and fold my arms across my chest. "What did you do?"

He leans back in the chair like it's his throne, all confidence and sexy sprawled body that I want to lick every inch of. "You'll learn that I like control in all things."

"That doesn't answer my question."

"You'll no longer be getting your meals from school. You either eat here with me—and what Gordon sends with you to school—or you don't eat."

I clench my teeth together, resisting the urge to stomp my foot. That's all I need, to act like the teenage girl I still am. Cole's so much older than me, I don't want to draw attention to our age difference and have him change his mind.

Ugh, I'm such a confused mess.

"I'll just call my dad and have him pick me up." Maybe what I need is space. Space and time to think.

Cole digs in his pocket and pulls out my phone. "With what? This?"

He wiggles it in front of my eyes and then slips it back in his pocket.

I hold out my hand. "Give me my phone."

"Sit down."

"Give me my fucking phone, Cole."

He glances up at me, that cold and impenetrable expression on his face, but underneath his eyes ignite. "Sit down or I'll make you."

"Whatever," I mutter and turn to walk away. I'll get dressed and walk to my dad's house. I bite my lip, thinking. I'll have to tell him I stayed at Waverly's last night so he doesn't question what I'm doing here instead of at school, but it'll be fine. I'll also tell him I lost my phone and need a new one.

Fuck Cole.

If he thinks he can suddenly take over my life, he's about to learn I'm not going to just sit and take it.

I make it all of three steps before his tattooed arm wraps around my waist and he drags me back.

But I don't go quietly.

I kick and scratch and seriously consider biting while he hauls me into his lap. None of it phases Cole, though. He waits me out, holding me tightly against his hard body that's turning me on even as I'm trying to resist, and I'm so mad I'm surprised I'm not bursting into flame where I sit.

I almost laugh. I bet he'd regret forcing me to sit in his lap when his ass was on fire.

When I realize it's stupid of me to try and physically overpower Cole, I decide to try a new tactic. He can't make me eat and he can't refuse me food at school. Even if the cafeteria won't serve me, Waverly will sneak me something. So I stare passively at him, giving him nothing.

He lifts his fork, spearing a piece of what looks to be asparagus that's sitting on the side of his egg white omelet. He holds it out for me, but I turn my head.

"So stubborn," he murmurs, but he only shifts his hand so he's clamping down on my thigh with his massive palm and his inked fingers slip between my legs. I hold very, very still even though the only thing I want to do is squirm.

But I don't give him the satisfaction.

Even though his dick is *definitely* hard underneath me.

He doesn't try to feed me again, and when he's done, he wipes his mouth with the fancy cloth napkin sitting beside his plate and pushes it away.

"Maybe I should have Gordon skip your lunch today, since you want to play these games with me. Eventually you'll come to see that I always win."

I scoff, but he grips my chin. "I don't want to punish you, but until you submit, I have no choice."

"That's such bullshit," I hiss, seething. "You have *every* choice."

"Not when it comes to you, I don't. Now, go get ready for

school, little lamb. Your things are in my closet, though I doubt Gordon's had a chance to unpack. Hurry, I don't want you to be late."

He releases his hold and I get up and try my best not to rush out of the room. I'm pissed off, but I don't want to give him my reactions. I'm used to being in complete control of my life, and Cole acting like I can't even make simple decisions for myself isn't going to work.

Fuck that.

For the first time, I'm starting to wonder if I'm in over my head with him. What's truly scary is maybe I never really knew Cole Callahan at all.

And the question I spend all day asking myself is whether or not I want to know him.

CHAPTER 19

FALLON

"Why are you acting like I just smuggled you a bag of drugs?" Waverly asks, as she watches me hide the blueberry muffin she just handed over under my jacket.

"Who knows if Cole has spies," I say, cringing the second the words leave my lips. I'm so hungry that I'm not on my thinking game, and I let Cole's name slip out.

She stops walking right in the middle of the hall and grabs my arm, her nails digging into my jacket to hold me in place. I slowly turn back while everyone's forced to move around us like we're rocks in the middle of a river.

"Cole? Cole Callahan? Insanely hot and scary best friend of your dad? The one you used to be totally in love with? The one who totally smashed your heart to pieces on your sixteenth birthday?" Her voice is getting louder and higher pitched with every question, and I drag her down the hall to the bathroom.

The door slams against the wall when we walk in and the girls in there all turn to face us. "Get out," I say and wait impatiently for everyone to leave. I've got a reputation as a bitch, and I'm totally okay with that if it gets people to do anything and everything I say.

Once the last person's out the door, I swing it shut and lean back against it so no one can interrupt. Waverly knows the drill and sweeps the stalls, making sure there's no one hanging out to listen in. When she's done, she moves back over and stands in front of me.

She grins and bounces on her toes. "Okay, spill. Tell me everything. When did you talk to Cole and what does he have to do with whether or not you can eat a muffin?"

My best friend starts rapid firing questions at me, and I hold up my hand to stop her.

"After practice yesterday, when I was walking to my dorm, Cole showed up and told me to go with him. At first, I thought maybe something happened to my dad, but then he took me to his house." God, was all of that just yesterday?

Waverly squeals and claps her hands. "Ohmygod, is this basically all of your dreams coming true?"

I glare at her. "How do you know about that?"

She tosses her hair over the shoulder with a glint in her eye. "Girl, you're so obvious about your crush on him. You thought you hid it from me so well. You tried to act like you were over him, but I know you better than that. The second he walks into the room, it's like he's all you see. You were practically drooling at your party."

Waverly leans against the wall, kicking her foot up and picking at her perfect manicure. "Now that we've established we're both well aware of your Cole obsession, can we get to the good part?"

I know she doesn't miss the way my face heats when I think about last night and the way Cole fucked me up against the window. I'm even a little sore today, and I want to press my thighs together with the reminder.

But my bestie, she's observant as hell and the second I do that she'll know what happened between Cole and me. I don't know if I want anyone to know. What happened between us, even with him being as infuriating as he is, feels private.

"So, you get to his house..." she prompts and gestures for me to continue.

"And he tells me I'm going to be living there with him now. That I'm *his*, whatever that means," I scoff, but inwardly my heart speeds up. It makes the feminist in me want to riot, but hearing the man I've been hung up on since I knew what a crush was claim me in that way is entirely too satisfying. I'm seriously worried for my emotional health and forget about the way my body reacts to him. There's something wrong with me and I should probably call a therapist ASAP.

"Oh, that's so hot," Waverly says, fanning herself. "Then what?" Her eyes are practically glittering.

"Then I spent the night," I say, averting my eyes. She's going to know what happened, but I don't want to get into it.

"Holy shit," she breathes. "Tell me everything."

"Nope, not happening."

She pouts and folds her arms across her chest. "Not fair."

"You know I'd normally spill it all," I say, thinking back to our detailed discussions about Misha's kissing technique. "But this feels private somehow. Let's just say it was the hottest experience of my entire life."

"Girl, you are *killing* me. I need details!"

"I've never come so hard, so fast, or so many times. He's just..." I shake my head and kill the smile that starts to form on my lips. "But then this morning he tries to tell me that I can't eat unless *he* feeds me."

She gasps. "He did not." Gotta love my friend and her appropriate level of outrage on my behalf.

I nod. "Oh, he did."

"But he can't do that. You're not locked up in his house like some prisoner."

"He drove me this morning, is picking me up tonight, and donated a ton of money to the school to get them to not serve me food unless he *commands* it." I roll my eyes.

"Who the hell does he think he is, God?" Waverly says, pushing off the wall.

"As a matter of fact he does. And in this town, he's not wrong."

She wrinkles her nose. "Narcissistic much?"

"Definitely, but… he pulls it off," I say, because I couldn't imagine Cole being anything other than what he is. A dark angel of vengeance. A fallen god. He seems untouchable, and maybe that's because he all but ignored me when I was growing up and I looked up to him. I'll never know for sure.

Waverly sighs. "He really does."

I adjust the books I'm carrying to my other arm, since the one I'm holding them with is starting to ache, taking a bite of my muffin when I switch it to my other hand. "Now you see why I needed you to sneak me breakfast. If he finds out, I don't know how he'll react, but I can promise you it won't be good." Or maybe it will. I shiver at the prospect of Cole's punishment.

"Babe, I think you skipped a few steps. Why didn't you eat breakfast this morning?"

I roll my eyes—*again*. At this rate, I'm going to strain a muscle. "I already told you. Cole said the only way I could eat is if he feeds me. Like off his plate." I take another bite of my muffin, this one huge and my next words are muffled because I'm chewing but I don't have time to use manners. "He already demanded I live with him, break off my engagement with Anton and go back on my word—"

"Which you'd never do and I'm sure you hate."

"Yep, I hate breaking that promise to my dad," I confirm. "I couldn't let him have this little piece of me this morning. It seems like all I have left that he can't totally control."

"Not with me sneaking you snacks," Waverly says, her smile lighting up her whole face. "I'll bring you whatever you want. Just say the word."

"Thanks," I say. "But there's something else we need to discuss. I'm going to need your help with a little revenge."

She rubs her hands together. "You know I'm in, but don't think I've forgotten about your engagement to Anton. You still haven't filled me in on that."

I wave my hand dismissively. "You knew I agreed to an arranged marriage, and he's who my dad picked. I thought he might've been okay, until I saw him the morning after my birthday, doing the walk of shame out of my pool house after *fucking my mother.*"

Waverly gasps again. "No!"

"Yup," I say, popping the *p*. "I'm not exactly broken up over Cole putting an end to that, but I haven't told my dad yet because I still don't really understand what Cole's even doing with me."

"What do you mean? He wants you to be his girlfriend." I don't tell her about how he said things like *wear his ring* and *have his babies*. Girlfriend doesn't seem like the right fit.

"This isn't a fairytale, Wave." My sweet best friend is totally a romantic and wants everyone to live happily ever after. I know real life doesn't work that way.

"Sure it's not," she says in a patronizing tone. Before I can say something bitchy back, she keeps going. "Talk to me about this revenge plan of yours. Who are we getting back? Misha's skanky cheating ass?" This is why I love my best friend. She's always got my back no matter what, and she's totally committed and in it with me, hardly any questions asked.

"Check our shared Cloud," I tell her, something we set up last year when Waverly's parents took away her phone and she wanted to be able to access everything from her laptop.

She pulls her phone out of the pocket of her uniform jacket and taps at the screen a few times. When she sees what's in there, her eyes widen and then her lips curl into a sadistic grin.

"Oh, hell yes. When do we drop the bomb?"

CHAPTER 20

COLE

The glass creaks ominously in my hand while I glare at the man across the room. The whiskey does nothing to improve my mood as I watch the man who falsely believes he has a right to be here.

Who thinks he has a right to Fallon.

Thoughts of my little lamb only darken my mood.

For two days, Fallon has defied me. She refuses to eat by my hand. I've let it slide to this point, thinking she'd eventually give in when she got hungry enough, but the lack of food doesn't seem to affect her at all.

It's as if she's getting food from somewhere else.

Naughty girl.

She stands on the other side of the room, speaking with her father but her eyes dart my way every few seconds. When I look away and back over at Anton, he's frowning while he watches her. His eyes drift away and lock with mine and I smirk, tilting my glass in his direction.

That only serves to piss him off, but by the end of this dinner he'll learn he doesn't have the upper hand in any of this, and he's going to walk out of here much, much angrier than he is now.

I'm looking forward to it.

I move to Tristen's side. "Mind if I borrow Fallon for a minute before dinner? I want to give her birthday gift to her since I didn't get a chance at her party."

"Go ahead, I need to catch up with Anton anyway," he says, giving me a meaningful look before slipping away and leaving me alone with his daughter—the same one I was balls deep inside just this morning.

The same one I plan to fuck again right now, right here, in his house. He doesn't need to know her birthday gift is my cock.

I can't let her sit next to Anton at dinner without my cum dripping from between her thighs, now can I?

Besides, according to the calendar I stole from her phone, Fallon's fertile body is practically begging for me to knock her up today.

"Where are we going?" Fallon whispers as I grab her hand and pull her out of the room and down the hall to the guest bathroom. I don't bother answering; she'll find out soon enough. I push her inside and shut the door behind us, the sound of the lock clicking ominous in the dark.

I flick on the light, and she blinks at the sudden brightness. Her eyes are wide and dart between me and the door, no doubt wondering what I'm up to.

"We can't be in here like this together, Cole."

"Don't worry, little lamb. This will be quick," I say, kissing her hard before backing her up to the sink and spinning her so she's facing the mirror. She watches me in the reflection, transfixed as I push her skirt up and run my hand down the curve of her ass.

"Stop. We're going to get caught," she whispers as her

cheeks flush, and her pupils dilate. Fallon can't hide how much she wants me, and I'll never deny myself when it comes to her.

"Good, then everyone will know you belong to me."

"Cole!" she whispers again, trying to spin to face me but my hands grip her hips tightly, holding her in place. I slap her on the ass twice in quick succession.

She whimpers, her fingers turning white where they're curled around the edge of the counter.

"I'm not about to let you sit through dinner next to another man without making sure he knows you're mine in every way."

Fallon stills and her eyes meet mine in the mirror. "What are you going to do?"

"Fuck you until you come so hard, you feel me still inside of you through this shitshow of a dinner. Until your pussy is full of my cum." She shivers at my words. I think she likes what's about to happen, even if she's afraid.

My little lamb has a naughty side I've watched from afar but haven't yet experienced myself. I'm looking forward to pushing her limits.

I lean forward until my lips brush her ear and whisper, "Don't let go of the counter." When her eyes flash with a challenge in the mirror, I growl out, "If your fingers leave this countertop, I'll tie your wrists behind your back with my belt."

I yank her panties to the side and run my fingers along her pussy. She's slick and hot, just how I like her. "Does the idea of getting caught make you wet? Or is it knowing you're about to be dripping with my cum?"

She whimpers but doesn't answer. "Answer me."

"Both," she whispers, but she won't meet my eyes in the mirror.

I reach down with my free hand and undo my belt, tempted to

use it on her even though she hasn't moved from the position I put her in.

"Please hurry," Fallon says as her eyes dart to the locked door.

"You want it fast and hard?" I ask, freeing myself from my slacks and rubbing my cock along her slick cunt a few times.

She pushes up onto her toes and arches her back, trying to maneuver me inside her. She still hasn't learned that she's not the one in control.

I grip my cock in my hand and slap it against her clit and she gasps. "Don't move."

Fallon has this ability to make me reckless. I'm always in control. Always. Except with her. Then I do things like fuck her in her father's guest bathroom where anyone could find out what's going on between us.

And I'm not going to stop.

I can't.

I take my time even though I know it's risky. It's not the end of the world if Tristen finds out about us, but I've got plans in place I'd rather not fuck with. For now, he needs to stay in the dark.

For a second, I think about that fucker Anton outside this door, waiting for Fallon. *My* little lamb. Thinking he has some right to her. That need to possess her almost overwhelms me and I thrust inside her hard. In the mirror, I watch as she bites her lip to keep from crying out as I fill her, denting the soft skin with her teeth.

Maybe if I can make her bite down hard enough, she'll bleed for me.

Her pussy is gripping me so tightly, I don't even want to move. The walls of her cunt clench, pulling me in, practically begging for me to unload inside of her. But then she shifts, and suddenly I *have* to move.

I'm fucking her like my life depends on it. Like I'll die if I don't make her come in the next thirty seconds. Her tits bounce, practically spilling out of her shirt and I reach up and pinch her nipple through the thin fabric before settling my fingers on her clit.

I may have only started fucking Fallon, but I can already tell when she's close to getting off, and right now, with her eyes fluttering closed, her lips parted, and her cunt trying to suck my soul out of my body, she's right on the edge.

I slow down, pushing my cock as deep inside of her as I can get it while I rub her clit just how she likes. "Cole... fuck," she chokes out, and just as she starts to come, squeezing the fuck out of my cock, someone knocks on the door.

She's not going to stop coming, so I shove my hand over her mouth to muffle the sounds of her pleasure and keep sliding in and out of her. When her pussy releases its vice grip on me, I let my hand slide off her mouth and grip her hips.

"Fallon? You okay?" Tristen calls through the door and her wide eyes meet mine in the mirror. I shrug and pick up the pace. The door's locked, and if he walks in while I've got my cock inside his daughter, shit's probably going to get bloody.

"I-I'm fine, Dad. I'll be out in a second."

"Okay, try to hurry. We're waiting on you to start dinner."

Her pussy ripples around me again, and I know with how close we came to being caught, I could easily make her come again, but we're out of time. She's perfect, her body begging for my come, and I finally let go, shooting my release so deep inside of her she'll never get rid of me.

I reluctantly pull out, tucking myself away, but when I see some of my cum slide out of her still-wet pussy, my dick twitches and I'm tempted to fuck her all over again. Instead, I drop to my knees and push it back inside of her, kiss the back of her thigh and slip her panties back in place.

She straightens from where she was bent over the sink, panting like she just went for a jog. Her cheeks are flushed and her eyes are glazed from the intense orgasm she just had. She looks absolutely stunning this way, and I want to take her home so no one else gets to see her like this.

But I have a point to prove.

I'm still kneeling, so when she turns to face me, I press a kiss to her flat stomach. For a second, I wonder if my baby's already inside of her. The thought of her carrying my child sends a possessive rush through my veins.

When I stand, her dazed eyes meet mine before she turns towards the door. Neither of us say a word, but that's one of the things I love about Fallon. She doesn't feel the need to fill the silence.

Her hand reaches for the door handle, but I stop her, snagging her fingers with mine. I reach into my pocket and slip my ring on her finger, the one that says she'll be mine by law as much as I'll own her body and soul, too. The one I had to pay a staggering amount of money for in order to have its creation rushed, so I'd have it for just this moment.

She looks up at me with those wide, green eyes. "What's this?"

"Your engagement ring."

"It's not the same one. Anton will know."

"I'm counting on it. I told you that you'll never wear another man's ring. You're *mine*, little lamb. So you'll wear my ring, and when we get married, you'll get another."

She blinks up at me. "*When* we get married? You haven't even asked me!"

I shake my head at her, disappointed. "I don't ask for what I want, and you're no exception."

"What if I don't want this?" she hisses, the flush on her cheeks no longer just from coming all over me, but now there's anger mixed in, too. My little lamb is pissed off.

I tilt my head. We don't have time for this conversation now, but I'll indulge her. "Do you not?"

"I didn't say that, but I'd like the choice."

"No, you wouldn't." I step forward so our chests press together, and she's forced to tip her head back to look me in the eye. "You want a man who's strong enough to rule in our little world. Who's happy to get his hands bloody for you. You think that kind of man is going to ask permission to have you?"

She bites her lip, considering, and then exhales. "How do you know me so well when you spent years ignoring me?"

"I may not have given you the attention you wanted, but I can promise you I didn't ignore you. Not even for a second."

She sways closer, letting her palm rest on my chest over my heart and I cover her hand with mine. "And what happens when Anton sees this ring on my finger? The one that's so clearly not his?"

I smirk. "He gets another lesson in what happens when he fucks with what's mine."

CHAPTER 21

COLE

Fallon leaves the bathroom before I do. She's got my ring on her finger, a blood red diamond set in platinum, big enough to send a message.

My life's always been marked, defined, and forged in blood. The ring she'll wear for the rest of her life and be buried in is no different. When this is all over, no doubt more blood will have been spilled, but she's worth it.

I straighten my cufflinks and button my jacket, covering the gun I have strapped to my chest underneath. Lucas will be out there and no doubt he came armed to the teeth, but I'm not taking any chances. Not where Fallon's concerned.

If Anton sees the ring and decides to start shit, I'll be ready.

By the time I get to the table, everyone's already seated. Tristen sits at the head of the table and eyes me as I walk in. He's got a masterful poker face and even I can't read him when I take my seat, sandwiched between his wife Erika on his left and Beckett on mine.

Fallon doesn't look at me once and it pisses me off.

All these people? This whole bullshit dinner? It's for nothing, because at the end of the day, Fallon's mine, and no amount of gameplay to gain the upper hand by Anton is going to change that.

This right here? It's a colossal waste of time.

Tristen gives a nod and the staff he's hired for tonight bring out the first course. Fallon's mom, Erika, sits beside me and I can't even smell my food over the choking scent of her overpowering perfume. I want to snap at her, to tell her to go take a fucking shower so I can breathe but I don't want to draw attention to myself.

Not yet.

"So, Cole," she purrs, sliding her chair closer to mine and batting her fake eyelashes up at me. She'd be beautiful if it weren't for that calculating look in her eye. I've met hundreds of men just like her—opportunistic and willing to do whatever it takes to gain power and money. For Erika, I think maintaining her youth fits in there somewhere, too.

Unfortunately for her, that's a battle she has no hope of winning no matter how many underhanded deals she cuts or how she whores out her body while she's still young enough to be able to.

If it wasn't for Tristen promising her father on his death bed that he'd take care of her for life, I'd have killed her years ago. Her father saved his family's fortune, so he owed him or some shit, and here we are.

Tris asked me not to intervene, so I don't. Doesn't mean I don't fantasize about all the ways I'd like to turn her into a corpse. He's a better man than I am.

"I haven't seen you around much lately," she pouts, leaning closer still until her plastic tits are pressing against my arm. Her fingernails dig into my thigh as she places her hand there, and my skin crawls. I smack it away and then slide my chair to the side, catching Fallon watching us out of the corner of my eye. Does my little lamb really think I'd fuck her mother? She doesn't understand the depths of my obsession with her yet, but she soon will.

"Then you're not looking very hard," I snap, lacking the patience to keep my tone civil. "I was here last week for Fallon's party."

I'll give her this—she's relentless. Erika pushes out her bottom lip into an obnoxious pout as she reaches for her wine glass. "Maybe next time you can come say hello." She lifts her glass to her hot pink lips and keeps her eyes on me as she drains the glass.

"You know what I think?" I say, leaning closer to her. Her lips start to curl up into a flirty smile at my close proximity, and I can hardly resist the instinct to recoil away from her. My dick couldn't be any more flaccid than it is right now. "You should stop trying to fuck your husband's best friend." I lower my voice so only she can hear it, though judging by Beckett's chuckle beside me, I'm not as quiet as I meant to be.

She gasps and then her entire demeanor changes to something much less sexual. Her chin lifts, her eyes narrow into slits, and she sits up straighter in her chair like she's preparing herself to fight back. I'm annoyed that she's distracting me right now and the need to spill her blood itches under my skin. I'm here for Fallon, to see what the hell Anton's up to, to gain information.

Instead, Tristen's whore of a wife is doing the same thing she does every time I see her—trying to convince me to fuck her. A disgusted shudder travels down my spine when I think of sticking my dick anywhere near Erika. Fuck only knows what she'd do to me if she managed to get her claws into me even once.

I glance across the table at Fallon. My little lamb is nothing like her conniving bitch of a mother. If she was, I'd have never touched her. She's talking with her dad, tossing her head back and laughing at something he said, and I'm completely captivated by her smile, by the sound of her happiness, by the expanse of her throat begging for my fist to be wrapped around it.

I shift in my seat, discretely adjusting myself so no one at this table recognizes my reaction to her. I can't help it—Fallon gets me hard without trying at all. If I had it my way, she'd be under this table with her plush lips wrapped around my cock right now.

A smirk plays across my face at the thought, and I let it. Anton glances in my direction and his expression darkens at the look on my face. Let him wonder what I'm imagining. That's the closest he'll ever get to seeing Fallon the way I do.

I fill my gaze with violence and the promise of his death, and I almost laugh when he sucks in a breath and breaks eye contact first. Pussy.

Once everyone's finished their first course and the dishes have been cleared, Anton gets his first real look at the ring I put on Fallon's finger. It's very obviously not the gaudy piece of shit he gave her with its cloudy, chipped diamond. He may have his foothold in the underbelly of Mulberry, but he's not a big player yet. He doesn't have the funds I do and if I get my way, he'll never be able to compete in the same league as the Savage Society.

When he really takes in the ring, his jaw clenches and his eyes dart around the table, eyeing every one of the Savage Six present—outside of Tristen—to see if any of us will give something away. I haven't made it a secret I don't like him, so he settles on me before he sneers.

Beckett elbows me and leans closer, so he's practically whispering in my ear. "Was this part of your plan? Pissing him off?"

I smirk. "It wouldn't be much fun purposefully fucking with him if it didn't piss him off, now would it?"

Beckett chuckles and shakes his head, moving out of my space. He grips his steak knife in his hand like he's about to stab someone while his most psychotic grin stretches across his face as he stares Anton down. Lucas catches my eye from across the table and raises his eyebrow. He's asking if I want him to do anything about the Fallen Angels leader, but I subtly shake my head. At this dinner, I've already made the first move putting that ring on Fallon's finger. Now it's time for his retribution.

Whatever it is, I'll be ready.

CHAPTER 22

FALLON

If Satan held a dinner party in Hell, I have no doubt it would be more fun than this.

I've been trying not to sit here staring at Cole the entire night, but I don't trust myself. So, I keep my eyes on everything but him. Remembering what we did in the guest bathroom earlier is enough to make my thighs press together and my stomach churn with both guilt and the overwhelming urge to *do it again*.

When did I become this girl? I've always been wildly independent, yet here I sit counting down the seconds until I can run off with Cole again.

I'm warm and sticky between my thighs, something he made sure of before I had to sit by Anton for this disaster of a meal. I'm learning that Cole's the jealous type, and I never thought that was something I'd like in a man, but here we are. My body is on fire for round two and the only way I can get through this thing, without anybody figuring out there's something going on between us, is to avoid all things Cole entirely.

Of course, I totally fail.

When I look up at him through the curtain of my hair I'm trying to hide behind, his eyes snag mine and hold them for a beat before the corner of his mouth tips in a sinister smirk that sends a shiver racing down my spine. God, he's so hot. His eyes are practically burning up as he shifts them down my body like he knows every single dirty thought I'm having.

I wouldn't be surprised if he did.

I tear my attention off him and try to focus on lifting my fork and putting food in my mouth. I'm not hungry, and what little appetite I might've had disappears when Anton, the man I'm supposed to marry, leans closer.

"I hope you're keeping out of trouble," he murmurs with his lips entirely too close to my ear. My fingers tremble as I wrap them around my knife and tighten my grip. Unlike Cole, Anton gives me the creeps, especially now that I know he's fucked my mom. Who knows? He might still be fucking her.

Why my dad puts up with her shit, I have no idea.

I want to lash out, stab him in the thigh and run from the room. No part of me wants to be this close to him, but until I can figure out how to handle telling my dad the truth, that there's no way I can marry Anton now, I have to play my part. My gaze flicks up to Cole again, only this time he's not focused on me.

The way he's looking at Anton... it's like he's trying to kill him with his glare.

"That's not really any of your business, is it?" I ask, turning slightly in Anton's direction and tilting my head to the side. I may want to get the hell out of here, but my dad didn't raise me to cower in the face of strong, aggressive men and I'm not about to start now.

Anton thinks he can tell me what to do? Yeah, fuck him.

Under the table, his fingers dig into my thigh where he's gripping it, and he's squeezing so tightly I'm going to bruise.

Beautiful Carnage

With how possessive I'm learning Cole is, I think he might actually murder Anton for touching me like this.

I don't even flinch when his nails break the skin and his grip tightens even more. Anton is watching me, studying my face for every tiny reaction and I refuse to give him the satisfaction of knowing he's hurt me. Even if I'm still forced to marry him, he's going to find out that I'm not about to just take his abuse lying down.

"You're going to be my wife, and until the day we walk down the aisle you'll be on your goddamn best behavior." He's whispering but his eyes are spitting fire in my direction. Where at my party he was charming and charismatic, now I see him for the monster he really is. He's let it slip out from where he keeps it hidden and now the mask he wears is obvious.

I give him an overly sweet, obnoxious sort of smile and bring my knife down to his lap, aiming the pointy end right at his dick. "Until the day I'm legally chained to you, you'll mind your own fucking business and stay out of mine."

Rage ignites in his eyes and his jaw clenches, but the plates are being cleared and the next course dropped in front of us. We're in a stare down and I refuse to break first. Fortunately, my dad clears his throat and captures Anton's attention.

"So, Anton, I heard some interesting news today..." my dad starts, and they get into a discussion about some business downtown. I immediately tune them out, exhaling slowly.

Anton releases his hold on my thigh, and I move my knife back to the table, sliding my body a couple of inches to the left, as far away from him as I can without making it obvious. I never let go of my hold on the knife.

My left hand shakes as I reach for my glass of water, forgetting about Cole's ring on my finger instead of Anton's. I still have no idea what happened to his stupid ring, and after the display he just put on, I almost want to rub it in his face that it's not his ring I wear anymore.

I hear Anton suck in a breath beside me when I lift my glass and take a sip, and I know—I just *know*—that he saw the ring again. Earlier, he got a glimpse, but he was distracted by Cole and I guess he forgot about it. This time I'm not so lucky.

"What the fuck is that?" he hisses, keeping his voice low enough that only I can hear it. "Where's my ring? What the fuck did you do with it, you stupid girl?"

One of my dad's other friends—Lucas—leans around Anton to look at me, scanning my face. He's wearing a frown and his eyes cut to Anton. I know Lucas works with Cole, and I wonder if he's sitting beside Anton on purpose. I dart my gaze across the table and if I thought Cole looked angry before, it's nothing on the homicidal expression he's got now.

I turn back to Anton. The anger is radiating off him in waves, and I'm surprised he doesn't spontaneously combust right here. He seems the type to lose his cool like that. Surprisingly, though, he reins it in. He swallows it back and I watch as the cool, calm, charming mask slips back over his face.

His eyes, though? They burn with the promise of retribution.

He turns to my father and lets a smile that appears warm cross his face. I know better.

"I thought it would be best if we got together tonight to discuss the wedding." He lifts his wine glass and takes a sip before continuing. "I was under the impression this discussion was for family only."

The subtle jab at my father's friends wasn't missed by anyone sitting at the table. Failing again in my attempt not to stare at Cole all night, I watch as he leans back in his seat with his glass hanging from between his fingers like a king sprawled out on his throne. He's enjoying pissing Anton off.

Beautiful Carnage

My dad's eyes harden. "You'll come to learn that these men are as much family as my wife and daughter are, Anton. The sooner you embrace that fact, the more cooperative and prosperous our relationship will be."

I'm surprised Anton even had the audacity to question my dad in this. Everyone in this town knows the Savage Six are closer than brothers. Confidants in everything they do, and with their hands in each other's businesses. Nothing can come between them. Nothing can break them apart.

A pit of guilt opens up in my stomach and the small amount of food I've managed to choke down churns when I think about what Cole and I are doing and how it might be the first thing to ever risk his relationship with my dad.

"Apologies," Anton says, obviously trying to salvage the situation. He takes another sip of his wine while the only sound around the room is the clinking of silverware on plates.

"Maybe you should save the business talk for after dinner," my mom chimes in, slurring some of her words. She's already clearly drunk and swaying in her chair—when she's not leaning so close to Cole she's practically sitting in his lap. I glare at her, but without making a scene there's not much more I can do.

My dad gestures to the man he hired for tonight, a silent signal to refill her empty glass. I sometimes wonder why he encourages her to act this way—why he stays with her at all—but the only thing I can think of is that he doesn't want to deal with her and getting her so hammered she passes out is the easiest way to get her out of the way.

"I don't think that's necessary," my dad says as my mom descends on her fresh glass of alcohol. He turns his attention to Anton. "Well, you called this dinner. What is it you want to discuss?"

Anton looks around at everyone sitting at the table as if he's weighing whether he wants them to be here for this. Or maybe he's savoring the moment, having the attention of three of the six most powerful men in the county all focused on him. Either way, he takes his time with what he says next.

And when he utters the words that will change everything? All hell breaks loose.

CHAPTER 23

COLE

"I'm marrying Fallon in thirty days."

I nearly choke on the words that are trying to burn their way up my throat. Words like *you'll be dead long before that happens.*

Tristen's gaze shifts over to me before he leans back in his chair, acting as if he's taking in Anton's words. There was no suggestion in them, no room for negotiation. He was making a statement, a move, a bold bid for power.

The bastard wants us to believe he's in charge.

The idea is laughable.

"We had an agreement," Tristen says, careful to keep his voice neutral though I can hear the slight tremble. He's as angry as I am, but for a different reason. Anton is a snake, and Tristen never intended to marry Fallon off to him. He needed to buy time, and now that plan has been upended.

I stare at Tristen, needing him to read my thoughts like he's done so many times before. On all things, we're usually on the same wavelength. We can spin this to be beneficial if we don't let Anton know that he's fucked up our plans.

"And I'm changing it," Anton says with a shrug. He lifts his fork and knife and cuts a piece of steak before tossing it in his mouth and chewing like he doesn't have a care in the world. Lucas meets my gaze and I know we're both wishing we'd gone ahead with the plan to fuck with Anton's food.

It might not kill him, but knowing he'd spend the night feeling like he wishes he were dead might bring me a small amount of comfort right now. Instead, we decided to wait. A small mistake, but a mistake, nonetheless.

There have been too many of those lately.

"You expect me to let you marry my teenage daughter before she's even graduated high school?" Tristen scoffs, and I know he's barely got control of his anger. The ice in his veins leaks into his eyes as he stares down our new nemesis.

It should bother me, hearing him talk about how young Fallon truly is, but it doesn't. When it comes to her, I have zero guilt. I would risk anything and everything to have her, even my friendship with Tristen or my place in the Savage Society. I hope it doesn't come to that but having her is worth giving up anything.

I built my life up once; I can do it again.

"Yes. I do." Anton is completely unapologetic. He finishes his food, wipes his mouth, and slides back from the table. "I'll give you until tomorrow to think it over. If you want the deal to proceed, you'll agree to my new terms."

"And I suppose I don't get a say?" Fallon says, and for the first time since Anton's announcement I look at her. She's furious. Her cheeks are tinted pink with her anger and her gorgeous green eyes are filled with bloodlust that hardens my cock.

Fuck, she's perfect.

Anton chuckles, this grating, sinister thing, and I bristle. I'd love nothing more than to throw myself across this table and choke the life out of him. Squeeze my fingers around his neck until the blood vessels in his eyes burst and his lips turn blue.

It would be so easy.

He ignores Fallon's question, focusing back on Tristen and his words break me out of my death fantasies. "Oh, and if you want this arrangement to continue, I'll be expecting payment for my ring, the one my *fiancée* has so clearly misplaced. I'll send you an invoice, but you should know it's not cheap like that replacement you tried to pass off that's on her finger now."

I bite my tongue so hard I taste blood so I keep my mouth shut. Anton's eyes glint as they settle on me before he turns and leaves the room. No one says a word, and the silence is oppressive. Lucas meets my eyes for a fraction of a second before he slides his chair back and follows Anton out. I know he'll make sure the prick leaves, or he'll get rid of him.

When the door closes behind Lucas, Tristen turns to me. "Want to tell me what the fuck that was about?"

So he didn't miss the way Anton looked at me with that ring comment. Shit. I quickly run through all the scenarios in my head about how to handle this next part. I'd originally planned to wait until Fallon was officially my wife, my child inside her, to tell Tristen so there'd be nothing he could do to stop me from having her.

But she's eighteen now and could already be pregnant. What can he really do? I decide there's no harm in telling him, other than the inevitable violence coming my way. I glance at Fallon and she's staring at me. We've always been drawn to each other, and now is no different. I wish I could spare her being here for this. She doesn't need to deal with the fallout of my choices.

Tristen's jaw is clenched so tightly, I'm surprised when his words come out sounding normal. "Fallon, take your mother upstairs and get her into bed, will you?"

She tears her eyes off me and moves them onto her mother, who's slumped in her seat beside me, eyes closed and breathing evenly. Fallon's nose wrinkles in disgust but she nods at her father and slides her chair back, moving to deal with her bitch of a mother.

Erika doesn't deserve someone like Fallon. To be fair, I don't either, but that's never stopped me from taking what I want before.

Once Fallon's dragged her mom out of the room, Tristen stands up and gestures for me to follow him to his study. Beckett moves at my back. His hand comes to rest on my shoulder while we walk, and there's no doubt he's taking on the role of peacekeeper for whatever's about to go down. I don't need protection from Tristen, but I appreciate the reminder that someone in the Savage Six always has my back.

Tristen moves inside and heads straight for the liquor cart, pouring three drinks. He downs his and pours another before he goes to stand by the floor-length window that overlooks the grounds.

"I want to know what the fuck that was in there," he says, not bothering to ask any questions but demanding an answer instead. It's how I'd handle it, too. If I was the sort of person who felt guilt anymore, my stomach might've been in knots having decided Fallon's the only woman I'll have.

I won't settle for anything or anyone else.

I decide to be blunt. There's no point in trying to sugarcoat shit. Tristen will see right through it. "Fallon is mine. Always has been, always will be."

Tristen stiffens, turning to glare at me while his fingers

tighten around his glass to the point his knuckles turn white. His body language screams brutality. "What the hell do you mean *yours*? She's eighteen fucking years old, Cole! And my *daughter*!"

I shrug. "Eighteen is technically legal." I don't bother addressing the daughter part. There's no good way to justify my actions, and I don't feel the need to anyway. The only reason Tristen's getting anything at all from me right now by way of an explanation is because he's my best friend and part of the Savage Society. He's one of the only people in the world I trust and respect, and I'm not about to throw that away if I can salvage it.

"Are you fucking my daughter, Cole?" he asks, his voice low and filled with the promise of pain.

Out of the corner of my eye I see Beckett shift closer to me. The guy doesn't look threatening, but he might just be the deadliest one of us all, and that's saying something.

I take a long sip of my drink, considering the right words to use. In the end, I settle for the simplest. "Yes."

"What the fuck?" Tristen explodes and he charges forward, his glass falling from his fingers and shattering on the floor as his drink's forgotten in favor of hurting me. Beckett moves like he's going to intercept Tris, but I hold up my hand, stopping him.

Tristen cocks his arm back and lets it fly right into my face. He needs this, deserves it even. I don't try to block the shot, and pain explodes from my right eye when his fist connects. But when he pulls back to hit me again, I grip his wrist tightly to hold him back. We're standing practically nose to nose and both of us are breathing hard with Beckett right beside us, ready to step in, a perfectly blank expression on his face like he's watching paint dry.

"She's *mine*, Tris. You want to keep up this bullshit fake

engagement thing with Anton, fine. But I'll be the one putting a ring on her finger. I'll be the one who gives you grandkids. And *I'll* be the one who protects her from everything and anything in this life that tries to hurt her, including what you're doing right now. You had your one shot, and you took it. Now you need to accept that this is happening. I'm not backing down."

I give him a second to let that sink in and when he starts to calm down, I let his wrist go. He steps away, running a shaky hand through his hair. His knuckles are cracked and blood stains the strands. My eye hurts like a motherfucker. It's been years since I had a black eye, but I'd gladly deal with that if it makes my best friend feel even marginally better.

He walks over and pours himself a new drink, and once he's finished it, his fingers curl around the edge of the drink cart.

His head hangs and he takes a deep breath. "Why my daughter, Cole? Why Fallon?" He spins to face me. "You could have literally anyone, and you have to fuck with my little girl?"

Beckett stays silent but watches me like he's curious about the answer to that, too.

"Do you know how long I've wanted her? You raised her to be perfect for me, for any one of us really. Our equal. There is no other woman like her. She's the most gorgeous woman I've ever seen, intelligent, clever. Strong. She's one of a kind and she's mine, whether you're good with it or not. I don't want to lose my brother, but I *won't* give her up. Not for anything, even you."

Beckett speaks up. "He has a point, Tris. No one can protect her like one of us, and you know Cole doesn't fuck around with women. If he says she's his, he means it. He's not going to let her go." His expressionless gaze slides to mine. "And he's not going to hurt her."

"I'd rather slit my wrists, and you both know I like myself too much for that."

Tristen eyes me but then the corner of his mouth tips up just enough to let me know we're going to be okay.

He grimaces and shakes out his hand. "Why the fuck is your face so goddamn hard?"

And just like that I know I haven't lost a single thing.

CHAPTER 24

COLE

T he room falls silent when Lucas steps inside.

He closes the door and leans back against it like he thinks someone's going to barge into our meeting. No one would dare—not if they wanted to keep breathing.

"He's gone, but there's something you should know," Lucas says, turning to me. "He put his hands on Fallon at dinner. Hard enough to bruise."

The rage swells up inside of me so fast, it's truly breathtaking. The fury is so massive I nearly can't contain it within my skin. "He left a mark on her?" I grit out.

"Marks, yes." A devious smile slashes across his face. "But she held her own. She threatened his dick with her steak knife if he didn't let go."

A trickle of pride works its way through the rage, and it's just enough to allow me to think more clearly. Nothing good has ever come from reacting in a moment of anger. The best vengeance comes from planning, plotting, and control. That's how you make it hurt the most.

"And what are you going to do about this, Cole?" Tristen turns his icy gaze on me. "You want to be the one to protect Fallon, so here's your chance. That piece of shit thinks he can order us around and come in here making demands. And *then* he has the audacity to put his hands on my daughter under my roof." His eyes glimmer with malice. "So let's hear your plan."

I drain my glass and set it on his desk, leaning back against the polished wood. "First, you're not paying him a cent for the fucking ring. He already has it back."

"What? How?" Tristen asks, but I ignore his question for now. We have more important matters to discuss than the way I gave Anton back his piece of shit ring.

Beckett rubs his hand over his jaw staring off into the distance. "You know, I should've thought about this before, but where did he get the money for that massive rock he put on Fallon's finger anyway? He's still too small to swing something like that."

"Someone's obviously bankrolling him," Lucas says.

Tristen hums in agreement and all their eyes turn to me. Technically, we're all equals but, in a room filled with powerful men, someone has to take charge and in the Savage Six, that man is usually me.

"Dig into that," I tell Lucas. "I want to know where he's getting his money."

"I'll meet up with Rome and we'll handle it," he says.

"How are we going to get around his ultimatum? I still need more time to get dirt on the Sheriff to get him back on my side, not to mention that fucker that manages the rail yard. Money's obviously not enough if Anton was able to flip him. I think the operation down there is going to need an entire system flush."

In Tristan speak, that means taking them out and replacing

them with men who are truly loyal to the Savage Society, who know if they flip on us it'll be the last thing they do.

"We hit him where it hurts the most," Beckett says with a grin the devil himself would be proud of, showing the first hint of true emotion all night. "His pride and his pockets."

"What do you have in mind?" I ask. I've got a few ideas, but they all tip toward the bloody, and I'm not sure that's in the best interest of the Savage Society, even if personally I think Anton's already been breathing too long.

Besides, sometimes it's fun to play with your prey before you slaughter them.

"You realize we're skipping over the easiest way to deal with Anton," Lucas says, pulling a knife out of somewhere and scraping it under his nails. "We could just kill him."

Tristen's shaking his head before Lucas even finishes his sentence, but Beckett looks like he's on board. "Not yet. I need to know if he's working alone. How a small-time gang nobody got it in his head that he deserves to be one of us. He doesn't strike me as smart enough to come up with that shit on his own."

"Fine," I agree. "But when the time comes, I'm the one that gets to end him."

They murmur their agreements, and I turn to Beckett. "Tell me your idea."

He grins again, setting his glass down to rub his hands together. He's incredibly enthusiastic about making people hurt. It's like his purpose in life is to inflict as much pain as possible in the most creative ways he can, and it's a gift being able to watch him work. Imagine watching Monet paint, but if his canvas was torture and his medium was blood.

"We start slow, hurt him enough to let him know we can. Then we see what he does. Does he come back and try to hit harder?" His eyes glint manically at the prospect of a full-fledged war. "Or does he back down? Does he get desperate and start to reveal things to us he wouldn't otherwise? Does he get sloppy?"

I look around the room at Tristen and Lucas, wishing Xander and Romeo were here to weigh in, too. They all look to me, but I value their opinions, even if I don't always listen.

"How do you propose we start? Go down to Mulberry and pick off a few of the Fallen Angels?" I ask.

Lucas chuckles. "Leave it to you to immediately go for the bloodier option."

I scowl at him, but really, he's not wrong. Threats are no longer an issue when they cease to exist. "You're one to talk. Your hands might be bloodier than mine."

He smirks and bows his head once in deference. We both know our souls are stained blood-red and will never wash clean. There's no saving us, not that we'd ever want to be saved. I almost laugh, thinking about Xander trying to save people's souls. He's more likely to convince them to sell them to him and burn in hell for eternity than save anyone.

"We cut him off. We wash out the railyard, steal a shipment or two, and get Rome to freeze him out of his accounts for a few days. Let's see what happens when he can't pay his debts or his men. Let's find out how loyal his Fallen Angels really are." Beckett's practically glowing at the prospect of mayhem to come.

Tristen laughs. "I like it."

I nod at Beck. "Talk to Rome. Get him on it."

Most people view Romeo as the brawn of the Savage Six. Brainless but scary as hell in the fighting rings he runs. What they don't know is he's a computer genius, and there's nothing he can't hack his way into. It's one of the many secrets we hold close to keep an edge.

"On it," Beckett says, pulling his phone out of his pocket and starting to tap at the screen.

Tristen moves to the leather couches, holding a fresh drink in his hand, and sits, gesturing for the three of us to join him. "Now which one of you is going to tell me what happened with Anton and his ring?"

CHAPTER 25

FALLON

"Is your goal to keep me so drunk on you I forget the rest of the world exists?" I ask Cole after I catch my breath. I'm currently sprawled out on top of him, and his dick is still hard inside of me despite having just come. My words are slurred, and I really do sound drunk. My body is so relaxed as his fingers trail up and down my spine, I'm on the verge of passing out.

When he chuckles at my question, his chest vibrates underneath me. "Not drunk, per se, but I'm absolutely trying to get you addicted to me and my cock. I'm going to spend so much time inside of you, you'll crave me when I'm not there. When we're apart for even a few hours, you'll seek me out like an addict looking for their next fix. I'm going to fall asleep with my dick inside of you every night, and you'll become as obsessed with me as I am with you."

I think a normal girl would be horrified by Cole's words but I'm not normal. In the world we belong to, the one I was raised in, having a man be so possessive over you is a good thing. It means he won't be out fucking everything that moves while you're stuck home, trapped behind barbed wire-topped concrete walls and lines of bodyguards.

Basically, I'm totally eating up every word and loving it. Little does Cole know I'm already there, consumed by him for most of my life. I shiver from the intensity behind his words, the ones made here in the dark of his bedroom. Or *our* bedroom, I guess.

This is our own little bubble where we can exist however we want without interference from anyone or anything. At least that's how I want it to be, but even as relaxed as I am, I can't help it when reality starts to trickle into my thoughts.

I lift my head and rest my chin on his chest so I can look up into those unreadable dark eyes of his, the ones that masquerade as blue but are really more like navy fading into black. "I've been obsessed with you since before I was sixteen, Cole."

"Maybe, but you haven't been addicted. You haven't needed me or craved me. Not yet, but you will. For the rest of your life, you will."

I hope he's right, but I don't say it. This feels heavy, and after a night where I had to face Anton, my drunk mother, and try to navigate an intense dinner without letting my dad in on the fact I'm sleeping with his best friend, I'm out of energy for heavy stuff.

Unfortunately, my brain hasn't gotten the memo, and since Friday's the day after tomorrow, I'm running out of time to bring up Carter's party invite to Cole. Just another thing to add to the list of crap heaped onto my plate.

I tense up and I know Cole feels it because his eyes narrow and his hand that was lazily stroking my skin is now holding me against his body like he thinks I'm getting ready to run. "What were you just thinking about? Tell me," he demands as his eyes narrow even further. Maybe he thinks if he glares hard enough, my brain will crack open and spill all my secrets out for him to collect.

But like I said... no energy to fight. Earlier, I tried to get Cole to tell me what happened with my dad and the other guys after Anton left and instead of answers, he distracted me with orgasms and now here we are. I haven't forgotten, but I also trust him enough to put off my curiosity until tomorrow.

I sigh, long and drawn out, while I gather my thoughts, turning my head back so my cheek rests on his chest. I have to be careful, because Cole already wants to kill Carter, and I don't think that's just something he says. I think he *literally* wants to kill him. "Friday's the day after tomorrow."

His eyebrows furrow and he nods slowly. "Okay..."

"I need you to let me go to the party after the football game with Carter." I hate having to ask for him to *let* me do anything, but I know how his world works, even as the words burn like acid on my tongue.

"No." His voice is cold, emotionless. A very *don't fuck with me* tone. What I'd imagine he uses when he's leading the Savage Society, but I don't know for sure. I really don't know exactly what Cole does, other than if he's involved with my dad, it's not legal and there's a good chance if I find out what it is there really will be no walking away.

"Don't you think I deserve to see his face as I get my revenge?" I ask, shifting so I'm sitting up, straddling him and looking down at his dangerously beautiful face.

His eyes soften just a fraction, enough for me to get a glimpse of the emotion inside. He's not unfeeling at all. It's actually the opposite. His eyes are *burning*, but then he blinks and it's gone. "I understand your need to see him suffer, but trust that I will handle it so you don't have to. The darkness of my world doesn't need to taint your soul, Fallon. Not when you have me."

"And what about your soul?"

The corner of his mouth tips up into a smirk. "I'd gladly rip out what's left of it and set it on fire if it meant saving you."

I laugh. "So now you're my hero?"

"Oh, no, baby. I am very much a villain, and I've got big plans for Carter Van Buren, and nothing about them is heroic."

"Please, Cole. I need to do this. Please." I lean forward so my hair's a curtain around us and my nose brushes against his. His hands go to my hips and he pushes his dick further inside of me. We both groan and I know our conversation is quickly coming to an end.

I know I'm being careless with him, but ever since Cole pushed me up against his bedroom window and fucked me for the first time, I can't get enough of him. He wants me addicted? Well, I'm pretty sure I'm already there.

When we're like this nothing else seems to matter. Not potential consequences or what the outside world might think of what we're doing. There's only us, and I've never wanted anyone like I want Cole.

"You can go for one hour, and Lucas will be your shadow," he finally relents, and when I open my mouth to argue, he cuts me off by wrapping his hand around the back of my neck and pulling me down to his mouth. He pushes his tongue between my lips and any argument I might've made evaporates.

He flips us so my back is pressed into the mattress and then he fucks me hard, as if he's reminding me exactly who's in control, but I haven't forgotten. And as independent as I always thought I was, there's something about Cole that makes me happy to let him call the shots. To submit. He seems untouchable, immortal, a god above men.

And maybe that's the scariest part of all of this, how easily Cole can make me forget who I am.

CHAPTER 26

COLE

I glare at Lucas over my desk at The Lodge. "The discussion is over."

He huffs out a laugh. "You know I'm not your little bitch, right? Why can't you do this shit yourself?"

I brush non-existent lint off the arm of my suit jacket, a nervous tic that Lucas doesn't miss. His eyes follow my every movement like the predator he is. Unfortunately for him, we're both at the top of the food chain so he only watches, like a lion flicking his tail in agitation but not moving from his spot in the shade.

He knows if he tried to strike out at me, I'd destroy him.

"I can't risk tying what Fallon's going to do tonight back to her, not with what I plan to do to the kid after she's finished with him. If anyone were to see me at this party and then see me later with her, it might become glaringly obvious what happened to him. I can't have that." I curl my fingers around the handle of the knife in the pocket of my slacks. "Nothing will touch her."

He sighs and lowers himself into one of the chairs in front of my desk, tapping his fingers on the arm. "Fine, but you owe me."

"Done." For any of the Savage Six, it's easy to hand out favors. I'd do anything for the five of them anyway, so whatever Lucas may want in the future I'm sure I'll have no issue doing.

"Why are you taking a hands-on approach with this kid, anyway? This seems way off your usual type of job. We can have one of the lower—"

"No," I snap, pushing out of my chair and standing up. I start to pace back and forth in front of the windows, unable to sit still. Not when I have so much rage coursing through my veins at the memory of Fallon's soft voice admitting what Carter Van Buren threatened to do to her.

"You'll follow Fallon and make sure she stays safe, and then take him and bring him back here. Leave him for me."

Lucas scowls. "I heard you the first time."

"Then why are you questioning me like you didn't understand what I wanted?"

"What I don't understand is *why* you're even bothering in the first place? We have bigger shit to deal with, like Anton for one."

Fuck, if I thought Tristen could get away with taking the kid, I'd have asked him instead of Lucas. Then I wouldn't be having to utter the words that make me homicidal because Tristen wouldn't question my need to protect Fallon. He'd be right there beside me, on the same page and wanting to make the kid pay.

But he's not stealthy or discreet. And everyone that goes to Emerald Hills Prep with Fallon knows who her father is. So, Lucas it is, but I still resent having to answer to him in any capacity.

"Because he threatened to rape Fallon." I say the words through clenched teeth and squeeze my fingers into fists so tightly, my nails break the skin of my palms. I barely feel the sting.

Lucas lets out a low whistle. "Well, fuck. That changes things." He stands up. "Consider it done, and we're square. You don't owe me shit. I'm happy to take out the trash."

I stop pacing and spin to face him. "His trip to The Icebox can be painful, but I want him alive. The only one disposing of him will be me. Understand?"

He nods, and when our eyes meet, I know we understand each other.

"Any word from Rome on Anton's finances?" I ask, happy to change the subject. While Anton pisses me off, he's so far beneath my level it's almost not worth my time to handle him myself. If it weren't for Fallon, he wouldn't even be on my radar. But when he attempts to take what's mine, I'm left with no choice.

"He's got Leven locked out of his accounts, and he dug around in his computer and cell and figured out when he's picking up his next shipment of guns. Tris is sending some of his guys to intercept, but I thought maybe you'd want to send some of ours as backups. Maybe pick off a couple of Anton's guys to send a message?"

I have to hand it to Lucas, he's as ruthless and bloodthirsty as I am, and it's one of the things I appreciate most about him. That and his attention to detail. I wouldn't trust anyone else to run Red Rum, the club I handle my contracts out of.

"Do it," I say, checking my watch before glancing back over at him. "Anything else?" I'm already standing, on my way out the door. Fallon will be out of school soon, and if Lucas has anything else to bring up, he can do it while we walk to my car. I won't allow her to wait even a second wondering where I am.

Punctuality is only one small tool in getting my little lamb to trust that I'll always be there for her no matter what.

"Everything else can wait. You still coming into Red Rum this weekend?"

"Saturday, if all goes according to plan tonight."

"I've got some new contracts we need to discuss," he says, which is normal business for us. When we formed the Savage Society, I stepped back from doing so much hands on wet work, but I still like to be kept apprised of everything going on. All it takes is one tiny mistake and everything could come crumbling down around me, and I'm not about to let that happen.

"Fine," I say as I step outside. He stays by the door, but I know his eyes are still on me, watching my back, watching everything. Lucas keeps the threats away from all of us, the ones even we don't always see in time. He misses nothing.

"You bringing Fallon with you?" he calls out and I hesitate but then I pull open the car door and slide behind the wheel without answering. I still haven't decided how much of my business to bring her in on. How much I want to tarnish her innocence with what I do, the things I enjoy. I'll never stop, so do I hide this part of me from her for her protection, or do I bring her in and let her be the queen she was always meant to be?

After tonight, what she's about to do, I'm going to make a decision that'll alter the course of both of our lives.

CHAPTER 27

FALLON

It's weird being back in my childhood bedroom. I never thought this place wouldn't feel like home, but somehow in the span of about a week, Cole's made himself my home. The center of my universe.

I don't know if I should be freaked out or not at how quickly he's totally turned my world upside down, but this is exactly what I've spent years wishing for.

Now that I've got it, it's almost like I'm struggling to completely give in and let go, let Cole sweep me away in his brand of over-the-top possessiveness, because I'm waiting for the bottom to fall out from under me. Maybe he'll say this was all a joke or a misunderstanding.

Or maybe someone will come along and be a better fit for him and take him away. Trying to figure out all the ways my relationship with Cole could go wrong isn't making me feel any better, so I grab my phone and text Waverly to see if she'll come over and help me get ready.

In only a few minutes, she's crashing into my room breathlessly, eyes bright as she throws her arms around me in a crushing hug. "I feel like I haven't seen you all week."

I laugh and hug her back. "I saw you at school today. We have four classes together."

She lets go and goes over to my bed, flopping down. "You know what I mean."

I sit cross-legged beside her and tuck a strand of hair behind my ear. "I know. Cole's sort of… a force. He's totally consuming all of my energy and attention. I barely got any work done this week at all."

Waverly sits up and gasps, her eyes going wide. "Oh, no! The perfect Fallon Ashwell missed a couple of assignments?" She scoffs. "You know you're already weeks ahead in the coursework, so it doesn't even matter."

My bestie knows me so well.

"Yes, but I don't want to lose momentum. What if something comes up and I need that head start I've been building all year? Prom committee was supposed to meet this week, and I totally forgot." I slump back against the headboard and let my head fall back.

All the responsibility I've taken on at school was never something I wanted, but when teachers or classmates would suggest I'd be good at something or ask for help, I couldn't say no. Besides, keeping myself busy helped distract me from thoughts of Cole and how he'd never be mine. Busy is better than depressed.

But now I'm regretting all my choices because I'm falling behind and the stress is piling up when all I really want to do is get lost in Cole. I've waited for this moment for what feels like forever, and I want to enjoy it without any other distractions.

Beautiful Carnage

I know it's not reality, but sometimes what we want isn't logical.

"Stop being so hard on yourself. Now," she says, leaning forward and looking at me with barely contained excitement glimmering in her eyes. "Tell me everything."

I may not have confessed how deep my crush on Cole ran all these years, but Waverly's not blind. And there were a few times where I confided in her how comparing high school boys to my dad's best friend was like ordering the knockoff version of couture. There really *was* no comparison.

So I let everything out. I tell her about Anton and the arrangement I agreed to, how I caught him leaving after spending the night fucking my mother, and how Cole's declared I'm his with an intensity that steals my breath even as I'm telling her about it.

"Wait. Hold on," she says, slapping her hand against the mattress. "You're *engaged* to Cole? *And* Anton?" Waverly's voice gets higher and higher pitched with each word until the last one is squeaked out.

"I don't know," I say, looking down at the blood red diamond on my finger. The one Cole put there and ordered me never to take off, not that I'd want to. It's stunning and something about wearing it makes me feel closer to him. Like when he says I'm his he means it enough to want the whole world to know.

"Do you *want* to be engaged? And, you know, have Cole's babies?" That last part she whispers while her eyes dart around the room.

I turn and fall onto my back, letting my arm drape across my eyes. "Do I want to marry Cole? You know how girls always have the fantasy about their dream wedding?"

She lays down beside me and rests her head on my shoulder so I feel her nod.

"Well I never cared about the wedding. What dress I'd wear or where it'd be or what flavor cake I'd have."

"Chocolate, obviously," she scoffs.

I grin because she knows me so well. "Obviously," I agree. "Do you want to know what I always pictured?"

"Tell me."

"Cole. Staring at me with those dark eyes of his, promising to love me forever. Nothing else mattered, but that was the one thing that I always came back to. The possibility that it could really happen? That he actually wants me—*me*—seems so surreal. It's scary to let myself believe it might be real."

"I saw the way he watched you at your party when he didn't think anyone would notice, and that man is completely head over heels. He was totally banging you with his eyes. Insecurity isn't cute, Fal, and if he says he wants you, maybe try believing him. What's the worst thing that could happen?"

I gnaw on my lower lip while I consider her question. "I let myself fall and he says *haha, just kidding* and walks away. I've wanted him for *so long*. I don't think I'll get over it if he breaks my heart. And oh, god, what will my dad say when he finds out? I gave him my word I'd marry Anton. He's going to think I'm a liar."

My stomach twists violently. My dad and I have always been super close, so the idea that this thing with Cole might make him look at me differently is really upsetting. I wonder if there's any way this ends with both Cole and my dad in my life.

"Cole's not going to let you go, babe. The man is obsessed. He didn't touch you until you turned eighteen. He waited, and there's even more at risk for him than there is for you. If things go sideways and your dad finds out he hurt you, he'll kill him."

I groan. "That can't happen. However things turn out between Cole and me, my dad can't lose him."

I feel Waverly shift on the bed beside me and I pull my arm away from my eyes enough to look up at her. Her body has stiffened and she's glaring in the direction of the door so I sit up to see what's got her looking so tense, and I almost wish I hadn't.

"Did you need something, Mom?" I ask, my back molars grinding together to keep myself from telling her to fuck off. The last thing I want right now is to deal with her petty shit and dramatics. She's worse than those daytime talk shows with the drama she brings to everything.

She sashays into the room like she expects all the attention to be on her, something she's no doubt practiced over the years and perfected. Unfortunately for her, it's just Waverly and me here and neither of us wants anything to do with her. But at this point I don't think she can turn it off.

My best friend hates my mother with the fire of ten thousand suns.

"I heard voices in here and thought I'd pop in and see what you girls are up to. Big plans tonight?" She lets her fingers run along the fabric of the dresses I have laid out at the end of my bed.

"We're getting ready for a party, Mrs. Ashwell," Waverly says, glancing down at me to make sure I'm not upset with her for sharing. I like my mom knowing anything about my life about as much as I imagine I'd enjoy getting stabbed in the eyeball with a pinecone, but whatever. There's not a lot she can do with this info.

"And did I hear Cole Callahan's name? Is he throwing a party?" Her assessing green gaze, so much like mine, unfortunately, studies us.

"It's not his party," I say, making sure to keep my voice flat. I don't want her knowing anything about Cole. When it comes to rich, powerful men, my mom's like a museum trying to acquire every single one for her collection. I wrinkle my nose when I think about her getting anywhere near Cole.

"Pity," Mom says, sticking her bottom lip out in an exaggerated pout. Then her gaze goes far off and wistful. "His last party was so... *satisfying*."

I sit fully up, my stomach writhing while a cold sweat breaks out across my body. She's not saying what I think she is... is she?

"Did you fuck Cole, Mom?" I ask, proud of the fact my voice doesn't shake at all.

Waverly gasps quietly beside me, probably at my audacity, but I *have* to know. If Cole slept with my mom, I can't be with him. Just the thought it might've happened makes me want to jump in a scalding shower and scrub my skin until it bleeds.

Erika laughs. Fuck calling her mom. I've tried to keep the peace by using her title, but if she ruins what I have with Cole, she can fucking forget it. "You think he keeps coming around for dinners because he likes your father so much?" She laughs harder. "Oh, honey."

When she gets herself together, she looks at me with pity and I hate her. I've hated her for a long time for how she's treated Dad, but in this moment? I've never hated anyone more than this woman—this stranger—who somehow shares my eyes and my DNA but is an actual monster who drags herself around in a human skin costume.

"Get out."

Her smile widens. "Is that how you speak to your mother?"

"Get. The fuck. Out," I yell, no longer able to maintain my calm façade. I'm shaking and Waverly grabs my hand to try to ground me. I squeeze her like if I let go, I'll explode because I think I just might.

"Fine, I'm going. If you see Cole at the party, tell him I'll see him at Red Rum later," she tosses over her shoulder as she saunters her way out of my room. When the door closes behind her, I launch myself off the bed and barely make it to the bathroom in time to empty my stomach of everything I've eaten today.

    She can't be telling the truth… can she?

CHAPTER 28

FALLON

After I've thoroughly brushed my teeth and rinsed my mouth out, I take a few deep breaths and try to calm down. As much as I'm freaking out over what Erika implied, I don't have time to sit in a corner and cry over it right now. Tonight's about dealing with Carter's threat.

I can't let it stand, and I need to make a statement.

A very public statement.

"You sure you're up for this tonight? We can skip and curse Cole over pints of ice cream while swiping through a dating app to try and find you someone new."

I love my best friend, but she doesn't get it. The all-consuming force that is Cole Callahan. There's no walking away from him, not intact anyway. Like he's sewn himself into the very fabric of my soul, I'll have to rip him out and risk losing chunks of myself in the process. That's not something I want to deal with tonight.

I don't even bother bringing up how we've been fucking

nonstop without protection and it's a very real possibility I could be pregnant with his baby right now. God, I'm fucking stupid.

I grab my phone and before I can second guess myself, I dial my dad's friend Romeo. He's closer to my age than my dad and Cole, and I know he's basically a genius with computers and tech. I need to push my doubts about Cole out of my head and deal with the situation with Carter. Hopefully Romeo will be willing to help me.

"'Sup, Baby Ashwell?"

"Hey, Rome. I was hoping you weren't too busy to do me a favor."

It sounds like he's moving for a second and then the background gets quiet. "For you? Anything," he says, and I can hear the smile in his voice. Romeo Hudson is the kind of guy who knows he's hot and has no problem flirting—and sleeping with—anything that moves.

"I'll owe you," I promise.

He scoffs. "Stop. It's fine. What do you need? Name it, it's yours."

I take a deep breath and blow it out. "I need you to build me a website, something that's not traceable. No one can know it's mine or where the posts come from."

Romeo chuckles. "Getting up to no good? I love it. Count me in."

"Just like that?"

"You want me to interrogate you about it?"

"Not really."

"That's what I thought. Now give me the details of what you need, and I'll hook you up." Keys are already clacking the background as I explain what I want to do.

When I'm done, he says, "Give me an hour and I'll send over

the login info and how to access it so you're protected." Then he hangs up, already lost in the job.

Now that things are in motion, my nerves settle. I'm focused, and Waverly looks at me in the mirror where she's doing her makeup.

"You know... since you have the website, maybe you should use it more than just tonight," she says, spinning on the vanity stool to face me.

"What are you thinking?" I ask, shimmying out of my jeans and chucking my t-shirt while I walk into my closet to grab a strapless bra. Normally, I wouldn't bother with the dress I'm wearing but the more layers between Carter and me, the better.

"This plan of yours with Carter is good, but it's just a start. Half the douchebags on the football team are just as bad as he is, and then there's Misha and Eden. You've got the video and you've been wondering what to do with it. Maybe this is the place to deal with all the assholes in your life."

The wheels start turning, and I hurry over and pick up my phone, firing off a text to Romeo.

Fallon: Can you dig into someone's medical history while you're at it?
Romeo: I like this new side of you, troublemaker.
Fallon: It's not making trouble if they started it.
Romeo: So revenge. Even better. Name?
Fallon: Eden Matthews.
Romeo: Consider it done.
Fallon: Thanks, I owe you.

I toss my phone back on the bed and grin at Waverly. "I asked Romeo to dig into Eden. Let's see what skeletons she's got in her closet that I can expose."

Waverly claps her hands. "I love it. What about Misha?"

I raise my eyebrow. "Don't you remember the video?"

She shakes her head.

I lean over and grab my phone, picking up my dress at the same time. I grin at the thought Mischa is so terrible in bed, Waverly actually forgot watching him bone Eden. It takes me a second to pull up the video and when I do, I quickly hand it off. If I never see that shit again, I'll still have seen it too many times.

While she watches, she looks more and more grossed out. "Imagine how I felt seeing that shit in person," I say, shuddering as I pull my dress over my hips. "He's got a small dick and no idea what to do with it. The video makes that more than obvious. There won't be a single girl at EHP who'll let him stick it inside her after they see that shit."

"Zip me up?" I turn my back and wait while Waverly tugs up the zipper.

When I spin, she's not looking at my phone but she's grinning at me instead.

"What?" I ask but she says nothing, instead lifting my phone and snapping a picture. She taps on the screen a few times before I can get it out of her hands.

"What did you do?" I ask, clicking into my messages to see who she sent it to and groan. "You didn't."

"Oh, I did. He needs to see what he's got to lose."

My stomach practically falls through the floor thinking about Cole and my mom. Gross. I should just ask him. It's what someone more mature than I clearly am would do, but I can't bring myself to do it. I know if he hasn't slept with Erika, I'll feel a thousand times better. But the possibility he has is too much for me to deal with right now.

All I want to do is pretend everything is fine until the end of the night. Then I can put the whole Carter threatening to rape me thing in the rearview and deal with Cole.

My phone buzzes in my hand and I look down at the screen.

Cole: My little lamb in wolf's clothing.
Cole: You look beautiful.
Fallon: Thank you.
Cole: Just a reminder you have one hour.
Cole: One. Hour.
Fallon: I haven't forgotten [eyeroll emoji]
Cole: If anyone touches you, they die.
Cole: Don't test me x

What is wrong with me that his words turn me on? His possessiveness is next level, and something I never thought I'd want in a boyfriend, but with Cole, it makes me feel safe and wanted. Invincible.

Light tapping on the door makes me jump, and I spin to find my dad standing in the doorway with a grin on his face. He's always loved trying to freak me out at every opportunity, and he's mastered the art of silently opening doors. When I was little, he'd hide around corners and jump out at me.

"Gotcha," he says, and then his gaze darts over to Waverly. Something flickers in his eyes, but I don't get a chance to analyze it before his attention's back on me. "What are you girls up to tonight?"

"There's a party at Isaac Masterson's house. We're going to stop in for a bit." I've never hidden anything from my dad. That's part of what makes this whole Cole thing difficult. Normally my dad would be the first person I'd run to and blab about my new boyfriend.

"Text me if you need a ride home," he says and then with one last glance at Waverly, he bails.

I spin and face her. "Why was my dad looking at you like that?"

Her eyes widen. "Like what?"

"You didn't notice?"

"No, should I have? I wasn't really paying attention."

Maybe I'm overreacting and that was really nothing. "Nevermind. Are you almost ready?"

I check the time before stuffing my phone in a clutch I grab out of my closet and slipping into a pair of black Louboutin's that complete my look. Skintight blood red dress? Check. Lips to match? Check. Sky high red bottoms? Double check.

One thing's for sure: Carter Van Buren fucked with the wrong girl.

CHAPTER 29

FALLON

"There you are," Carter growls into my ear like a fucking animal. His arm snakes around my waist and his fingers dig into my hip. The two red cups I'm clutching in my hands jostle and beer sloshes over the sides.

I grit my teeth and grin up at him like I'm happy to see him when all I want to do is rip his balls off for touching me. If Cole finds out he's laid a finger on me, I have a feeling that threat he made by text earlier wasn't something to take lightly. I just can't seem to find the will to care whether he hurts Carter or not. After I show Carter he can't get away with the way he treats women—especially me—I don't care what happens to him.

"I was just doing a lap and grabbing us drinks," I shout over the music and Carter snatches one of the drinks out of my hand and guzzles it down like I'm supposed to be impressed. When he's done, he crushes the cup in his meaty fist and burps loudly before snatching the other cup and downing it, too.

I wrinkle my nose and when he sees, he blows his disgusting

belch in my face. "C'mon, babe. Lighten up. Isaac's over there and I want to say hey, then we can go upstairs."

Ugh, this disgusting creep thinks I'm going to fuck him. I look around the room, searching for Waverly and when we lock eyes, she gives me a slight nod. She's ready, and when Carter finally crashes, everything will be in place. I just hope he doesn't talk to Isaac too long because if the drugs from the beer he guzzled kick in before we're upstairs, I don't think I'm strong enough to haul his massive mountain of a body up them.

Reluctantly, I let him drag me across the room and I scowl while his sexist friends sit around rating all the girls in the room on a hotness scale from one to ten. It's degrading and makes me wish I could humiliate all these idiots to teach them a lesson.

Maybe Waverly's onto something with this new website of mine.

When Carter sways and starts to lean more heavily against me, and his words begin to slur, I decide it's time to move so I tug on the sleeve of his t-shirt and look up at him from underneath my lashes with what I hope passes for a flirty smile. It feels all kinds of wrong looking at anyone but Cole this way, but I've got to use all the weapons at my disposal if I'm going to pull this off.

"Can we go upstairs?" I murmur, and Carter's unfocused eyes drop to my lips and then to my boobs. He's not exactly subtle, but that's okay. I know I've got him.

"I'm about to fuck the ice queen!" he yells loudly and all his friends cheer and clap him on the back, offering high fives. God, I wish I could go around the circle and rip off their cocks and shove them down their throats while they bleed out.

But I don't do anything except let Carter van Buren drag me upstairs. At the top, he sways again, and I hurry us into the closest room that doesn't already have people fucking in it. Isaac lives in a house about half the size of my dad's and Cole's, but there are plenty of rooms to go around.

Carter stumbles over to the bed, turning at the last second before he sinks down onto the comforter. "C'mere," he slurs, eyes half-lidded. His head keeps dropping like it's too heavy for him to hold up and I don't think he's going to be able to stay upright much longer.

"How about before I come over there, I give you a nice…" I say, dragging my finger down between my breasts. I watch in thinly veiled disgust as his unfocused gaze follows the motion. "Sexy…" I move my fingers down to my thigh and slowly move upwards, stopping just before I get to the short hem of the dress at the top of my thighs. "Show?"

"Fuck, yeah," he mumbles before losing the fight and falling back onto the bed. I spin and crack the door open, spotting Waverly right outside. She hands me a set of handcuffs and my lipstick, and I toss her my heels and silently close the door.

When I climb up onto the bed, Carter is totally out of it. His eyes are closed and he's breathing evenly like he's passed out. I grab one of his wrists and lock one of the cuffs around it, and then cuff him to the headboard with the other end. Once that's done, I shove his shirt up, so his chest and abs are exposed, and pull the lipstick lid off with my teeth.

Finally, I scrawl the word *RAPIST* across his chest like a blood-red tattoo screaming his sins and truths to the world. When it's done, I lean back and admire my handiwork.

I let myself enjoy a second of satisfaction. This asshole thought he could scare me into letting him put his pathetic dick inside me, and I have no doubt he would've drugged me to make it happen. Now he's getting a taste of his own medicine. Lucky for him, I'm not the raping type or he'd be waking up with a nasty hangover and a cucumber shoved up his ass.

Finally, I take out my phone and open the camera. Then I slap him across the face. Hard. "Carter! Wake the hell up," I snap, hitting him again until his eyes crack open. I don't think he's really conscious, but eyes somewhat open is enough for me. "Smile," I say, and he lifts one side of his mouth in an attempt to do what I say.

I snap a few pictures, and then when I'm done, I don't bother saying anything else. It's not like he'll remember anyway. My point will be made when the entire school gets a look at Carter van Buren exposed for the manipulative dick he is.

Cracking the door open, I check to make sure no one but Waverly's around and slip out of the room, leaving him handcuffed to the bed. Let him try to explain that.

She hands me my shoes, and heart pounding, I grab them and we get the hell out of there. Once we're outside, we run barefoot for her car, breathlessly laughing as the adrenaline floods our systems. The grass is icy and crunches underneath my feet, but it's invigorating instead of painful.

"I can't believe you actually pulled it off," Waverly says, panting when she slides behind the wheel.

"I know, me neither. I thought for sure he'd insist on getting his own drink." I roll my eyes. "But of course he wouldn't dream someone would drug him."

"His overconfidence was his downfall," Waverly agrees, starting the car so we can get the hell out of here. She turns up the music, "Unholy" by Hey Violet blasting while we both sing along. And on the way back to her place, where Cole's picking me up later, I use the login info Romeo sent me earlier and post the photos of Carter.

I also confess how he blackmailed me with threats of rape to be his date, keeping everything vague and anonymous, of course. He takes a different date to every single party and social event, so hopefully no one knows it's me. Then, I do something I may live to regret, but I add a submission form where people can submit their own experiences, ones that I'll post publicly.

The way he just casually threatened me leads me to believe I'm far from the first girl he's pulled this shit on, and I'm counting on others wanting to share their experiences.

Once I'm happy with everything, I publish and pull out the burner phone I asked Waverly to buy earlier today for just this occasion. I plug in the numbers for the most popular kids in school and text them the link to the website so they can do the work of spreading it like wildfire to the entire student body.

When it's done, I text Cole that I'm on my way back to Waverly's then sit back against the seat with a satisfied sigh.

Too long boys like Carter Van Buren have gotten away with terrorizing us, and now it's time for the court of public opinion to take its pound of flesh.

CHAPTER 30

COLE

"It's done," Lucas says. "He's waiting for you in The Icebox."

He disconnects the call, and I press down on the gas, running a red light. No cop in this town would dare pull me over, and it's late enough that there's not a lot of traffic on the streets of Emerald Hills anyway.

Fallon's check in text came half an hour ago, and I've been crawling out of my skin all night with the need to see her. To see for myself she's safe and no one hurt her tonight. Lucas would've told me if anything happened, but it's not the same as using my own two eyes.

The tires squeal as I take a corner faster than I should, but my car sits low to the ground and can handle it. It's only minutes later when I swing into the circular driveway at The Lodge and jog up the steps.

Security takes seconds to clear, and I impatiently tap my foot the whole time. It's not like me to be so wound up, to have all these *feelings* inside trying to claw their way out. I've spent years suppressing any emotion that might be used against me or seen as weakness.

But Fallon's cracked me open and I'm not sure I can shove everything back inside. Or that I'd want to even if I could. Thinking of her grounds me, brings me back to center as the doors swing open and I step inside the Savage Society headquarters. The red haze of rage settles over me like a blanket, weighty and familiar.

It's almost comfortable, this need to dole out violence.

My heart slows, my breathing deepens, and I take a moment to check the weapons strapped to my body. There's a selection in The Icebox, but I prefer to have my own in case things go sideways.

There's a creak from behind me, and in the window beside me I see Beckett's reflection as he steps out of the shadows. "Are you losing your touch, or were you trying to announce your presence?" I drawl, checking the clip of my handgun before sliding it back into its holster.

He's wearing his glasses tonight and pushes them up his nose before he smirks. "I think we both know if anything I've only gotten better with time."

"What are you doing here so late? Couldn't sleep?" I ask, and he chuckles. It's not a nice sound, more like what you might imagine the nightmare under your bed sounds like as he drags you into oblivion. Beckett parades around looking like a human, but his disguise only barely manages to mask the monster hidden within. To be fair, the rest of us are the same. It's why we all work so well like this.

"I'm working on a new plot idea," he says. His eyes glint behind the frames of his glasses. Beckett's a best-selling horror novelist, but that's only the parts he lets the world see.

"Anything I can help with?" I ask as I start to move towards

The Icebox. Beckett sees where I'm heading and his expression lightens to something closer to excitement, if he were capable of such an emotion.

"I didn't think so, but... is that your project in the Box?"

I nod.

"Mind if I tag along?"

"On one condition," I say, gripping the door handle to the walk-in freezer we use to torture and kill people and store bodies in until we can get rid of them. "He leaves here broken but alive."

I've been considering how far to take things with Carter since the moment of Fallon's confession. Death is too easy an outcome for someone who leaves scars on women that will never fully heal. So, I've decided that will be his penance—living broken. I'll take his pride, his manhood, his ability to hurt a woman. It'll be his punishment. My retribution for Fallon.

He'll live with his scars for the rest of his natural life, and the memory of how he got them will haunt him for years to come. I'll make sure of it.

"Since when do we let rapists live?" he asks, flashing me a look of disgust. That's one emotion he's more than capable of feeling.

I don't even bother asking him how he knows about Carter and why he's here. Beckett has an uncanny ability to pick up things around him most people miss. In this case, I doubt it was hard considering he was lingering in the shadows and Lucas had to drag Carter past him to get to The Icebox.

But how he knew Carter was a rapist? Beckett always makes it his business to know those kinds of things about Emerald Hills. It's what fuels him, the sins of others, so allowing him to come along and observe what's about to happen doesn't bother me.

As long as he doesn't touch. Carter is mine to destroy.

"Since it'll make him suffer more to have to live with the consequences of his actions. I don't plan on letting him leave with the ability to hurt any more women."

He goes to step through the door, and I grab the sleeve of his black Henley. "Masks."

Normally when people step into The Icebox, they don't come out alive. There's not really a need for hiding our faces, and if for some reason they live, there's a reason and we want to leave a lasting impression. With Fallon involved, I can't chance Carter linking what's about to happen back to her through me.

Especially after seeing the website Romeo forwarded me earlier and Fallon's handiwork. Pride slashes through my chest, but I don't let it linger. Not when I've got a point to make before I can go to her. It's strange, being proud of someone other than myself, but if anyone could surprise and impress me, it would be her.

Beckett takes off his glasses and tucks them in his pocket before he pulls a black and white skull mask over his face, and I do the same. We match so neither one of us will offer anything discerning, and I slip my suit jacket off, hurriedly unbuttoning my shirt and hanging everything up. Beckett tosses me a Henley like his.

The hallway outside The Icebox is stocked with everything you might need for torture, including clothes to be unremarkable in. It's just smart conducting ourselves this way, and it's one of a thousand small reasons why we're better than everyone else who's attempted to do what we do.

I eye the shining tools lining the walls like a grotesque museum. They've seen more blood than a slaughterhouse, but they shine like they're brand new. Plucking a scalpel, a switchblade, and a saw off the wall, I watch as Beckett studies my choices and silently adds a blowtorch to my collection.

The guy's fucked up but he has good taste.

I do one last check to make sure that both of us are covered before I slip on a pair of leather gloves, covering the black *VI* tattooed on the back of my hand. Some people might prefer latex, but there's something about the buttery softness of leather when it crinkles as I flex my knuckles that feels more permanent. More sophisticated.

Like what's happening is inevitable.

I turn to Beckett with my hands full and without exchanging even a word he knows what I want him to do. He grips the metal handle and swings the heavy door of The Icebox open with a clunk.

Lucas left Carter perfectly positioned and tied down to a metal chair that's bolted to the floor above the drain. He's got a hood over his head so he can't see, but his body jerks at the sound of Beckett and I stepping inside. Our footsteps echo off the empty walls.

"Good. You're awake. Now the real fun can begin," I say as Beckett swings the heavy door closed behind him with an ominous *thunk*.

CHAPTER 31

COLE

"Hello?" Carter calls out, his voice muffled through the hood over his head.

Idiot. What kind of moron draws attention to themselves by calling out to the monster who hunts them?

I hand off my tools to Beckett and stride over to my captive, gripping the top of the hood and ripping it off his head. His lips are blue from the cold and his teeth chatter together. He blinks furiously, trying to adjust to the sudden brightness.

When his gaze settles on me and then slides to Beckett, that cocky stare he often wears in his obnoxious social media pictures is nowhere to be found. In its place is cold, hard fear. The kind of terror I relish inciting in my victims. I side-eye Beckett, knowing he gets off on this shit, too.

Who needs drugs when fear's such a potent high?

"W-who are y-you?" he asks. His teeth chatter, making the words disjointed and halting.

I don't bother answering. Whatever his mind is conjuring up

will only make this more fun. Besides, I'm worse than anything he can imagine.

"I've g-got m-m-money."

I turn my back and calmly walk over to Beckett, grabbing the scalpel he holds out. My fingers curl around it, the leather of my gloves creaking. I breathe in the icy air and expel a cloud of white.

When I'm standing in front of Carter again, he trembles and tries to shy away from me. To sink into the unforgiving metal chair. There's nowhere to go. No escaping this fate. He's lucky I've already decided he'll live. People don't change and the world would be a better place without him in it, but the heat on Fallon would be unacceptable.

But first, I'm going to have some fun.

In a lightning quick movement that comes from years of practice and skill, I slice his shirt down the middle without nicking his skin. He jerks back like I've cut him, but not a drop of blood has been spilled... yet.

"Fuck! S-s-stop!" he yells. "What do you w-w-ant?"

The tears start then, dripping down his pathetic face and freezing to his skin. He's an ugly crier and snot drips down from his nose. My lip curls, but he can't see it.

"What I want," I say, dragging the scalpel along his chest. I don't press down, only let the cold metal scrape along his skin. "Is for you to stop being a rapist piece of shit."

He stiffens like I've slapped him. "I haven't r-r-aped anyone! I s-swear!"

Beckett scoffs from somewhere behind me and I have to say, I agree with his assessment. Every word out of the mouth of someone being tortured is useless. They'll only tell you what you want to hear. That's why torture's only really good for two things: Punishment and fun.

"Unless you want to lose your tongue, I'd stop with the lies."

When Carter opens his mouth this time to argue, or maybe defend himself, I press the blade into his skin, beginning my work. Once the blood begins to flow, he no longer cares about anything but the pain. His mind shuts down and his only focus is escaping the torment, but there's no getting away. Not until I'm finished making my point.

When I step back, his chest is heaving and glitters crimson. Blood drips and oozes out of the slices I've made, the brand that will become a permanent title warning everyone away.

RAPIST.

Right on top of the scarlet lipstick left over from Fallon's revenge, I made her declaration everlasting.

"I t-t-old y-y-ou," Carter slurs, all fight gone out of him. "I'm n-not a r-r-apist."

I don't need him to admit to his crimes. I've had Romeo dig up all sorts of disturbing shit off Carter's phone and laptop that tells a different story. One of harassment, entitlement, and blackmail. He deserves everything he's going to receive by my hands today and more for the things he's done.

Beckett moves up beside me and I hold out the bloody scalpel. He takes it and passes me the saw. It's got jagged teeth and Carter's drooping eyes widen when he sees it. His shivers have become so violent, his muscles are locked up and I'm surprised his teeth aren't breaking off from the force.

"W-what are y-y-you going t-to d-do with that?"

Using the saw would be too much if I want to keep him alive. You know that saying *my eyes were too big for my stomach?* Same deal here. I had grand visions of the torture I'd inflict on Carter once I got him in here, but the reality is he's more delicate than I'd like. He won't survive if I start hacking into him the way I imagined when I grabbed this tool off the wall.

"Saw off your cock," I tell him in a flat voice.

He pales even further, and now his skin's got a blue tinge to it. If I'm lucky, he'll lose a few fingers to frostbite before we're done.

"You don't want to chop off his dick," Beckett says, pushing off the wall and adjusting the gloves on his hands. He drops the blowtorch on the ground before picking up the scalpel and handing back to me. The switchblade he slips into his pocket.

Beckett tilts his head, studying Carter. "Go for the balls, but don't cut them off, either." He looks up at me. "You want him alive, right?"

I nod.

Carter starts sobbing again, but he brought this on himself. When I think of what he could've done to Fallon, the rage inside me flares to new heights.

"Make an incision and pop his balls out of the sack before you sever them, then sew him up so there isn't an open wound."

I don't want to know how he came by this information, but I trust he knows what he's talking about.

"I didn't bring a suture kit." We don't tend to sew up the people we cut into in this room. Beckett spins and leaves while Carter begs me to reconsider. I don't. I won't. I can't.

He took things too far, and if I let him go without suffering enough, he'll go right back to doing what he was before. Like I said, people don't change.

When Beckett steps back into the room and hands me the sealed suture kit, I get to work. I do what Beckett suggested while Carter screams until his voice gives out and then passes out from the pain. He's not going to get off that easily, missing out on a second of this because of unconsciousness, so I wait for him to come around before finishing the job.

Once it's done, I admire my handiwork while I toss the

scalpel aside. Blood still drips out of the letters carved into Carter's chest announcing to the world what he is in a way he'll never be able to get rid of.

At least not without extensive skin grafts.

And for the first time since I stepped inside this room tonight, my lips curl up into a smile. Carter Van Buren has fucked with my girl for the very last time.

CHAPTER 32

FALLON

I don't know when I got so addicted to Cole.

I lived the first eighteen years of my life without knowing what it's like to have him look at me the way he does, like he wants to devour me. Like he wants to steal me away from the world and hoard me for himself and never let anyone else come near me again.

I shouldn't want him to treat me that way, but… it's Cole. He's always been like air to me—necessary for survival. Now that I'm getting to experience him up close and personal, it's like my whole life was in shades of gray before and now it's an explosion of color.

And for some reason, I want to share everything with him.

I can feel myself falling, fast and hard, and I'm totally helpless to stop it.

I don't think I *want* to stop it.

It's slowly starting to sink in that maybe Cole isn't playing with me. Maybe he's serious when he says he wants everything. And maybe I want to give it to him. Cole's the kind of man who stands out in a magnetic, hypnotic way. I'm drawn to him like a moth to flame, and I can only hope my wings don't get burned off in the process of loving him.

Because I think I might love him.

My stomach flips as I think the words, but there's no denying the effect he has on me. Is it possible to love someone and feel like you don't really know them?

My first thought when Waverly and I ran out of Isaac's place after dealing with Carter was how I wanted to tell Cole what I did and how it went. But I knew he was busy doing whatever it is he does, so now I'm pacing Waverly's room like a caged animal while she flips through a trashy magazine.

"You're going to owe me a new rug if you wear that one out," she says, not bothering to look up from what she's reading.

I glance out the window that overlooks her driveway again before checking my phone for messages. Nothing.

"How many views is it up to?" Waverly asks, setting aside her magazine and sitting up.

I pull up the website with the pictures of Carter on the front page and check the stats. "Five thousand."

Waverly claps her hands and laughs. "Holy shit. We don't even have half that many kids at school."

"If it weren't for how good Romeo is at what he does, I'd be freaking out right now," I tell her. "With that many views, someone would eventually track it back to me."

She waves her hand around dismissively. "They won't, and even if they did, Cole wouldn't let anything touch you."

There's a look in her eye that means trouble. I know she's about to start the inquisition, but lucky for me headlights flash across the front of the house. The speed of my pulse skyrockets. "Gotta go," I say, rushing for the door.

Her laugh carries out of the room as I practically throw

myself out her bedroom door. "Don't think this got you out of the talk you owe me!"

As my best friend, Waverly's always been there for me, and she's never judged me once. But things with Cole… my feelings for him and what's happening between us have always felt sacred. I never told her the extent of my obsession with him before all of this happened, and I'm not sure how much I want her to know now.

I'm not sure how much I want *anyone* to know.

The way things are now, it's like Cole belongs only to me. I know it's stupid because he's the kind of man who's larger than life. Who casts a huge shadow, and who everyone in this tiny town thinks they can have a piece of. But when we're alone? Just the two of us? It's like there's nothing else.

I've been fighting my whole life to be strong enough to stand in my father's place someday, but with Cole, all of the sudden I don't have to fight at all. He's there, taking control, taking charge of everything and I can just exist. There's something undeniably freeing and addictive about the whole thing that I never want to lose.

I'm not insecure, but there's always that small voice of doubt in the back of my head wondering why he's picked me. Why now? What if he changes his mind? I don't think I'd ever recover all the pieces of myself if he tossed me aside.

When I step outside, he's leaning against the passenger door of his sleek, black sports car. The second our eyes lock across the driveway, my blood ignites. It's after midnight and the darkness is thick like ink, but his eyes glimmer with hunger as he watches me come to him.

He holds out his hand without saying a word, and I slide my palm against his. He pulls me into his hard body and wraps his arms around my body, trapping me right where he wants me.

When I breathe in the scent of his cologne, my body unwinds, and I sink into his hold. One of his hands splays across my lower back and the curve of my ass, and the other tangles in my hair while he grips me tightly, like he missed me as much as I missed him. Like he needs this as much as I do.

Eventually, we pull apart and he opens the door for me to get in. When he's behind the wheel, we take off.

I want to ask him where he was, what he had to do that was more important than being with me at the party. The idea of Cole at a high school party is laughable, and he's running a literal empire. I don't want to come off immature and insecure, but I've grown up watching my mom fuck around on my dad constantly. I refuse to exist in a situation like that.

"Where were you tonight?" I ask after gathering my courage. My stomach is knotted, and I swallow hard around the urge to say *nevermind* and pretend the words never left my lips.

He glances at me but instead of the irritation I expected in his expression, his lips curve up into a devilish smile. "Why? Did you miss me?"

I meet his gaze head on. "Yes."

The grin on his face only widens at my blunt honesty and he chuckles darkly. "I didn't expect you to admit that so easily."

"Maybe you don't know me as well as you think you do."

"Tell me what happened at the party," he says, instead of bothering to respond to my barb.

"Tell me if you've ever fucked my mom," I say, instead of giving in to his demand. My heart is beating faster than a hummingbird's wings as I try not to stroke out while I wait for him to respond. I didn't mean to say anything because I honestly don't know if I want the answer, but now the words are out there. They're hanging between us like a noose swinging in the wind waiting for its next victim.

"What the fuck makes you think I'd ever touch your mother?" Cole's lip curls.

"She might've implied that your last party was *satisfying*. Her words."

"I'm sure she got fucked, but it wasn't by me." He side-eyes me. "Or your dad."

I exhale, my body sinking into the seat as the tension melts out of me, but Cole's the opposite. I can almost feel the rage shimmering in the air around him.

After a couple of seconds of silence, I say, "Tell me where you were tonight."

"Taking care of the trash."

"What does that mean exactly?"

He glances over at me again, letting his gaze search my face. "Before I answer that question, you need to think about how involved you want to be in what I do."

Cole doesn't live all that far from Waverly or my father, so it's just hit me that we're aimlessly driving the streets having this conversation. Maybe there's something about the darkness, the empty streets, and the tiny slivers of pale light cast down from the streetlamps that make the atmosphere feel cozy. Intimate enough to share secrets.

"Did you mean everything you said before? About wanting everything from me?"

He grips the steering wheel and twists it to the right, pulling off the road. I jerk forward as he slams on the brakes. Then he unbuckles me and yanks me across the console and onto his lap like I weigh nothing.

The space is tiny and uncomfortable, and I have no choice but to straddle him.

His large hands hold me in place while his fingers dent the skin of my hips. "Do I seem like the kind of man who has to lie to get what he wants?" he asks in a low, dangerous voice.

I consider his question, but ultimately shake my head. If Cole wants something, I have no doubt he takes it with no need to explain himself or ask permission.

"Good girl." A shiver streaks down my spine, and it doesn't escape his notice. "If I could, I'd consume you until there was nothing left. Nothing I'd have to share with anyone or anything else. You'd exist only inside of me. Since that's not possible, I want everything you have to give. I want you tied to me permanently. I'm only going to ask this once, and it's only because of what you mean to me that I'm asking at all, but do you want this? Me?"

The look he gives me then is open and vulnerable unlike anything I've seen from him before. The walls have dropped and he's letting me see all his feelings in a clarity and depth I didn't know he possessed. A gasp slips past my lips and I'm nodding before I even have a chance to consider the ramifications of this decision.

But does it really matter?

In the end, hasn't it always been Cole?

The air crackles between us with everything too intense to give words to, and then we're crashing together like a storm, clinging to each other while we get lost in what we're becoming.

And I realize the only place I ever want to be is right here, with him.

CHAPTER 33

FALLON

When I wake up, Cole's hovering over me. His nose brushes against mine and all I can see are his eyes, dark like the bottom of an endless ocean.

As soon as my lashes flutter open, he pushes inside of me before I can register that he's between my thighs, like he was waiting for the second I regained consciousness to fuck me into oblivion.

"Your cunt was made for me," he groans with a voice gravelly from sleep. He rests his forehead against mine while he holds himself still inside of me. That careful control he wields like a weapon looks like it's in danger of shattering as his eyes burn and his jaw clenches.

"Cole," I breathe, gripping his biceps and digging my nails into his skin.

He may be possessive, but I am, too, and I love leaving marks all over his body. I hold on while he fucks me, never dropping his gaze from mine. He fills me to the point of ecstasy, and then moves his body in the perfect rhythm. He's hitting my clit with every stroke of his thick cock.

Cole's already learned how to perfectly work my body.

I shouldn't be surprised—he's the best at everything he does. Cole doesn't have to worry about wanting to own my body—it's already his. He commands it with his touch, bends it to his will, and as he fills me as deeply as he can go, I combust.

It's like lightning strikes me and I'm turning to ash, blowing away on the wind of a hurricane. I'm coming, but I'm also coming apart at the seams, and Cole's here to catch me and put me back together, reforged into someone worthy of his love and obsession.

He pushes deep, groaning as he comes hard. I wrap my legs around him, pulling him closer and he collapses on top of me, but I don't mind his weight.

"Fuck, I never want to leave this pussy," he eventually mumbles against my neck.

"Then don't."

He chuckles and pushes up so he's holding himself up on his forearms. Then he pushes his hips into me again, his still hard cock twitching. I arch my back to try to get him to move but he lets the weight of his hips settle against me, holding me down.

"Greedy little lamb," he says with a grin and then kisses me. "This was just a taste of what you're in store for today."

I reluctantly let my legs drop from his waist when he pulls out of me, but then he slides down my body and uses his long fingers to push his cum back inside of me. The first time it happened, I think I might've died from embarrassment, but now I'm used to it. He does this every time we have sex.

"You have no idea what watching my cum drip out of your perfect little cunt does to me."

"What does it do?"

He runs his hands up my legs and bends my knees while he moves up my body until my thighs are resting against my stomach. Then he runs his still hard cock up and down my core, every now and then catching on my clit. The damn thing is *tingling* because I'm so turned on.

"Turns me the fuck on."

He thrusts against me again, pushing inside one, twice, and then pulling out completely. He groans and rolls over onto his back next to me. I let my legs drop but he turns and glares at me. "Keep your legs up."

"What? Why?"

"To help you get pregnant faster."

I open my mouth to say something but close it when I realize I don't know what the hell to say to that. I'm still in high school, for fuck's sake. What am I even doing?

"I'm not ready for kids yet, Cole!"

The look he gives me could start a wildfire. "You're having my baby."

"No. I'm not."

His glower turns into a wicked grin. "We've been fucking nonstop, little lamb. It's only a matter of time, unless..." His palm spreads across my stomach. "It's already done."

I shiver at the possession in his voice even though I'm mad as hell. Not only at him but at myself, too. It's not like me to be so irresponsible, but Cole makes me forget about everything but him.

"I'm getting on birth control," I tell him.

"The fuck you are." He moves on top of me, pressing me into the mattress. His dick is hard and heavy against my thigh while he glares down at me.

"You can't stop me, Cole."

He lifts his eyebrow in a silent challenge. "If you get on the pill, I'll throw them away. If you get an implant, I'll cut it out. If you get an IUD, I'll tie you to this bed, bring in a private doctor and make him remove it." His eyes glint. "You don't want to test me on this, Fallon."

"I'll get the shot. You can't do anything about that one." I stare right back at him, defiant as hell. I'm seething, but more than that, I'm *wet*. My body has betrayed me because it loves every stupid, dominating word coming out of his mouth. So much that my heart's pounding, and straight up *need* pulses between my legs. It's gone so far beyond want that I'm wrecked.

Cole Callahan has destroyed me, and I hate that I love it.

His hips shift and then he's inside me. It's only an inch, but it's enough for my eyes to roll back and any argument I was about to make to die on my lips. "I can chain you to my bed and fuck you until you've got my baby inside of you," he says, but it sounds more like a threat.

I shiver as he slides another inch inside and one of his big hands comes up to wrap around my throat. My eyes pop open and I'm falling into the vastness of his wild stare. "You wouldn't do that. People would come looking for me," I argue, but it sounds weak and breathless even to me.

"And they wouldn't find you. Not until I want them to."

His grip tightens while he slides the rest of the way in, and he stays there while I'm so full of him I can practically taste him on my tongue. I arch my back, trying to get him to move but he doesn't. "You want me to fuck this pretty little cunt?" he coos, running his nose along my jaw up to my ear. "Then you're going to have to beg for me to fill you up with my cum."

"Never."

He swivels his hips, grinding his pelvis against my clit while I bite my lip to hold in my gasp. Sparks flash under my skin when he does it again, smirking down at me because he knows what he's doing. He's reading every tiny reaction on my face.

When I clamp my mouth shut, biting my cheek to keep from saying the words that will end this torture, he ups the ante. He pulls his dick out of me and uses it to rub against my clit, back and forth. Back and forth. The tip catches with every stroke, so close to pushing back inside me where it belongs.

But then he pulls back and I'm going mad with the need to come. To feel him everywhere. I no longer feel whole without him as deep inside of me as he can get.

See? Wrecked.

"You only have to say those three," he murmurs, using his cock to slap my clit. "Little." *Slap.* "Words." *Slap.*

I can't help the moan that tumbles free. Shit, I'm totally going to cave. I'll deal with the consequences later if they happen.

"Please, Cole," I finally whisper, not giving him the words he really wants.

He grips my thigh and wraps my leg around his hips, still thrusting lazily against my slit. I'm so wet, it's dripping everywhere, smearing all over both of us and making a mess neither of us cares about. "As much as I love to hear you beg for my cock, baby, I'm going to need you to say the words."

Fuck. "Come inside me," I murmur, and he freezes.

"Say it again. Louder," he demands.

"Put that monster cock inside of me and fuck me until you come," I yell, digging my nails into his arms hard enough to draw blood. Our eyes are locked together in battle, and he doesn't even blink as he thrusts into me so hard the headboard slams against the wall.

He fucks me hard and ruthlessly. His rough fingers pluck at

my nipple and I'm about to come when he slows his movements and the orgasm that was *right there* drifts away.

"Tell me you want to have my baby," he orders. His eyes burn into mine as if by sheer will, he can rip the words he wants out of me.

"I want to have your baby… someday."

"Today."

"Cole—"

"Right. Fucking. Now. Say it."

"Please, I need—"

"I'll give you everything you need if you say the words, Fallon."

"Put your baby in me, you psycho," I snap, detaching my nails from his arms and grabbing his ass to force him deeper. Fuck, right now I'd promise him anything if he'd just make me come. My nails dig into his perfect, sculpted ass while he thrusts into me wildly.

"Look at me when I come inside of you," he demands, tilting my chin up with a tight grip on my throat so there's no escaping the gravity of his attention. "Watch while we make a baby."

And then he shifts so he's hitting the perfect spot and I start to come. I'm clenching and convulsing around him, squeezing him and he stops moving and groans. "Fuck, you're going to milk the cum right out of me."

He lets go of my throat to reach between us and plays with my clit, making one orgasm roll into another and then he's groaning my name as he empties himself inside of me.

"If we didn't have important shit to do today, I'd keep you in bed all day, filling you up over and over and over again while you're still in this part of your cycle."

All the blissed out post-orgasm floaty vibes from two seconds ago evaporate. "Um, what? How—"

"I have my ways," he says, back to being a mysterious asshole. "Now go shower and get dressed. We're going to be late."

I'm so lost for words, I find myself following his orders before it even registers what I'm doing.

For the first time since all this began, I'm starting to think I'm in *way* over my head.

CHAPTER 34

COLE

Clouds hang low and heavy in the sky, but the steps to the courthouse are dry. Fallon deserves more than a spur of the moment wedding, but I can't wait anymore. Not after last night with Carter.

Not knowing Anton thinks he has some claim on her.

I'm putting an end to it all today.

Within the hour, Fallon will be my wife even if I have to drag her in front of the judge and force her to sign on the dotted line. Hopefully it won't come to that, but nothing will stop this from happening—not even her.

When I park and step out of the car, Tristen is there to open Fallon's door. Her eyebrows furrow when he helps her out of the car. "Dad? What are you doing here? What am *I* doing here?"

Tristen shuts the door and pins me with a look over Fallon's head. Yeah, I should've told her what's happening, but that'd only give her more time to fight me. This way she's caught off guard and less likely to slit my throat over not asking her first.

I wouldn't put it past her. I know for a fact Tristen brought her up to be pliant but deadly if the need arises.

And she's perfection.

I round the car and take her hand from her father. She looks up at me with storm clouds gathering in her eyes. "Someone better start talking. Now."

My fingers tighten around her hand and the blood red diamond of the engagement ring I put on her digs into my skin. "We're getting married."

Her eyes widen and dart over to her father. He's not about to throw me a bachelor party, but he doesn't look like he wants to murder me, either. I'd say he's doing better than I expected.

"He knows, little lamb. He's known for a while."

"I— You—"

Tristen grabs her other hand. "I need you to know I never intended for you to marry Anton. I only needed to buy some time and I used you to do it, but I never would have let you tie your life to such an undeserving scumbag."

Fallon's momentarily stunned, but it doesn't last long. She cuts her narrowed gaze in my direction. "Did you say we're getting *married*? That's funny because I don't remember you asking."

Then she shifts that fiery glare to her father. "And you... you're just okay with this? Me marrying your best friend?"

Tristen laughs and lets her go to turn in my direction. "Did you think Fallon would be this upset about my acceptance of the two of you?"

I ignore him, scanning the street. Lucas and Rome are standing by the doors to the courthouse strapped head to toe with weapons, but we need to get inside. In this town, people fear us enough not to try to start shit they know they can't win... but that's not to say some new asshole with a misguided idea about his importance might think today would be a good time to make a move.

I look down at her, tugging her closer so she's pressed up against me. Her chin tips up so she can glare at me properly. "I never ask for what I want, little lamb. You know this. I take, and you're no different. You've always been mine, now we're going to make it official."

Before she can protest, I pull her with me toward the door with Tristen at her back. This isn't going to be pretty, but that doesn't matter. Not now, while Anton thinks he has some right to her. There's an overwhelming itch beneath my skin, one that won't be satisfied until Fallon is tied to me in every way possible, starting with this one.

Today she'll take my name, wear my ring, become my wife.

Today she'll promise her life to me, this one and beyond. Eternity.

I won't be satisfied with anything less.

"Sometimes I hate you," Fallon mutters as I drag her inside.

"But most of the time, you love me." I'm confident in her feelings for me, even if she hasn't realized them for herself yet.

We step into the sterile marble lobby of the courthouse and when the doors close behind us, she tugs on my hand, and I turn to face her. Tristen raises his eyebrow at me but is smart enough to know we need a minute.

The look on Fallon's face is guarded, and to someone who doesn't know her as well as I do, they might not be able to read her. But I can see every thought running through her head as clear as the surface of Crescent Lake.

"Cole." She has my full attention as she nibbles on her plump bottom lip, and I'm transfixed as her teeth leave tiny indents. She's gathering her thoughts. I don't think she knows how to describe the way she's feeling right now, but that's okay. I don't need her to think, only to move forward. To get through this day, and once she's mine, she can process what it all means later.

We can work through it together if that's what she wants.

If she doesn't, even better. Fallon's a smart girl, and she'll figure out the way things are going to go between us in time.

But I won't leave any doubt here today about my intentions or what our future holds. And I won't have her questioning whether I mean all the things I say to her. If she won't believe my words when I say them, I'm going to have to take action to prove them to her. Soon enough, she'll come to understand that when I speak, it's not just bullshit spewing out of my mouth.

I check my watch noting we're going to be late. Fuck, I hate being late.

Her pretty green eyes finally look up at me from under her lashes. "I probably shouldn't give in to you right now."

"Why not?" I ask with every ounce of haughty arrogance I can pour into the words. Fallon needs to understand she's mine. It's as simple as that.

"It sets a bad precedent." Her lips flatten.

I can't help it; I laugh, which only makes her eyes narrow into a withering glare that could melt the paint off the walls. "I thought you understood. I'm in control here, not you. But you don't want to be, do you, little lamb?"

I run my fingers down the side of her face and she shivers. Her eyes flutter closed for a second as she leans into my touch before she catches herself and straightens her spine. My lips tilt up. "I want to have a say in my own life."

"You think that, but are you unhappy to be here right now? It may not look like you expected or dreamed about, but the end result will be what you've always wished for, will it not?"

Her pensive gaze flicks over my shoulder to where Tristen is standing with Lucas. They're murmuring quietly enough that I can't hear them even with the echo in here. "Did I hope someday you'd pay attention to me? That maybe we'd end up getting married and living happily ever after?" She refocuses on me, and I fall into the emerald expanse of her eyes. She's staring at me completely open, letting me see everything.

Every piece of her heart that I now own, and I make a silent vow to guard it from pain with my life.

Every hope and dream she has for her life, even if she doesn't know what they are yet. I see them.

"Yes. I did." Her words shock me back to reality. "But I didn't think we'd be here so soon. I'm only eighteen, Cole."

"And I'm thirty-six. What's your point? When you know, you know. You're it for me, Fallon. Have been since that goddamn wish when you turned sixteen, but fuck, I tried to push you away. To forget about you and move on because you could do so much better than me. But then you fucked up, little lamb. You didn't let me go. You put yourself in my path every chance you got, and this here? This is what happens when you tempt the devil. Now you have to live with the consequences."

She steps into me then, wrapping her arms up behind my neck and pressing even closer. She touches her lips to mine but doesn't kiss me. They linger there as I breathe her in, our eyes colliding so close I swear I'm staring straight into her soul. "I love you," she whispers, and I feel the words on my lips.

"I'm sorry," I whisper back, and then I kiss her. I let her taste the truth on my tongue, the obsession, the pain of loving her even if I haven't said the words. Her loving me is like ingesting a slow-moving poison, one that will taint her and strengthen in her blood until eventually it kills her.

But I can't step back. I can't let her go. Even if this ends in tragedy, there's no walking away for either of us.

When I pull back, her eyes are wide and shining with understanding. She knows. She felt it all, the depth of what I feel for her. There aren't words to adequately describe everything she is to me but vowing my soul to hers for the endlessness of forever is a start.

"Come, little lamb. Our wedding awaits."

CHAPTER 35

FALLON

Cole's right.

I *hate* that he's right, but there's something about him taking control that I like. That I want to sink into like a hot bath and let him take away all the stress, worries, and fear I'm carrying around with me. When he's making decisions, I don't have to. I don't have to think about consequences or what the right move is. He takes care of it all, and there's something incredibly freeing about that.

And I never thought I could trust someone as easily as I do him, but he's honest with me almost to a fault. Sometimes that honesty is hard, but I appreciate it all the same.

So standing here, before the Justice of the Peace while Cole and I pledge ourselves to each other, is almost a surreal experience. My father stands on my other side, and I'm almost as surprised to have him here today as I am to be getting married at all.

Seriously. How the hell is this my life?

A month ago, I was hopelessly crushing on Cole with no idea

where I'd be standing today. Say what you want about the man, but when he knows what he wants he's relentless and impatient and I kind of love that about him.

This whole thing may turn out to be a disaster, but maybe it won't.

Maybe there's a tiny sliver of hope that this all works out in the end.

Cole smirks at me when I repeat the word *obey* in our vows before I notice he's slipped it in there. Bastard. There's a cough to try and cover up someone's laugh from behind us, and I imagine lighting Romeo and Lucas on fire with my glare as I turn it on them.

I hear myself saying *I do* and Cole slips a ring onto my finger, but it feels like I'm outside my body hovering somewhere nearby. None of this feels real. Even as I rip my gaze away from him and look down at the band that matches the engagement ring he gave me, I can't believe I've just married Cole.

Cole Callahan.

My dad's best friend.

My *husband*.

When he looks at me after he says his vows, the possessive gleam in his eye isn't lessened. If anything, it's actually worse. For a second, I can see the monster inside of him lurking in his eyes. I shiver from the intensity of that look. With him I never know what he's going to do next, and the way he's watching me, like the rest of the world can fuck off for all he cares, sets my body on edge.

He wouldn't fuck me in front of my dad… would he?

Cole's trained me so well to anticipate his touch that now all he has to do is look at me and my body responds. My nipples tighten and his eyes flick down hungrily. But then he's on me, kissing me like he's trying to devour my soul and with Cole, I wouldn't be surprised if he is.

I'm ripped away from Cole by a hand on my arm. "Enough. Jesus fucking Christ, I don't need to see that," my dad snarls over my head at Cole.

Cole's breathing hard and his eyes are almost demonic looking, they're so dark. His fingers twitch beside his gun, and for a second, I think he might shoot my dad. I step in front of my dad and Cole's deathly stare shifts to me.

"Move, Fallon," he growls.

I lift my chin. "No. You're not shooting my dad."

Quicker than I can track his movements, Cole strikes, pulling me against his body, my back to his chest and one of his palms pressed against my stomach. My heart's beating erratically, and I can't catch my breath.

"No one gets between you and me," he breathes into my ear, and I shiver again. The possession in his voice sinks under my skin and pools between my legs. "I don't give a shit if he is your father."

Cole rips his gun free of the holster under his jacket and levels it at my father's head. My legs start to shake. No way would he shoot my father on my wedding day. I'd kill him.

"This is your first and last warning. Don't try to come between me and my wife or I'll pull the trigger. I don't give a fuck who you are to me, no one keeps Fallon from me, not even you."

Cole grips me tighter and swings the gun around the room, aiming at all his friends in turn with a murderous expression on his face, one I've never seen before. None of the other powerful men in the room seem phased by it. Lucas even looks mildly amused, with his lips turned up at the corner.

"That goes for all of you. I suggest you heed the warning and don't test me."

"Put the gun down, Cole. We get it," my dad says, buttoning his suit jacket in a symbolic gesture of putting away his guns. My dad always, always, always has weapons strapped to his body somewhere. He wouldn't be the most powerful arms dealer in the state if he didn't, and he wouldn't have lived as long as he has if he wasn't ready for anything at any time.

I suspect my new husband is the same way, though I still don't know all the details of what he does. I'm going to have to fix that now that we're tied together for life.

When I glance up at Cole and see the possessive fire in his gaze as he stares down at me, I know that it won't matter what he does. Now that I've said *I do* there is no escaping him even if I wanted to.

Even if he's a monster who hunts the streets at night killing and terrorizing the citizens, it won't matter.

"What now?" I ask, almost in a whisper.

The flames in Cole's eyes nearly incinerate me with their intensity and his tongue drags along his lower lip. "Now we're going home so I can fuck you."

My gaze darts over to my dad as my cheeks burn. There's no way he didn't hear Cole's crude declaration. Lucas loses the battle and I hear him chuckle from over by the doors.

"For fuck's sake, Cole. That's my daughter." My dad's lip curls up in disgust.

"If you don't like it, don't listen."

"You're such a fucking asshole, you know that?" my dad says. "Remind me why I let you marry my only daughter again?"

Cole tucks his gun away. "As if you had a choice."

"Yeah, but *I* have a choice, and if me being with Cole means the two of you are going to fight, I'll walk out right now."

I didn't think it was possible, but Cole pulls me even tighter against his body. So tight, in fact, I can feel the steel pole he's packing digging into my lower back. I ignore the goosebumps popping up all over my skin, but Cole doesn't. He smirks down at me, and I elbow him in the stomach. His abs are rock hard, and I think it hurts me more than it hurts him.

"You're not going anywhere," Cole murmurs in my ear, his soft lips brushing the shell. I know he's not just talking about right now but means it in a forever way.

"Let's get the hell out of here before I see something I won't be able to unsee," my dad says, striding for the doors. Cole loosens his hold and I follow, but before I take two steps, he's slapped my ass.

When I whip around to glare at him, his gaze is focused firmly on where his hand just made contact, and it slowly crawls up every inch of my body until I feel like I'm totally exposed to his penetrating stare. My mouth closes without a word.

"Good girl," Cole says with a smirk. "I've got big plans for your perfect little pussy, wife, so move your ass before I throw you over my shoulder."

And fuck I want to defy him just to show him that I can.

But that look in his eye? The growl in his voice?

I've never been able to resist Cole's attention, and now that he's my husband I don't stand a chance in hell.

CHAPTER 36

COLE

"Nevermind," I say, changing course. Suddenly even the drive home is too much.

I'm trembling as I drag Fallon into the office at the back of the room. I'll never make it home with the raging hard on I've got and every cell in my body demanding I fuck my wife. She tries to protest, but I can't hear anything over the blood rushing to my cock.

My head spins from a lack of blood flow.

When I throw the office door open, the man who just married us, *the Honorable* something or other's head snaps up and his eyes narrow, but I won't be stopped.

"Get. Out."

My voice barely sounds human. All pretense of bravery falls away from the man, and he ushers his assistant out in front of him, nearly tripping in his rush to get out of his chambers.

Fallon stands before me breathing hard, her chest rising and falling rapidly but she's as desperate for me as I am for her. Even though her eyes are wide and fearful, her pupils are blown, and her nipples stand out behind her dress.

I close the distance between us, gripping the back of her neck and dragging her toward me. She's so fucking beautiful and now she's all mine. The need to be inside her, to put my baby in her is riding me hard and I kiss her, needing a taste of her on my tongue, before letting her go and stepping back.

She sways forward looking dazed when I'm not there to hold her up anymore. "Climb up on the desk and lay down."

I could bend her over it, but I want to see her face when she comes. I want to watch the way the light in her eyes shifts, how her soft lips part as she screams my name.

She doesn't hesitate to obey, knocking off the judge's paperwork and office shit while she spreads herself out for me, arching her back to entice me closer. I move to one side, gripping her thighs and dragging her to the edge.

Fallon's wearing a dress, so I push it up. My gaze drops to her cunt, barely covered behind lace but even that barrier pisses me off.

"Don't you da—"

But I'm not listening. I grip the fabric and rip it from her body, tucking it into my pocket. My hand shakes as I reach for my zipper, yanking it down so hard it rips but I don't give a fuck. All I can think about is getting inside my wife.

I fist my cock, yanking it out of my boxers and rubbing it against her soaked pussy. It's slippery and warm and my will to resist is shot, so I push inside of her as far as I can go.

Once Fallon's filled with me, I grip her thighs and widen her legs so I can lean over her. We're staring at each other, not moving, frozen in this perfect moment where we're connected as much as two people can be. I reach up and rip my shirt open as buttons fly around the room, too impatient to try and unbutton it, and my wife's stare falls hungrily to my inked chest and down to my abs.

"Tell me you love me," I demand while I dig in my pocket for the blade I keep there.

Her eyes shift to the knife in my hand before meeting mine. "I love you, Cole."

I exhale. "What I feel for you... it goes beyond love. Beyond obsession. You've infected every atom of my being. You're toxic, the kind of poison that can never be cured and only tempts me to beg for more even if it means death. You, Fallon, are every-fucking-thing, and I will never let you go."

I'm still inside of her, but neither of us are moving. She shifts, but I let go of my hold on her thigh and grab her hip instead, digging my fingers in and keeping her still. Her eyes blaze with defiance, but then I flip the knife open, and that fire turns to fear.

"What are you doing?" She shifts again, but my grip keeps her from moving away.

"Showing you how I feel." The inner walls of her cunt tighten, gripping my cock while I find a blank space over my heart where no ink touches and I dig the blade in, carving an *F* into my skin that will never fade.

Blood drips down my chest and Fallon watches it with blown pupils and parted lips. When it's done, she tightens around me again and I toss my head back and groan, closing my eyes and relishing in the feeling of being inside of her. Being owned by her so completely.

Her fingers wrap around my hand, prying the blade free and I open my eyes and look down at her as she pulls the top of her dress down. Her tits pop free, but they barely register. I'm fixated on the blade in her hand and the way she's carving a *C* in the same spot I did, right over her heart.

Blood wells in the wound, soaking into the edges of her white sundress. I brush my fingertips over my initial sliced into her flesh, her blood mixing with my own. My skin's stained with it.

"Now do you see? You're not the only one obsessed, Cole."

Fuck. The bloodlust buzzes in my veins better than any high from any drug, and I thrust my hips forward, slamming them against her again and again. I'm unhinged, feral as I fuck her, leaving bloody fingerprints all over her dress in every place I touch.

"Harder, Cole," she gasps, and I climb up on the desk on top of her, granting her wish.

The wooden legs scrape against the tile floor and our skin slaps together, and still she cries out for more.

"You're just begging for me to corrupt you, aren't you, little lamb?"

She moans and I wrap my fingers around her throat, tilting her chin up so she's forced to stare into my eyes. "You want to be destroyed, ruined for anyone but me, don't you?"

She gasps when I roll my hips so I hit her clit with every thrust. "Answer me."

"Yes," she moans as her eyes roll back and she squeezes my cock so hard as she comes, it's like she's trying to suck it into her body. Fuck, it's so good that I come right after her, emptying everything I have into her tight little pussy.

"Look how greedy you are for my cum," I murmur, staring down at where we're still joined. "So full, just how you're going to be every day from now until forever."

I let go of her throat, brushing the hair off her face. The blood on my chest drips down onto her dress, but it doesn't matter. It's ruined. It's also the hottest thing I've ever seen, her spread out

Beautiful Carnage

beneath me with my cum dripping between her thighs and our blood mixed all over her skin.

I pull out of her even though it's the last thing I want to do. But this was just the warmup, and I plan to spend the afternoon fucking my little lamb until she can't take anymore. Until she's so full of me, there's no room for anyone or anything else.

I help her stand on shaky legs, stripping my shirt off and dropping it onto her shoulders. The top of her dress is stretched out, ripped, and covered in blood. We look like we just murdered someone, but she doesn't care. She just grins up at me with a lazy, satisfied smile that has me smiling back. Fuck, when was the last time I really smiled?

I tuck myself into my boxers and pull up my pants, shoving the bloody knife back in my pocket.

"Now what?" Fallon asks as I throw my arm around her, using my other hand to hold my pants together as we leave the office. The judge is nowhere to be found. In fact, the only person we encounter on the way to the car is Lucas, and he knows better than to say shit.

Doesn't stop the fucker's smug grin, though.

"We go home and get started on my wedding gift to you."

Her eyebrows furrow as she slides into the car. I reach in and buckle her up. "Gift?"

I close the door and move to the driver's side, slipping behind the wheel. "The hundred and four orgasms I'm going to give you, one for every week I had to wait to make you mine."

She blinks at me, and I smirk.

"One down… and you're not leaving our bed for at least a week."

CHAPTER 37

COLE

Eleven orgasms down… and Fallon's unconscious in our bed.

Tonight she choked the absolute fuck out of my dick, and I never wanted to stop.

I slip out from between the sheets, careful not to wake her. Her messy hair is splayed across my pillow and her naked body's tangled in the sheets. She smells like me and it's only that knowledge, and knowing she's too sore to keep fucking her, that's pulling me away from her on our wedding night.

I haven't been to Red Rum in days, and I'm needed there tonight. Besides, I promised Lucas I'd show, and when I give my word to one of the Savage Six, I keep it.

I should shower before I go, but I won't. I like having Fallon on my skin. I did bandage up my chest in between fucking my wife, so I'm not bleeding anymore.

When she carved my initial into her skin? That was unexpected, but so fucking hot. My head falls back and my eyes close as I breathe deep and savor the moment, replaying it in my head.

The slippery feel of our blood mixing, the metallic scent of it in the air while Fallon's pussy clenched around me. It takes next to nothing to get my dick hard where she's concerned, and it presses against my zipper now, the insistent fucker.

But I've got matters that can't wait, so I ignore it, pushing reminders of my wife and her body wrapped around mine out of my head. Now's the time to focus, and I can't let Fallon be a distraction that could mean my death.

She's not getting rid of me that easily.

I bend and kiss her forehead, filling my lungs with her one last time before I leave. After a stop in my office to load up on weapons, I'm out the door.

Red Rum's my bar—the one I run my business out of. It's mostly just a front. All the important shit gets done at The Lodge, but I need a place clients can come to submit their contract requests. Red Rum is it.

I pull up to the valet, tossing the keys of my Pininfarina Battista without looking, trusting that if he wants to keep his job, he'll catch them. It's not often I take my baby out of the garage, but tonight I'm making a statement.

Sometimes people need reminding who holds the power in this town, and I'm all too happy to demonstrate.

"Callahan!"

I ignore whoever thinks they can gain my attention by throwing my last name out in that tone, but they call out again and again—each time more angrily than the last. The guard at the door flicks his gaze my way, waiting for instructions, but I decide to handle this myself.

I'm here to make a point, after all.

When I spin, I can't say I'm surprised to come face to face with Anton. He's dragged himself out of the gutters of Mulberry and into my territory, and there are only two things that could've accomplished such a feat. Unless one of the men I trust with every aspect of my life opened his mouth, Anton isn't aware that Fallon's my wife. Not yet.

I'm holding onto that card for later.

Which means he's here about—

"Where the fuck is my money?" he growls. I'm towering over him. Not only am I taller, but I'm up a couple of steps. I've got the high ground, literally and figuratively.

I smile at him, a shark's smile. The kind I wear when I'm hunting prey. When I scent blood in the water. He's attracting a crowd which can only be good for me. Let him make a fool of himself publicly. It'll only make my victory that much sweeter.

It's almost a pity how unworthy of an opponent he is. I'd welcome a true challenge, but at this point he's really just a nuisance. Still, I'll play with him for a while until something better comes along. Sadly for him, he doesn't realize he's already lost.

Fallon is *mine*.

Unless he's plotting something else. I tilt my head to the side and study him. I shouldn't be surprised, but he looks a mess. His hair's sticking up in every direction, his clothes are wrinkled and stained as if he's been wearing them for days, and his eyes are bloodshot. My nose wrinkles as I stare down at him.

How could he think he deserves to stand with us? To be a part of the Savage Society? It's laughable and insulting in equal measure.

"I didn't realize I was your accountant," I finally drawl, buttoning the jacket on my suit.

"Stop fucking around. You know what I mean. My money. Give it to me."

I click my tongue. "You know, you should really learn to keep better track of your things. Otherwise someone might just come along and sweep them right out from underneath you when you're not paying attention."

I can practically hear his teeth grinding together from here, and I turn to continue inside. At the last second, I turn back. "And take a fucking shower. You stink of desperation."

"I'm going to kill you for this," he says, grinding the words out through clenched teeth.

"You can certainly try," I toss out over my shoulder as I move inside, already forgetting about his threat. He won't be able to follow me, and even Anton isn't cowardly enough to shoot me in the back on the steps of my own club. The aftermath of that would mean his end, and it wouldn't be quick *or* painless.

It's too public. Anton is more of a snake hiding in the grass. He'll wait and strike out at you when he thinks you don't see him coming. I've gone up against his type time and time again, and I like to think I know how to handle him. Accosting me outside my club isn't going to get him anywhere with me besides in a shallow grave, so I don't know what he hoped to accomplish.

I guess it's that desperation clinging to him, making him act out of character.

As I step inside, Lucas comes out of fuck knows where and moves to my side, never breaking stride. He looks every inch the serial killer he is. "We need to watch Anton. He's getting desperate."

"Like a cornered animal," Lucas agrees, gesturing to one of my men. If Anton's still outside, he'll be thrown off my property.

The music is loud and sultry, the sort of beat you feel pulsing in your bones. The sort of beat people fuck to. The people packing my bar, writhing hedonistically, part for me and Lucas as we pass. Instinctively, they know to keep out of our way.

In the VIP lounge, it's quieter, a place better suited for meetings and discussions about contracts and non-Savage

Society business. It's held for me and the Savage Six at all times, and only the highest paying, most powerful clients ever gain access.

Before we're even in our seats, the waitress drops off our drinks of choice. Lucas gulps his down, looking like he's about to dive into some heavy shit, but then Xander slides into the booth beside him. He's wearing that shit-eating grin he likes so much because he thinks it makes him look less threatening.

He's not wrong. He's the best of all of us at getting people to do his bidding.

"Dude, do you have a death wish?" Xander asks. The waitress drops off his drink and he winks at her before she turns and rushes off. He takes a sip and then settles his attention back on me. I haven't bothered to answer his question because we both know the answer. I wouldn't be in my line of work if I was afraid of death.

"I can't believe you married Tristen's daughter. How has he not murdered you yet?"

I smirk but smother it by sipping my Balvenie single malt. "He would've if he knew how hard I've been trying to knock her up."

Lucas shoots me a look that screams *what the fuck?*

I shrug. "What? It's true."

"So your murder's impending then?" Xander's grin widens as he lifts his drink in cheers.

"You think Tristen could take me out?" I scoff, spinning my glass between my fingers.

"While we're all still breathing," Lucas drawls, shifting his gaze from Xander to me. "How about we discuss something a bit more pressing."

"Hit us with it," Xander says, and I watch my second expectantly.

His cool gaze settles on me with a weight I haven't felt in a long time, and then he speaks. "Someone took out a contract."

I don't bother stating the obvious. Killing people for money is what we do, so a contract isn't exactly newsworthy.

"I could be in bed with my new wife right now," I snap when my patience disintegrates. "Enough with the dramatics. Spit it out."

"The hit's on you."

CHAPTER 38

COLE

A laugh bursts out of me, taking all three of us by surprise. When was the last time I really laughed? I can't remember, and it feels foreign doing it now.

"Who the fuck is idiotic enough to take out a contract for my demise *in my own club*?" The laughter is starting to subside, and it's quickly being replaced by slow burning rage. It's not a wildfire that blazes out of control, more like embers waiting to spark against something flammable.

"They may not be as stupid as you think. The contract came in right after the wedding, when I wasn't here to intercept, and two of our guys have gone rogue," Lucas says. His words are clipped, and his body language screams fury. There's no doubt in my mind he's pissed right the fuck off that not only did someone get past him with this, but that he's now going to have to hunt and take down two of our own men.

Even if they deserve it.

It's not as if there's another company like mine in the area, but even if there were, my hitmen are well compensated. It wouldn't be an effective way to run a business where you corral literal murderers and not pay them well. I'd have quickly found myself on the wrong end of a deadly weapon years ago if I handled shit that way.

Xander whistles. "How much is the contract for? What's our Cole's life worth these days?"

"Shouldn't you be out terrorizing your sheep?" I drawl, tracing the rim of my glass with my finger.

Xander leans back in the booth looking smug. "I don't necessarily need to be present to make sure they suffer. It's called *passive torture*."

Lucas looks like he's about one second from jumping across the table and strangling Xander. "Passive torture? Doesn't that take the fun out of it?" he finally asks after he contains his anger.

"No. If anything it makes it more fun, prolonging the hurt. Stretching it out so in the end, they're begging you for death. But, of course, you don't give it to them, not right away. No, that's when the real fun begins." The psychotic glimmer in Xander's eye is something he works hard to keep buried deep inside himself, at least around everyone but us. This right here is his true self, the one he doesn't allow out because if he did, they'd no doubt lock him up in a ward somewhere.

He'd never survive it if he were caged.

As it is, he uses his psychosis for good... sort of.

"We'll come back around to that," I say, turning back to Lucas. "Tell me about the contract."

He closes his eyes, nostrils flaring as he breathes deep. He's gathering himself, and I can't blame him. My life's the one at stake, but it's his job to handle our assassins and the contracts. Mostly I'm above the day-to-day shit because Lucas has my back. This is something that never would've slipped by him if he wasn't at my wedding earlier today.

"Obviously I didn't take the meeting," Lucas grits out through clenched teeth. The glass cradled between his palms cracks from the strength of his hold, and Xander reaches over and plucks it out.

"Let's just get this out of shattering range, shall we?" Xander murmurs while downing the amber liquid, giving zero fucks as to whether there may be shards of glass floating inside.

I lean forward, slipping my elbows onto the table. "Who did?"

With nothing to occupy his hands, Lucas rakes them through his hair, ruining its perfect style. "Fuck if I know. I came back to the goddamn thing on my desk with the payment wired into the company account. The only signature on the fucking thing is an *X*."

"I think it's reasonable to assume one of our two traitors took the meeting, but what's interesting is they didn't keep the funds." I run my fingers along my jaw, absently noting the rough stubble and making plans to rub it all over Fallon's thighs when I get home. "Who are we hunting?"

"Yeah, Luke. Whose blood's getting spilled?" Xander asks, rubbing his hands together like some D-list supervillain.

Lucas shoots Xander a sharp glare that could turn coal into diamonds. "You two aren't getting involved in this. It's my mess. I'll be the one to clean it up."

"That still doesn't answer my question."

Lucas lifts his eyes to meet mine. "Matteo and Clint."

"Fuck." That slow burning rage inside of me heats up. "I thought those two were loyal."

"Just goes to show, you can't really trust anyone outside of the Society," Xander says, his tone uncharacteristically somber. When he looks over at me, there's madness and anger swirling in his eyes in equal measure, and it helps settle some of my irritation.

Knowing you've got people behind you who are pissed off on your behalf, who'll gladly dive into a war with you, without you even needing to ask, is something I've never taken for granted. I'm reminded now what family really means, and as memories of my father try to surface, I shove them back down in the empty hole in my soul and chain them up so they can't break free.

"True, but we have protections in place for this kind of thing. Namely, an ironclad noncompete clause everyone signs that essentially forfeits their life if they take a job outside of Red Rum." I wave my hand dismissively. "It's not enforceable in court, obviously, but they know the score going in. To take that risk, they must have been offered something they couldn't refuse."

"Or they thought they could get away with it, that we wouldn't find out," Lucas muses.

"If they thought that, why leave the contract behind? Why not take it and the money for themselves and not leave a trace. They wanted us to find this."

"Fucking idiots," Xander says under his breath. "Why would they taunt you like that? They have to know their deaths aren't going to be quick or easy when you come for them. Maybe they're just that stupid. They forgot to grab it on the way out."

I take a second to think it through before answering. "It's clear someone offered them protection." I laugh. "As if that will keep us away."

"We all know who's behind this," Lucas says, signaling to the waitress for another drink.

"Anton." I nod. "But I don't think that's the full picture. If it were just Anton, he couldn't afford to lure two of our own away.

He has neither the power nor the finances to do such a thing. Particularly with us confiscating his accounts and latest shipment."

The three of us sit in silence, sipping our drinks and contemplating what this all means before Xander speaks up.

"I wouldn't mind popping in for a little *confession* with the slithery fucker, maybe get him to repent a bit and see what he might reveal." Xander flashes his teeth.

"Easy, Father." Lucas rolls his eyes. "You've got a role to play. You can't exactly go flaunting the fact you'd happily devour the souls of babies for breakfast to your flock."

Xander pouts. "Remind me why I agreed to this bullshit again?" He stares down at his clothes with disgust.

My lips twitch. "You said, and I quote, *I'm going to find out who's stealing kids off the streets, and when I'm done turning their insides out, I'll stick my dick in every single nun I can find. My dick will be drenched in the holy blood of all those virgins, and I'll be saved.*"

Lucas snorts. "I think there was an *amen* in there somewhere."

Xander leans back in his chair and smirks. "That's right. Sometimes it helps to be reminded of your goals."

"So, Anton," I start, and Lucas holds up his hand. I allow it, only because of who he is to me. No one else could get away with that shit, but I make sure he knows he's on thin ice when I shoot a look filled with the promise of his death.

"Rome's already on his finances. Eventually, he'll sniff out a trail and follow it to the source. For now, I'll handle it."

"And if you fail?"

Lucas lifts his eyebrow mockingly. We both know he never misses.

"If he fails, I get a crack at the wannabe," Xander unhelpfully chimes in, cracking his knuckles.

I move my gaze from Lucas to Xander, so they understand the gravity of the situation. "Anton wants me to believe he can get inside my defenses, but he truly has no idea what I'm capable of. What *we're* capable of. He's playing a game he has no hope of winning but let me make myself clear." I pause for dramatic effect. "If Anton ends up dead before we know who's funding his power trip, things are only going to get worse. Hurt him, ruin him, but leave the motherfucker alive." I lick a drop of aged bourbon off my bottom lip, wishing it was Anton's blood.

"Because when this is all said and done? His life is forfeit, and I'm going to be the one to collect."

CHAPTER 39

FALLON

"I'll do it after I graduate." I glare at my husband even as I obediently open my mouth and let him push a bite of pancake inside. He thinks he can bully me into changing my name, but it's not happening.

Approval flashes in his eyes, but only for a second because he's gearing up to try to force me to submit to him in this, too. The fact that I'm sitting on his lap while he feeds me breakfast isn't a win to him, it's just the way things are.

"You'll do it today." His tone, of course, leaves no room to argue. Cole's not used to people pushing back or defying him, and even though I've struggled to tell people no my whole life, Cole makes me want to challenge him. He brings it out in me.

"No, I don't think I will." It definitely undermines the steel I'm trying to inject into my spine that I'm perched on his lap while he feeds me, but I've still got to try.

I love Cole but getting married while you're still in high school is weird. People are going to look at me like I'm crazy, and I'd rather just keep my head down and not draw even more attention to myself if I can help it. I may have an image to maintain at school, a reputation I've built over the last four years, but it's taken a couple of hits lately and marrying my dad's best friend isn't going to do me any favors.

Cole sets the fork down and pushes the half-finished plate of food away. I open my mouth to protest, and he shoves his finger inside. My lips close around it automatically, and I suck, scraping my teeth along his skin. He groans and then stands so fast, I don't even know what's happened until I'm sprawled out on the table and dishes are clattering to the floor.

Cole stands between my thighs, the custom Italian wool slacks he wears doing nothing to hide how turned on he is as he presses his massive cock against me. "One last chance, little lamb. Change your name."

His eyes spark, and his voice… it does things to me when he's like this. His words are husky and demanding. When he speaks, shivers trail down my spine as if they were his fingers carving into my skin.

I stare up at him defiantly through hooded eyes because I have a feeling whatever torture he's about to use to get me to agree will be worth the fight. "No."

He grins, and it's a wolfish grin that bares his teeth like that was what he was hoping I'd say all along.

"Cole," I warn, trying to sit up, but he presses down on my chest in the place between my boobs, careful to avoid my wound. "I'm going to be late to class."

"If you're that concerned, you can just agree, and I'll let you go." Even as he says it, his fingers trail down my stomach until he reaches the hem of my plaid uniform skirt. They dive underneath, sneaking up my inner thigh.

Heat coils inside of me, pooling between my legs and I arch my back trying to get him to move faster. But Cole does what he wants and won't be rushed. He chuckles darkly, stroking the tips of his fingers over my underwear. His touch is so light, it's only a tease but in the most perfect way that leaves me wanting more.

Wanting all of him.

"Ready to surrender yet, little lamb?" Cole purrs, increasing the pressure of his fingertips as he circles my clit. Around and around and around. He stays outside of my underwear for now, but it's only a matter of time before he takes things further.

"Never."

"Hmm." He dips his fingers beneath the fabric and brushes the tips across my pussy where I'm already slick and heated. Then he inches up until he's circling my clit again, only this time he rubs it directly.

I bite my lip to stifle the moan I feel climbing up my throat. I don't want to give him the satisfaction of knowing he's winning, though from the cocky smirk on his face, he's reading the signs from my body just fine.

Cole's playing my body like an instrument, or maybe one of the weapons he loves so much. He strokes me and I'm climbing higher and higher with every touch. I'm helpless to resist him, and we both know it. It's only a matter of time until I concede, but I'm going to make him work for it.

"Give me what I want," he demands, as he pushes one long finger inside of me. My toes curl when he pulls it out and pushes it back in again, his thumb finding my clit.

"No." I don't sound convincing, my resolve wavering with every stroke of his fingers. He's moved so he's sprawled out in the dining room chair now like a king, cold gaze fixed on his fingers moving inside of me.

Goosebumps break out across my skin even as I'm overheating. Cole leans forward, pulling his finger free and swiping his tongue across my slit. He laps at me like he's starving, not missing a spot before he settles over my clit and sucks in a pulsing rhythm. My eyes cross before rolling back and I reach down, blindly gripping at the strands of his hair to pull him closer.

His rhythm is teasing, a taunt to force my hand and even knowing that, I'm helpless to resist.

I'm shaking now, trembling under his touch as sweat dampens my skin. I can't catch my breath, but that's just what he wants. I'm craving him, knowing with one thrust he could end this torment and make me come. He knows it, too.

"Cole," I plead, knowing it's playing into his hand. Knowing he's getting what he wants, but I can't stop.

"You want me to fuck you, Fallon?"

I whimper, no longer able to form words.

"Then be a good girl and give me what I want. I'll make you come so hard you'll feel me the rest of the day." He tilts his head, putting his pouty lips on me again and this time he sucks. *Hard.* I'm right there, and one stroke of his tongue will throw me over the edge, but he pulls back, and I whimper.

Whimper like a fucking helpless fool.

But that's what Cole does to me.

"Fine," I finally concede. My voice echoes off the walls and before the last reverberation finishes, Cole's thrown the chair back and ripped his slacks open. He thrusts inside me so brutally, so perfectly, it hurts but I wouldn't have it any other way.

He's so hard, so big, that I'm stretched to my limits, and it only takes seconds before I'm coming so hard, I black out. When I blink my eyes back open, clearing the haze, Cole's right there, leaning over me and gripping my chin with one hand so I'm forced to stare into the abyss of his eyes as he finishes as deep inside of me as he can get—without a condom.

Fuck.

It's hard to be upset with him when my body's perfectly relaxed and every ounce of tension has been bled out of me by my very own monster.

Still inside of me, he shoots me a devilish smile, one full of ego and smug satisfaction. He got exactly what he wanted like he always does.

Cole drops a soft kiss on my lips, one at odds with the devil in his eyes, and then stands, pulling out of me and holding out his hand to help me up.

"Better go change, little lamb. We wouldn't want you to be so late you can't stop by the office on your way to class."

Even though I'm boneless from my orgasm, he didn't play fair, so as I step by him on my way up to our room, I shoot him the finger over my shoulder. All he does is laugh, but I'll never give him the satisfaction of letting him see the smile stretching across my face.

CHAPTER 40

FALLON

It only takes a few minutes in the office and a flash of my marriage certificate before I'm officially Fallon Callahan at school. The people who run the office give me funny looks, but thankfully no one comments.

I can't wait to see what my classmates have to say. *Hashtag sarcasm.*

When I'm in this building, I can't afford to care what people think. They need to think they don't affect me, that I'm above them all. They can hate me from afar and fear me in equal parts. I'm happy with the arrangement because it means I can do whatever I want and if what I want is to be left alone, all I have to do is snap my fingers or give someone an icy glare and they bail.

Waverly meets me at my locker while I grab my books for first period. I'm immediately hit by a wave of guilt when I remember I got married this weekend and didn't even tell my best friend. She's going to kill me when she realizes she didn't get to be my maid of honor.

I'm quiet when I stack my books in my arms and slam my

locker closed. I can feel the weight of her stare on the side of my face. "Soooo," she pushes off the locker so we're facing each other. "How was your weekend? I didn't hear from you."

"Yeah." I glance around but everyone near us has already taken off for class, not that they won't find out soon enough. "I've got news, but you have to promise you won't freak out."

Waverly's eyes brighten and then narrow. She shifts her books to the other arm so she can lean closer. "Does this have to do with a certain tall, hot psychopath?"

I nod. "I kind of… got married."

Her eyes widen. "What?" she screeches.

"Shh!" I grip her sleeve and yank her into the nearest alcove. We're definitely going to be late for class if she can't keep it together.

"Holy shit, Fal. You married Cole? What the hell?"

"I know. It's insane, but you know how he is."

She cracks a tiny smile. "Wouldn't take no for an answer?"

I brush my hair over my shoulder and avoid looking at her. "Understatement of the century. But honestly, I didn't even try to say no. Not really," I murmur, admitting out loud for the first time how much of a pushover I am, especially when it comes to my brand new husband.

"He didn't actually force you, did he? Because I will go up there right now and rip his balls off and serve them to him for lunch." Waverly looks like she'd go conquer the world on my behalf, and I can't help but grin since I'd do the same for her.

"No. He's excellent at pushing me way outside of my comfort zone, but if I'm honest with myself this is what I've been dreaming about for the last two-plus years, only better because it's real."

"God, I'm so jealous," Waverly sighs, leaning against the wall before she straightens back up when the warning bell rings.

"Okay, so two things you should know." She holds up a manicured finger. "One, everyone's talking about your website and the pictures of Carter all over it, and two," another finger pops up, "he hasn't shown his face yet this morning, so we need to be on alert for him to retaliate."

"Damn. With everything else this weekend, I already put Friday out of my head." I frown, fidgeting with the corner of one of my textbooks. "Do you really think he'll come at me today?"

"If he shows. What you did was a huge blow to his ego, not to mention I bet the cops are going to want to have a nice, long chat. If his parents haven't shipped him off to some foreign boarding school somewhere to hide the scandal, I'm sure he'll be back before you know it, being his typical douchebag self."

"Well, let's hope he's off in some remote wilderness somewhere far, far away from here where we never have to see his rapist ass again," I say, stepping out of the alcove.

The halls are mostly deserted as Waverly and I make our way to first period, but as soon as I step through the classroom door, the teacher, Professor Harris, waves me towards his desk.

He looks flustered, even more than usual. His thick, wavy hair falls over his forehead and he pushes his glasses up his nose when they slip down. He teaches my ancient civilizations class, which is boring as hell, but there's a waiting list to take it because all the girls want to seduce poor Professor Harris into their beds.

I might've noticed if I had the ability to see anyone other than Cole. As it is, I can admit objectively he's got the hot geeky professor vibe going for him, but it does nothing for me. For the most part, Emerald Hills Prep doesn't hire old, decrepit teachers. We've got all the young, fresh, idealistic instructors who still care about making sure we learn, even if it's wasted on most of the student body.

My fellow classmates are destined to either blow their trust funds until they have to beg daddy for more or follow in their parents' footsteps and run multinational and Fortune 500 companies that are part of their family's legacy.

None are like me—determined to do well just to show I can and trained by my father to rule over the underbelly of Mulberry County someday. Whether or not Cole's going to fight me to stand at his side as an equal is still a mystery, but one I hope I'll have the answer to soon.

"What's up, Professor H?" I ask, as I step up to his desk. That's the other thing with Emerald Hills Prep—the teachers are all super informal. Some even go by their first names.

"You've been summoned to the principal's office." He hands over a slip of paper and I sigh. They couldn't have told me when I was down there twenty minutes ago?

"You'll be able to find the link and assignment information from today's class in the cloud server," he says, already distracted and shuffling through the piles of paperwork on his desk.

"Okay, thanks." I turn to leave but he calls out for me and when I look back, he's got a small grin on his face.

"I saw the name change. Congrats."

My gaze darts around the room but nobody's paying attention. I might not be able to care outwardly about what these assholes think, but that doesn't mean I want to deal with the gossip, especially when I see everyone crowded around their phones and keep catching Carter's name floating around. Thankfully no one knows that I was the one who fucked with him, but if he comes back, I'm sure he'll be all too happy to fill in the blanks. Just another reason to hope he stays away.

"Thanks, Professor."

I don't stick around, afraid if I do, he'll ask me questions and someone will catch on. Like the Carter situation, it's only a matter of time before it gets out.

My attention shifts to what the principal could want. He's new, Dr. Collins, and I haven't met him yet. I'm the student body president and cheer captain and have never been in trouble a day in my life. It's not that I shy away from trouble, just that I'm good at not getting caught.

My dad taught me well.

When I step back into the office, I give my name to his assistant and wait. For the first time since I put Carter on the website, I go on my socials, scrolling through dozens of posts from people blasting Carter. There are tons of women revealing that he did the same thing to them, and of course the small group of people defending Carter and his actions are attacking right back.

God, sometimes I fucking hate people.

Dr. Collins's assistant—*Matthew*, according to the sign on his desk—ushers me into his office before closing the door as he leaves. The principal sits behind his desk but stands and grins at me. "Welcome, Miss Ashwell."

"Actually," I say, heart pounding because I'm about to correct someone for the very first time. Cole would be beside himself with glee right now if he knew. "It's Callahan now. *Mrs. Callahan.*"

Dr. Collins's eyebrows raise in surprise, but he doesn't say anything. Unless you live under a rock, if you're from Emerald Hills you know who the Savage Six are. "Right, have a seat. I won't keep you long, but I wanted to introduce myself and also ask a favor of you."

Crap. I already know I'm going to say yes. Sometimes I wish I was better at setting boundaries.

"Sure. What do you need? I'm happy to help." I hear the

words coming out of my mouth and wish I could grab them as they float his way and shove them back inside. I have so much on my plate right now it'll be a miracle if I hold on to my valedictorian spot, though with Carter possibly out of commission my odds are looking up.

"Excellent." He leans back in his chair with a glint in his eye that reminds me of that Mr. Burns Simpsons gif. I'm pretty sure it's just the way the light from the windows on either side of his desk is hitting him because when he sits forward it's gone. "I've just gotten approval to increase the number of scholarships we offer students who wouldn't be able to afford to attend EHP otherwise, and rather than wait until next year, I've decided to start the program now with some new transfer students."

My stomach flips for those poor souls. The kids at EHP aren't for the faint of heart and will eat them alive. "That's going to be a great opportunity for them," I find myself saying instead of what I really want, which is that he's throwing these kids to the sharks and they probably won't last more than a week.

"I'd like for you to welcome the students to our school when they start next week, show them around, sit with them at lunch. Help them get settled."

I nod. "Sure, I can do that." And I mean it. I'll, of course, have to keep my persona intact, but if I can keep these new kids from suffering at the hands of people like Isaac and Carter, I'll do what I can.

"Great." He claps and then stands up and I get the distinct impression I'm being dismissed. "Check in with Matthew and he'll get you a pass back to class."

I walk out of his office hating that I can't seem to say no, because the last thing I need right now is the responsibility of making sure these new kids aren't destroyed by my world.

CHAPTER 41

FALLON

Over the last two weeks, I've settled into what I'm hoping is my new normal. A couple of scholarship kids showed up at school to take the heat off the fact that Carter hasn't been back yet.

It's a little hard to return to school when you're wanted by the police for all sorts of sexual crimes. I have no doubt his family's hiding him somewhere and he won't dare show his face in Emerald Hills again.

Now that the gossip surrounding the new kids and Carter has passed, I can finally take a second to breathe. I'm lounging on the couch in Cole's office in front of the fire while he works. The heat from the flames licks against my skin and chases away the chill in the air.

Emerald Hills doesn't really start to warm up and show signs of spring until it's nearly summer, so I've claimed this spot as my own. Cole and I haven't talked about it, but neither one of us likes to be very far away from the other.

Is it unhealthy? Probably, but I don't care and neither does he.

My phone's in my hand while I stare down at it, wondering if this is the right time to post what I've got on Misha and Eden. Romeo got back to me a week ago with something on Eden and it's been hard sitting on it for the last seven days. But I want to time the release for maximum impact.

"Why do you look like you're on the verge of ruining someone?" Cole asks as he lifts my legs off the cushion and sits beside me, draping them over his lap. "And why does that make me so fucking hard?"

I turn to take in the perfection that is my husband with his messy dark hair and straight nose, and just the barest hint of a five o'clock shadow dusting his sharp jawline. It's still so damn weird to think of him that way, as my husband, but I'm starting to adjust. At least my mom still doesn't know. The first thing she'd do is run to her little fuck buddy, no doubt, and the last thing I want to deal with is Anton.

It's gotten easier to believe this is actually my life. My dad even came over for dinner a couple of days ago and it wasn't even awkward.

It was like this was the way it was always supposed to be. Totally normal and natural, and it's hard to accept that I'm *this* lucky.

"You're always hard."

"Around you, yes."

I groan as Cole digs his thumb into the arch of my foot, massaging the ache of wearing heels all day at school away. "And it's probably because I'm trying to decide if it's the right time to post what I've got on Misha and Eden on my website."

No one would believe how sweet and attentive Cole can be, in his own way. Then again, I think he's only like this with me. I love that he saves this part of himself for when we're alone together, that I own parts of him no one else will ever witness or experience.

What can I say? I'm just as much of a psycho when it comes to him as he is with me.

"Don't you think you've left this long enough?" he asks, moving from my feet up to my calves with his magical fingers. "You could always let me kill them."

"And miss out on their public humiliation? No. They tried to make a fool of me, and I can't let that stand."

"That's my girl," Cole praises, flashing me his cockiest grin with a bit too many teeth showing. It makes him look like the apex predator he is. "Sometimes it's better to let your victims wallow in their mistakes, to live with the consequences of fucking with you."

"I love the way your mind works," I murmur as I slide my hand along his jaw and up into his hair. The strands are silky between my fingers, and he leans into my touch.

"You love my crazy, little lamb?"

"I do."

"And how insane am I to drag you into my world?" His eyes cloud over for a second like he's gone somewhere else but then he blinks and he's back. "Have you given much thought to how involved you want to be in my business once you graduate?"

I'm surprised by his question, but I shouldn't be. He told me to consider how much I want to know. Cole's not the type to shy away from the hard questions and conversations that need to be had, but I appreciate his giving me the option to keep my head in the sand, even if I'd never take it.

I nod. "I'm all in. We either share our lives with each other or we go our separate ways." He glares at me, tightening his hold on my foot like he thinks I'm about to run away.

"I thought I made myself clear. There is no escape for you, little lamb. No going back on your vows. If you tried to leave me, I'd hunt you to the ends of the earth. I'd chase you into the afterlife. You. Are. Mine."

"Then no secrets, Cole. I mean it. Don't keep things from me because you think you're protecting me."

"Then I should probably tell you what I did to Carter." The expression on his face can only be described as *gleeful*. He doesn't look the least bit sorry, and honestly? What did I expect when I confessed what Carter threatened to do to me? I knew Cole had darkness inside of him that he fully embraced and gave zero fucks about holding back.

That monster peeking out of his eyes right now shouldn't turn me on, but it does. So much. "Did you kill him?"

"No, but I made him wish I had."

I shift, not sure I want him to know what his darkness does to me. The way I can almost feel it on my skin, dragging my own up from inside of me. Tempting it to the surface. My nipples tighten and I press my thighs together, but of course Cole misses nothing. His gaze snaps down to my chest and his lips tilt up into a wicked smirk.

He drags his tongue across his pouty lower lip before forcing his eyes up to meet mine. "You're fucking perfect." He leans forward and brushes my nose with his and I breathe him in. "You want to see what I do, little lamb? Feel the hot splatter of blood on your skin as you watch the life drain from someone's eyes?"

Suddenly I'm all too aware of where Cole gets off walking around like he's got the biggest dick in the room. Taking lives must make him feel godlike. The power he wields over life itself must be intoxicating, and it strikes me just how much of a psycho he really is.

And what does it say about me that I love it?

That I love this part of him as much as every other part?

That a tiny part of me wants him more because of it?

I find myself nodding. "Yes," I breathe against his lips when they brush mine. "I want to see, but first…"

I lean away and pick up my laptop, clicking *publish* on the video of Misha and Eden, plus the juiciest bits from Eden's medical file along with a short caption:

Poor Misha. Looks like that tiny dick isn't getting the job done and fucking him is less fun than staring at the wall. Right, Eden? And speaking of Eden… hopefully Misha wrapped it up. Wouldn't want another secret summer baby, would you?

Once I'm done, I send the same text blast from my burner phone that I did when I posted about Carter and let my classmates do the rest. With a satisfied sigh, I shut my laptop and slid it onto the table and turned my full focus onto Cole.

"Fuck, I love it when you're devious," he says, tugging me onto his lap so I'm straddling him.

I laugh, and for the first time in my life, I feel like I can be myself. He sees who I truly am deep down inside, and I don't have to hide. It makes me want to be wild. Reckless. Free.

And I grasp his face between my hands and let myself fall into his dark eyes. "Show me how much."

CHAPTER 42

FALLON

I usually sleep like the dead, so when something wakes me up in the middle of the night, I know it's not going to be anything I want to face at two a.m. I'm blearily looking around the room when a hand slips over my mouth, masking my gasp.

"Shhh," Cole breathes into my ear.

With a shot of adrenaline that could rival a hit of amphetamines, I'm wide awake. He slowly moves his hand away from my mouth and I can barely make out his dark eyes in the pitch-black room. The only light comes from the hazy moonlight falling through the wall of windows as it reflects off the surface of the lake.

There's movement by the door as someone steps into the room and Cole slides out of bed so quietly, he might as well be a ghost. If I wasn't watching him, I wouldn't have heard a thing. Even then, it's more a sense of his movement than actually seeing it.

The shadow by the door steps further into the room and with

each nearly silent step they take, my pulse accelerates. I'm panting, but forcing my lips closed to try and keep the sound inside. I don't know what's about to happen, but I'm smart enough to recognize if the person invading our bedroom knew I was awake, it would destroy any advantage Cole might have.

And if there's anything I trust, it's my husband's ability to keep me safe.

Reminding myself that it doesn't matter who's attacking us right now helps. Cole will always be the most dangerous man in any room, and there's comfort to be found in that. My fingers tremble as I curl them into the sheets, gripping onto something tangible to try and keep still.

I want to throw myself out of bed.

Launch myself at whoever dares to step foot in our bedroom.

Scratch their eyes out and tear their skin from their body.

But I have to trust that whatever's about to happen, Cole will handle it. He's more prepared than I am right now.

I watch as the man creeps further into our room, still totally unaware of the fact that Cole and I know he's here. It's clear he's a man by the size of his form as he slinks into our bedroom, and whoever he is, he's not very observant.

Maybe it's too dark for him to see.

But Cole and me? We have such an intense connection, it's like I can sense him and he me. It's because of this connection I know he's circling around the edge of the room while the man moves towards the bed. There are pillows under the blanket that could be mistaken as Cole or me because it's so dark.

The hulking man reaches the bed and rips the blanket off. I let out the gasp I've been stifling, but in the time it takes the man to register the sound, it's already too late. Cole moves behind him up into his space, gripping the man's head with one hand and ripping his other across his neck.

Blood sprays out from the gaping wound in his throat while the man desperately tries to hold it back. Hot splatters hit me in the face, the chest, the legs. I barely feel it as I watch him drop to his knees, making sure the intruder doesn't somehow make a miraculous recovery and go after my husband.

But of course Cole would never allow that to happen. He stands over the man, staring down at him. I can't make out the expression on his face as he checks that the man is dead, but as soon as the awful gurgling sounds end, he turns my direction.

Cole climbs onto the bed and grips my face between blood-soaked hands. "Did he touch you?"

My heart rate is beginning to slow, and even as the metallic scent of blood still hangs in the air, I'm not afraid. This is the first time I'm seeing Cole for who he really is. The beast inside of him is fully untethered and free, and when I stare into his dark, fathomless eyes—the eyes of a killer—all I see is the consuming way he loves me shining back.

It's at this moment I realize I'm not normal. A normal person wouldn't be okay with her husband murdering someone in front of her. A normal person would be freaking out or having a panic attack or some kind of trauma response appropriate to seeing a life taken in front of them.

But not me.

I knew growing up my father was involved in some illegal shit, and that his friends must be, too. It's not like I'm stupid, and to amass and hold onto the kind of power my father and his friends have, there's no way everything they've done is legal.

Somehow, it's different seeing it for myself. It's almost better knowing the worst of it. My imagination can stop filling in the blanks because I know exactly what Cole's capable of now. He didn't hesitate. He acted like he'd done this a hundred times before. A thousand. A million.

I shake my head. "He only grabbed the blanket."

Cole lets me go, stands up, and kicks the corpse on our floor as hard as he can a couple of times. "He got too," *kick*, "fucking," *kick*, "close," *kick*.

"I don't think he was here for me." I untangle myself from the ruined sheets and stand up, starting to strip them off the bed. Cole grabs the sheet I just removed and lays it over the dead guy. "He went right for your side of the bed."

"It's Matteo. He's obviously been watching me. I should've waited to kill him until I got some answers, but when I saw him getting close to you, I couldn't take the chance," Cole mutters, moving to the nightstand and grabbing his phone. The light illuminates his face, and for a second, he looks like the nightmare everyone thinks he is.

Cold.

Harsh.

Unforgiving.

A shiver runs down my spine, but not from fear. He must notice the movement because he tilts his head to study me and then smirks. "Look at my naughty little lamb," he purrs as he stalks around the bed, tossing his phone aside as every step brings him closer and closer to me. Cole's still in his tight black boxer briefs and his pale skin is spattered with crimson.

He's never looked hotter.

"You like seeing me coated in blood, don't you?" he asks, his eyes gleaming in the moonlight. "It turns you on."

"What? No," I say with a nervous little laugh that totally gives me away.

He moves closer so his chest is pressed against mine and his fingers slide against my hips. His right hand moves down between my thighs. "Liar," he whispers as he runs his nose along my jaw and the side of my face. "You're soaking my fingers."

As if to prove his point, he lets one bloodstained finger slide across me while his other hand presses against my back, holding me against him so I don't fall. I let my head fall back and close my eyes, giving in to the pleasure.

A moan falls from my lips as he toys with my body, but all too soon he's pulling back. I protest, gripping his biceps to try and pull him back but all he does is let out a dark chuckle that does absolutely nothing to ease the ache between my thighs.

"You want me to fuck you with a corpse on the floor?" he murmurs in my ear, and I nod. Fuck it, watching Cole in all his bloodthirsty glory gets me hotter than anything I've ever seen in my life. I'm willing to admit how depraved and fucked up I am.

"Christ, Fallon." He moves away and my body cools without his heat to warm me. He grips my chin and tilts my head, forcing me to look at him in the dark. "You really are perfect, aren't you?"

I know he doesn't expect me to answer, so I don't. His phone buzzes from where he tossed it onto the mattress, and after it stops and then starts again, he finally lets me go. The trance that kept me focused on him and him on me breaks, and he releases me to pick up the device.

"Go shower," he tells me while he answers his phone. "Wash his blood off your skin, and by the time you're done, he'll be gone. Then we can finish what we started."

Cole's eyes are locked on my body as I turn to walk away, even as he's speaking to someone else on the phone—ordering them to come clean up his mess. I should be terrified right now.

Horrified at myself for what I've become.

But then I realize... this is who I was always meant to be.

CHAPTER 43

COLE

The last week crawled by as I barely contained the need to strike out against Anton in retribution for what he'd done. Sending a nearly untrained man into my home to try and murder me was just insulting. The fact it was my own assassin in training just makes it worse.

Matteo was new, greedy, hungry to prove himself and still terrible at the job.

Now I'm biding my time, letting the suspense build. There's something to be said about playing with your food, and Anton's at the bottom of the food chain as far as I'm concerned. Let him wallow in the stress and anticipation for a few more days.

The mug resting against my thigh burns my bare skin as I lean against the headboard catching up on emails on my phone. Periodically, I sip the bitter coffee and stop my scrolling to stare down at Fallon. She's still asleep, hair wild and untamed against the sheets.

She has no idea how far gone I am for her. How devastatingly ruined I am. She's shown me her soul and it's just as twisted as mine, even if it's not as tainted. In time, standing by my side, it will be. A good man would hide that side of his life from her. A good man would protect her innocence.

Good has never been a word I'd use to describe myself.

Great, sure, but never good.

If I tried to hold parts of myself back from her, Fallon wouldn't stick around. She wouldn't forgive me or let me have her the way she does now. She's all in, just as captivated by me as I am her.

The phone in my lap buzzes and I tear my gaze off my wife and look down. A grin spreads slowly across my face as I read the reminder notification that popped up seconds ago.

Fallon's period is a week late.

My dick likes that idea a whole lot and hardens. I don't even attempt to talk it down, even though its job is likely technically done. We can start practicing for the next one if my suspicions are confirmed. And if not... well, I'll double down on my efforts to make it happen next month.

But I don't think I'm wrong. I think my wife is pregnant.

Tristen is going to chop my dick off. I nearly laugh out loud at the thought.

First, I have to know whether I'm correct in my assumptions.

I set the mug and my phone on the nightstand and slip out of bed as quietly as I can. Fallon's a heavy sleeper, but I don't want to risk her waking up before I'm ready. In preparation for this moment, I had Gordon stock up on pregnancy tests, so I grab one out from under the sink and set it on the bathroom counter.

I'm too impatient to wait for Fallon to wake, so I stalk across the room and lower myself to the mattress beside her. My fingers drift along her spine and even in her sleep she shivers at my touch. I watch in fascination as goosebumps rise along her skin in the wake of my fingertips and the tiniest ghost of a smile falls across her lips.

"Wake up, little lamb," I murmur near her ear as I lean over her. Her scent drugs me and in seconds I feel like I'm drunk on her. The day's barely begun, and I've already forgotten everything but her. If I'm not careful, I could easily let everything go and allow myself to be wrapped up in all things Fallon. Every second of every day of the rest of my life belongs to her, and if I want to maintain what I've built, the power I've amassed, I need to carve out a place for everything else. Restrain myself, though it seems impossible here and now on the cusp of something life altering.

It's with that thought I lean back to try and clear my head. But then I remember why I'm insisting she wake up in the first place, and fuck it, I throw my reservations straight out the goddamn window. Eventually this obsession with my wife will wear off and I'll return to a more normal state.

Maybe.

If not, I'm going to welcome the chaos and change she brings because there's nothing on this earth more important to me than her.

"Cole?" she mumbles into the pillow before turning and blinking those enchanting green eyes up at me. "What's wrong?"

"Nothing's wrong. Now get up, you have a test to take." The sheets slide off her body as I tug them away and she turns to face me. I try to ignore that she's naked and I'm harder than ever.

"Am I in a nightmare right now? One of those ones where you stand up in front of the class and have to take a test or give a report you didn't study for?" Her eyes narrow as she watches me.

I laugh. "Not that kind of test. Come on." Her hand fits in mine as I drag her impatiently out of bed.

"What the hell, Cole?" Fallon says as we move into the bathroom. She yawns and rubs her eyes. I grab the test and push her toward the toilet. When I'm ripping into the box, she yanks it out of my hand, studying the front. "I'm not taking this. I'm not pregnant. I told you I'm getting on birth control."

The smirk that I give her isn't nice or patient. "Your period is a week late, Fallon. Now sit your ass down and pee on the goddamn stick."

Her eyes widen as the color drains from her face. I give her a second to do the mental math, but she'll come to the same conclusion everyone does: I'm right.

"Fuck," she finally mutters, snatching the test out of my hand. "Can I have some privacy?"

"No."

"Cole." She glares up at me.

"Fallon."

"Get out."

"We can argue about this all day, but I'm not moving from this spot until we know the results of that test. You can't physically force me out, and I told you before, there will be no space between us. So, pee on the fucking stick. I'll set a timer."

She huffs, but eventually she gives in and when she's done, she sets the stick on the counter before washing her hands and brushing her teeth while we wait. This is the longest three minutes of my entire fucking life, and Fallon is silent throughout it.

I know she's completely stuck in her own head. She didn't want this, not yet, but I can't find even an ounce of guilt inside of me. This is the way things are supposed to be between us. Existing on one another, creating our own family. She'll come around.

The timer on my phone goes off and I swipe the stick off the counter before she can, narrowing my eyes as I read the single word etched across the digital screen.

Pregnant.

"Well?" Fallon asks, hands on her hips. Her voice is laced with hysteria and something I can't place.

"We're having a baby," I tell her, handing her the test. She takes it and stares down at it so I can't see her expression. That doesn't work for me.

"Tell me what you're thinking," I demand, stepping into her personal space and pulling her against my chest. I don't give a single fuck about if she thinks she needs space to process. She doesn't. We created a life together, and we're going to see it through together.

"I thought I'd be freaked out or upset if this happened," she mumbles against my skin before lifting her gaze up to mine. I stiffen, waiting for the inevitable rejection of me or our baby. If she says she doesn't want to go through with the pregnancy, I'll just make sure to change her mind.

But I want her to be as happy as I am. Even now, even while I'm braced for the negativity, bursts of joy erupt inside of me like I've never felt before. The monster inside of me slams against its cage, demanding I unleash it so I can keep Fallon and our baby safe.

"And?" I prompt when it doesn't seem like she's going to say anything else.

I stare down at her, the tears shimmering in her eyes but not quite falling, the tiny freckle on the left side of her nose, the way her bottom lip has a soft dent right in the center, and I wait for her to speak.

It's like the universe is holding its breath, waiting for her. The air is thick with anticipation, and I tighten my hold, afraid she'll slip free. That I'll lose her somehow. That her next words will destroy something inside of me.

Her hand slips between our bodies and slides along her flat stomach while her sweet lips stretch into a smile, one that gets brighter and brighter by the second. "I'm freaked out, but not in the way I thought. I want this, Cole. I didn't think I would, not for ten more years at least," she narrows her eyes in a glare that makes me chuckle because that was never going to happen. "But it feels right. I'm... happy," she settles on.

Then she grabs my hand and splays it across her stomach, and I don't think I've ever felt as content in my entire life. If only my father could see me now.

CHAPTER 44

COLE

"I'm surprised you didn't bring Lucas with you for this," Tristen notes, staring out the passenger window of the SUV I'm driving. It's a rental reserved under an alias I'll never use again.

"I have a feeling you're going to need a bit of murder and mayhem in your life," I mutter, hoping he doesn't hear me over the bass of "Straight Shooter" by Skylar Grey pouring out of the speakers.

Unfortunately, he does.

He turns his attention away from the dark, empty streets and toward me.

"And why's that?"

Fuck it, we're almost there. Now's as good a time as any for this little confession. I turn down the music and smirk. "Because you're about to become a grandfather."

"Fuck you. That's not funny."

"I'm not kidding."

I take my eyes off the road long enough to look at Tristen, to make sure he's not about to grab his gun and blow my brains out. He's radiating fury, and his jaw is ticking, but all in all, I don't think my death is imminent. At least not until I park.

"Fallon is eighteen goddamn years old, Cole. You couldn't give her five years?"

"Eighteen is an adult, Tris, and no. I couldn't. Maybe if you weren't married to a blood sucking demon, you'd understand. I can't let her leave me once she finds out how dark shit can get."

There. I confessed my ultimate truth, the one I didn't even want to admit to myself. Yes, I'm obsessed with Fallon, but the truth is I could've given her more time if I was normal. But I'm not. And to ensure she could never leave me, I needed her pregnant and in love with me.

Mission fucking accomplished.

I'm a thirty-six-year-old man terrified of what an eighteen-year-old girl will do to me if she ever tries to leave. Fallon is my one weakness, one I'll never give up for anything. It might paint a target on her back—and mine—but nothing will ever touch her as long as my heart still beats.

It's weird as fuck talking about this shit with her father, but it's times like these I need him to be my best friend first and her father second.

"How much longer?" Tristen grits out from between his locked jaws. His hands are balled into fists on his thighs, so tightly the skin is turning white.

"Two minutes." I turn the music back up. It's not that I mind explaining myself to Tristen but talking isn't what he needs right now. I know him better than anyone else, outside of my wife. Right now, he needs to burn shit down. Destruction will be his release.

We pull up a couple of blocks down from Nine Circles, the Fallen Angels' shitty home base. The dive bar no one but them will miss once it's gone. The place looks to be about half full tonight, with dozens of motorcycles out front.

Tristen and I get out of the car, closing the doors gently so we don't draw attention. We're both decked out in head to toe black, and I round the back of the SUV with Tristen on my heels.

From the back, I pull out a can of gasoline and Tristen grabs a heavy-duty chain with a heavier duty padlock attached.

We slowly stalk toward the building, hanging back for a few minutes while the burly leather-clad bikers out front snub out their smokes and head back inside. The more men we can take out, the better.

When the doors swing shut behind them, Tris secures the handles with the chain and padlock. The windows in this place are nearly non-existent, just one in the back office and it's only big enough to maybe fit one small person at a time. The bar is a bunker and there's no way they pass safety inspections without bribing the fuck out of whatever official conducts the thing.

This is an execution, a message to Anton for sending that amateur into my house, my fucking *bedroom* to try and kill me.

He's about to find out what a professional kill looks and feels like.

While I cover the door, Tristen grabs the gas from me and takes off around the back of the building. The Fallen Angels didn't want anyone getting too close, so their bar is on the outskirts of Mulberry and sits on the corner of a street with alleys on either side so you can almost walk around the entire building.

The gasoline fumes drift on the air as he dumps it on every surface he can reach. I take a lighter out of my pocket, flicking the lid open and closed. Open and closed. Tristen finishes and comes back to stand at my side. He takes the lighter out of my gloved hand and flicks it open, holding it up to the gas can.

It ignites instantly, and he tosses it at the row of motorcycles where he ended his trail of fuel. They go up in flames within seconds, but it's not like in the movies where there's a massive explosion. At least not until one of the gas tanks catch. Then there's a *boom* and the heat of the flames licks at my skin.

"You're right. I needed that," Tristen says with a grin as he watches the chaos, the inferno reflecting in his eyes. "If you ever call me grandpa, I'll slit your throat." He grumbles, "I'm only thirty-six goddamn years old, Cole. I hope the stress of being a father gives you gray hair and erectile dysfunction, you dick."

I chuckle as smoke fills the air over the destroyed building, sparks flying up towards the overcast night sky. Even the moon doesn't dare show its face tonight in the face of so much death.

We take off back to the car to watch the show just until we hear sirens in the distance. The building burns, and I only get a chance to hear the start of the screams before Tris and I have to take off, but they soothe something in that place where my soul should be.

Backtracking the long way to our part of town, we ditch the rental with a chop shop Tristen uses and swap it for a ride back to my place. "You want to tell me why we had to turn Nine Circles to ash tonight?"

Yeah, Tristen went along with my plan without asking any questions or needing an explanation. That's the kind of ride or die friend he is—all of them are.

"Anton put a contract on my head, and one of the guys who took the job came into my bedroom, where Fallon was sleeping, and thought he'd try and kill me." I shake my head at the sloppiness. I need to talk to Lucas about upping our vetting standards if this is the caliber of assassin we're hiring at Red Rum.

"I recognized the motherfucker because he used to work for me." Can't say I'm upset over that loss.

"Did he touch Fallon?" Tristen's no longer relaxed, his body strung tight with tension all over again.

"Fuck, no. But he scared her." I don't tell him that watching me murder the guy had her more turned on than I think I've ever seen before.

Some of the stiffness bleeds out of Tristen. "Did you make it painful?"

"Well, I didn't draw it out, but I don't imagine it felt good when I slit his throat and let him bleed out on my hardwoods. I wasn't about to take any chances with my wife right there or I would've dragged him to The Icebox and really made him regret his life choices."

"Mmm," Tristen hums, staring out the window, and if I know my best friend as well as I think I do, I can only assume he's imagining all the ways he would've killed Matteo for fucking with his little girl.

CHAPTER 45

FALLON

Pine needles crunch under my boots as I stomp through the woods behind Cole's house. Well, I guess *my* house now. Time passes so quickly, it's hard to believe it's already been several weeks since we found out about the baby. It's been months since I've had the weight of my camera around my neck and the clean scent of earth, pine, and rain in my nose.

I've missed this.

I lift my camera and adjust the aperture before snapping a picture of the soft green moss that grows along the rough bark of an ancient tree. The juxtaposition makes my heart happy.

It's late spring in Washington which means I'm wearing about ten layers, ready to strip them off as the day heats up. The sun is hiding behind a solid marine layer of clouds, so it'll be a while before they burn off and let the streaks of gold filter down through the canopy, but I don't mind the wait.

So far with this pregnancy I'm not feeling much different. Maybe a little sleepier, but otherwise good. Well, except I want to jump on Cole the second he walks through the door or picks me up from school, but that's not much different than usual when it comes to him.

He's always been irresistible to me.

These woods are the same ones I grew up hiking every inch of, but at the same time not. Cole lives about half a mile away from my father, so while I can walk deeper into the forest and find my usual favorite places, there are also plenty of new ones to discover, too.

The sound of water rushing catches my attention and draws me deeper into the unfamiliar parts of the forest. I can already feel myself relaxing as the stress of everything that's happened since my birthday starts to fade.

I need this.

I stop a couple of times on my way to the river I can hear but not see yet, snapping pictures of mushrooms growing on a rotten log and a whole field of ferns. If I could just do this for the rest of my life, take pictures of the world around me and lose myself in living, I'd be one happy girl.

I don't think Cole would like that I'm out here alone, especially now that I'm pregnant, but he doesn't get to control every aspect of my life. That's why I wait until I'm already out here to send him a text letting him know where I am. He can come try and stop me, but he's going to have to strap on some hiking boots to do it.

It's been quiet since the attempt on his life, and the man wasn't there for me, only Cole, so I think I'm safe. Spending time in the woods is better than therapy, and I'll never stop. It doesn't hurt that he's busy with Savage Society business for the next few hours and probably won't be able to track me down.

The strap for my camera digs into the back of my neck while I let it hang and check the time on my phone. My service is crap. Zero bars, and I hope my text to Cole got out. I frown down at it, but I grew up in these woods. For the next hour or so, I won't need it anyway.

I inch closer to the river, now getting glimpses of rushing water broken up by boulders and frothy white peaks through the trees.

There's no trail out here. I'm carving my way through fallen trees, rocks, sticks, and plants so dense I can't see the dirt underneath my feet. The people of Emerald Hills—particularly this neighborhood—aren't your traditional outdoorsy Washingtonians. This place is practically untouched by the outside world, the wild edge creeping up on the civilization at its borders, itching to take it back over.

Finally, I step right up to the bank of the river, my toes touching the place where the land cuts away and below are only swift water and rocks. I stare down into the swirling, churning water and think about how everything's changed in such a short time.

Cole doesn't like to give me time to process, probably because he's afraid if I do, I'll run. If only he could see into my head, read my mind. Sometimes I think he can, but it's only because he pays attention.

But if he really *could* see inside my thoughts, he'd know there's nothing short of death that would make me leave. It seems like I've always known he was supposed to be mine in some way. I just didn't believe *he* thought that. Now that I know he does, I'm not going anywhere. Ever.

I'm so focused on my thoughts and feelings, sorting through everything, that when the muddy bank gives way and my feet tumble out from underneath me, I don't even have time to reach out and grab something. I'm freefalling three feet into a frigid river with a current so strong it immediately sweeps my feet out from under me, slamming my head into a rock.

There's no saving my camera, but that's the least of my worries as my elbows, knees, and hips crash into the slippery rocks. I finally manage to reach out and snag a branch from a fallen tree that's close to the riverbank and sticking out of the water, but when I go to stand, the rocks are so slick my ankle twists the second I put weight on it, and I collapse back into the icy water.

If it wasn't for my ironclad grip on the branch, I'd have been swept away again. The water is so cold it's like needles of ice stabbing every inch of my skin, and my teeth chatter while I shiver violently. My clothes are heavy, and my ankle throbs. At least the cold water will keep it from swelling too much, but if I don't find a way to get out of here soon, I'll get hypothermia and die.

Fuck. *The baby.*

My phone is still in the back pocket of my jeans, but not only do I not have service, but it's soaked and probably completely dead from the damage. Moving slowly, I grab onto another branch a little higher up and pull myself up a little further out of the water. I try to ignore the way my hands cramp from the cold and eventually get to the top of the log, which is actually the roots of a fallen tree.

I'm curled into a ball, shivering and panting. I'm so cold, it's impossible to take in a full breath and I'm slowly going numb. My eyelids are heavy and I'm pretty sure I have a concussion so I refuse to close them.

I don't know how much time passes, but my muscles ache from the involuntary tremors wracking my body and I'm tired. So, so tired.

"Fallon!" I hear off in the distance. It's a man's voice, still so far away that it's too quiet to tell who it is. It could be Cole, my father, or any of the other Savage Six.

It could also be another assassin.

I shouldn't have come out here alone. It was stupid, and I wasn't thinking. Now that I've got another life to worry about and not just my own, I can't take risks like this. Not without a satellite phone or at the very least watching where I put my damn feet.

Ugh. Cole's never going to let me out of his sight now.

I open my mouth to try and yell back, but nothing comes out. I still can't catch my breath even if I could get my voice to work.

"Fallon! Where the fuck are you?" Another voice yells, closer this time. I also know it's Cole because of the way the ball of ice that's made a home in my chest thaws just the tiniest bit and makes it so I can take my first full breath in what feels like eons.

"He-r-r-re!" I choke out, barely loud enough to hear myself over the raging river. "I'm-m-m her-r-re!" I try again, a little louder this time.

I try to sit up, but I can't. I'm weak and numb and my hands and feet feel like they're on fire. "Fuck!" Cole bites out from somewhere behind me, I'm guessing on the riverbank over my shoulder. I can't turn my head to look, though.

"Tris! She's over here!" Cole yells, and my lower lip trembles as tears slide down my face. I held onto hope he'd find me, even if I didn't know how he'd know where I was or if he got my message. I should never doubt my husband's obsession with me.

"Shit, sweetheart. Are you hurt?" my dad asks as he catches up to wherever Cole's standing. They're close enough that I can hear them clearly now, but when I try to move my head to look, my neck aches and cramps and all I can do is whimper pathetically while I shiver like a chihuahua.

"I t-t-twi-i-sted m-my an-n-kle." My teeth are chattering too hard to form words.

I close my eyes and listen to my husband and my father discussing how to get me out of here, and I finally let myself drift knowing no matter what, they'll make sure I'm okay. That my baby is okay.

And with that thought, I sleep.

CHAPTER 46

COLE

"I'm putting a fucking tracker in her," I bark the second we walk through the door. Fallon's curled up in my arms shivering and so cold it hurts me to touch her skin.

Which is tinted blue for fuck's sake.

She's also unconscious and there's a lump on the back of her head. I can't even let myself think about the baby without spiraling into pure chaos in my head—chaos that can only be cured by bloodshed.

"Dr. McCarthy's on his way," Tristen says, slipping his phone into his pocket. He wisely says nothing about me chipping his daughter.

By the time we're in my bedroom, I'm shaking nearly as badly as Fallon is. She's exhausted and won't wake up and I need to get her warm as soon as possible. I can worry about how infuriated I am at her for taking such a risk once I know she and the baby are both okay.

"Start the shower," I order and Tristen hurries past me into the bathroom. I lay Fallon out on the bed and strip her down before wrapping her in the sheet. She and Tris may be close, but I know she wouldn't want him to see her naked. Fuck, *I* don't want him to see her naked.

He steps out of the bathroom and leans against the wall out of the way. "It's ready."

Fallon fits in my arms like she was made to be there as I haul her dead weight up off the bed and into the bathroom, stepping into the walk-in shower without bothering to take off my clothes. I hold her under the warm water while it soaks into my clothes, but I hardly notice.

Nothing matters but getting Fallon warm and making sure she's safe.

My pulse hasn't slowed since I spotted my wife clinging to that goddamn tree in the river. I thought she was dead, and I was on the verge of jumping right in beside her. Without Fallon, there's no reason for me to go on.

Her shivers are beginning to subside and she's heavy now that her body and the sheet are completely waterlogged, so I kneel and finally sit on the floor of the shower, making sure the water keeps hitting her. It splashes onto my face and drips down my hair, my eyelashes, my nose. I blink it all away, uncaring about anything as I stare at Fallon's pale face and wait for her to stir.

Time passes, but I have no idea how much. It's not until Fallon's cheeks have regained some color and her trembles have stopped that I start to relax. Tristen steps into the bathroom, his eyebrows drawn together, and his forehead creased with concern for his only child. I tighten my hold on her, making sure the sheet is still covering her naked body.

"How is she?" he asks, though he keeps his voice quiet

enough that it's hard to hear over the endless stream of hot water pouring out of the waterfall showerhead.

"Better, I think," I tell him, though I don't know. I'm transfixed by her breath, watching her chest rise and fall to reassure myself she's still alive. My hand is wrapped lightly around her throat so I can feel every steady beat of her heart—the heart that belongs to me.

"Dr. McCarthy is here. He's waiting in your study."

"Give us ten minutes and send him up to the bedroom," I say, dismissing Tris. Fallon's eyes flutter open at the sound of my voice, finding mine just for a second, before she passes back out. That tiny bit of awareness eases some of the terror coursing through me.

I manage to get Fallon and myself up and turn off the water, not giving a single fuck as we drip all over the floor. I let the sheet slip off her and lay her on the bed, leaving her to go find her one of my t-shirts and a towel to dry her off.

I need her surrounded by me, wearing my clothes.

She snores softly as I towel off her body then slip the t-shirt over her head and tuck her into bed. Once she's handled, I strip out of my soaked clothes and leave them in a pile on the bathroom floor before changing into dry ones.

I don't take my eyes off Fallon for even a second.

Just as I'm pulling a sweatshirt over my head—something I'd never normally wear outside of the gym—Dr. McCarthy knocks lightly on the door.

"Come in," I call out, keeping my voice low so I don't wake my wife. I'm torn—I want her so badly to open her eyes again so I know everything's fine, but I also know she needs her rest.

Dr. McCarthy steps into the room and his white eyebrows raise in surprise at me hovering over my little lamb. He's patched up my bullet and knife wounds for years but never seen me with a woman. He's been the hired doctor for the Savage Society for years, so he knows us all well.

"What happened to Miss Ashwell?" he asks, as he moves around the bed to stand beside Fallon. I know he needs to examine her, but I find myself wanting to shove him out our bedroom door and away from her. The idea of him touching her is almost enough to have me reaching for my gun. My fingers twitch at my sides with the need to feel the weight of a weapon.

"It's Callahan now. Fallon's my wife," I finally say, though I'm still fighting an internal battle on whether or not to let him touch her. In the end, my need to know she and the baby are okay wins out and I take her hand in mine but move out of the doctor's way.

Dr. McCarthy nods as he sets his bag down on the edge of the bed and digs inside, pulling out everything he'll need for his exam.

"She fell into the fucking river." Even getting those words out enrages me all over again. "I think she hit her head."

Dr. McCarthy hums in acknowledgement as he checks Fallon's blood pressure.

"She's pregnant," I tell him, and he nods as he checks her temperature, his mouth turning down into a frown. "What? What's wrong?" I ask, the grip on Fallon's hand tightening like if I'm not holding on hard enough, she might drift away.

"Nothing really. Her core body temperature is just lower than I'd like." He turns and eyes me, not unkindly, and I stare right back.

"What?"

"Maybe you should wait outside."

"I'm not leaving."

"Then I need you to stand to the side and keep your comments to yourself until I'm finished."

Under normal circumstances, he'd be dead before he finished that sentence, but I need him, so I let it slide for now. If Fallon's not okay, I'll make sure he understands the depth of my wrath.

Tristen steps into the doorway and leans against it, jerking his head toward the hall. I reluctantly drop Fallon's hand and follow him out to let Dr. McCarthy finish his exam, but I never take my eyes off her. Not for a second.

"What?"

I'm not even looking at Tris, but he'd be an idiot if he expected me to.

"We need to deal with Anton. After what we did to him, I'm surprised he hasn't retaliated yet. Let me set a meeting. I'll inform him marriage to Fallon's off the table and we'll deal with the fallout then and there instead of waiting for him to come at us." When I glance over at him, Tristen's watching his daughter as closely as I am. "I've taken care of the rail yard and it's back under my control, though I doubt he realizes it yet."

I'm sure we're both thinking the same thing—if he came for her now, in this state, he might stand a chance of hurting her.

Dr. McCarthy is setting up a complicated machine I'm assuming is a portable ultrasound. He must've come prepared for everything, judging by the amount of equipment he hauled into my house.

"Fine. Set it up." I start to walk back inside but turn back. "But I'm going to be there with you. If Anton plans to fuck with my wife, I'll end him."

"Done," he says.

And then I tune the rest of the world out while I walk toward my little lamb. A sense of excitement bubbles under the surface of my anxiety as I take my spot on the side of the bed beside Fallon and stare at the black screen where I'll see my child for the very first time.

The end is in sight, and once it's done, nothing will ever come between Fallon and me again.

CHAPTER 47

COLE

Fallon needs rest.

I need bloodshed.

Dr. McCarthy left—after putting the tracker in the back of my wife's neck—and I paced around my bedroom until Tristen came up and told me Anton agreed to a meeting tonight.

Fallon's barely been conscious since we got home, but Dr. McCarthy assured me that's normal, especially at this stage in her pregnancy and with what she's been through. Her body is depleted and the best thing for her right now is sleep.

Not to mention the fucking concussion she has.

The last thing I want to do is leave, but I can't relax like this. Not with the anger coursing through my veins, the helplessness Fallon forced on me earlier today. I'm *never* helpless or powerless. I've made sure of that.

Except today I was.

I need to purge this feeling. To expend the helpless energy festering inside of me.

Anton Leven is the perfect target for my wrath.

Xander sits on a chair in the corner of my bedroom with a rifle lying across his lap. He twirls a knife around and between his fingers as he lounges, and I know nothing will touch Fallon with this psycho watching over her.

The trust I have in him and the other four men I consider brothers will allow me to face Anton tonight with my focus intact. Well, mostly. Without having my own eyes on my wife, it'll still be a struggle, but this needs to be done.

"Why are you leaving my daughter with Xander and not Beckett?" Tristen asks me the second I step outside the door.

I chuckle. "As if one of them is better than the other. They're both certifiable."

"And my question is still valid. Father ADHD in there is going to come across something shiny that he wants to chase down and murder and he'll forget all about keeping an eye on Fallon."

"Beckett's working on his latest book tonight. He couldn't make it." Tristen flashes me a look because we both understand what *working on his manuscript* means and fuck knows we won't interrupt unless it's absolutely necessary.

With Xander able to step in tonight, it's not. So, we'll leave Beckett to his murderous plots and hope Xan is up to the task of protecting my wife when I can't be there.

"I can't wait to see that fucker's face when we tell him," Tristen says once we're outside as he jogs around to the driver's side of his car. I stop and look up one last time in the direction of my bedroom. I can't actually see the window from this side of the house but knowing I'm leaving Fallon here doesn't sit right.

It's not like I'd take her along for this. Not while she's pregnant. I need to suck up my issues and get through this. Showing weakness in any way to Anton Leven is about as appealing as using a nail gun on my eyeballs. I've tortured someone that way before and it's fucking disgusting. They pop like a water balloon.

You can imagine then that letting Anton in on how essential Fallon is to me isn't something I'm going to do tonight.

I slip into the passenger seat and when we pull out of the gates, another car moves in close behind us. "Romeo and Lucas," Tris supplies and I relax back against the seat.

"Where are we meeting Fuckface tonight now that he doesn't have a home base?" I ask, smirking as I remember burning his men alive inside Nine Circles. It's one of my happier memories and I've certainly been enjoying reliving it.

"My warehouse at the end of East twenty-second," he says and then grips the wheel harder. "I wish we could just kill the motherfucker."

"We will, but he needs to suffer first, and we need information. Is Rome any further along the money trail to Anton's source?"

"He said it was like a rusted chain. There are all kinds of links and shit that break off when he tries to follow them and some lead nowhere. It's a mess, and he's trying to untangle it as quickly as he can, but he's not a miracle worker."

I scoff. "Could've fooled me. He's turned shit into gold for us before."

"I didn't say he can't do it, just that it's taking longer than any of us would like. He'll find the answers we need, but that means leaving Anton breathing a little longer."

"Oh, look. A welcoming party," I say as Tristen parks outside of his warehouse. Anton's already there, flanked by his leather-clad biker clan. There aren't as many men as I'm sure he would've liked, and when I climb out of the car, I meet his stare and smirk.

Fury sparks in his eyes which only widens my grin. He can't

prove it was me who burned Nine Circles to the ground—thanks to his sketchy as fuck lack of security cameras—but he knows the truth. Unfortunately for him, without proof he can't do shit—just how I like it.

Lucas and Romeo pull up behind us and we walk into the warehouse shoulder to shoulder—a fortified wall Anton and his men have no hope of going up against.

Once we're inside, they follow, and Anton's minions spread out behind him blocking the exits. Lucas stands beside me and casually aims the rifle he's holding at the man standing in the main entry point. Romeo keeps his gun trained on Anton and Tris and I are armed but don't bother showing off our arsenal. There's no need.

Everyone in this room knows if Anton or his men fire on us it'll be their end.

"Give me back my money," Anton demands. "I'm done waiting."

I chuckle and Tris grins at him. "Well, you're right about that. There's no need to wait when you're already about to get everything you deserve."

"And for the record, since we're just diving in, the wedding is off."

Anton's mask of calm slips and the rage he's feeling rushes to the surface. "What the fuck do you mean? We had a deal!"

"Yeah, well, you broke that deal before we even made it by luring the shipyard manager away from me, didn't you?" Tristen drops his taunting smile in favor of a murderous stare down. "And let's not forget about how you fucked my wife on my daughter's birthday—the night of your engagement."

Anton pales and his mouth falls open as if he's about to defend himself, but then snaps shut because what the fuck could he possibly say?

Tristen chuckles darkly. "You think I don't have every inch of my property wired with security cameras?" I know he's bluffing. The inside cameras only cover the main living spaces, but the bedrooms aren't under surveillance.

Thank fuck or he would've killed me for fucking around with Fallon before I had a chance to explain.

"And finally, you tried to make demands and when they didn't work, you came after Cole." Tristen clicks his tongue like he's scolding an errant child. "Did you really think it was a smart move taking out a contract on Cole in his own fucking company?"

"I don't know what you're talking about," Anton says, shifting his weight to his other foot. It's clear he wants to run, but the second he turns his back before we dismiss him, he's a dead man.

"Well, either way. This is your official notice that the engagement with Fallon is off and that we know what you've been up to. If I were you, I'd pack up my shit, dissolve my gang, and get the fuck out of Mulberry before we come for you."

Anton's clearly not smart, though, as evidenced by the fury still rolling off him and his next words. "You promised her to me, and I've got plans for her. She's mine."

"See, that's going to be a problem seeing as how she's already married to *me*," I drawl, reaching into my blazer and slipping my gun out of the shoulder holster concealed under my jacket. I casually flick the safety off, never wavering in the eye contact I'm maintaining with a trembling Anton.

Whether it's from fury or terror is hard to say.

"I'd suggest you take Tristen's advice and fuck off. Hunting our prey is so much more fun than catching it in a trap and putting it out of its misery."

Anton's eyes narrow in a glare and his men step closer before he holds up his hand. "I know you burned down Nine Circles," he says, trying to get in one last shot, scrambling for any leverage he can get.

I grin, baring my teeth viciously. "Prove it."

"This isn't over," he says as he turns to leave and quickly steps in front of his men so their backs are to us, not his.

"Fucking coward," Romeo spits as we watch them leave.

"Odds that he'll run and leave us the fuck alone after this?" I ask, tucking my gun away when the sound of tires squealing on pavement makes its way inside the warehouse.

"Low," Lucas says, but we exchange a look. Both of us have been looking forward to Anton's demise, and now we're closer than ever.

CHAPTER 48

FALLON

Graduation is less than a month away. It used to be the most important milestone in my life, the one I knew would change everything once it was here. That girl feels like a completely different person than who I am now.

Now I couldn't give a single shit about it.

Three months ago, I married Cole, and life has been blissful ever since. Maybe we're still in our honeymoon phase or whatever, but we've settled into our lives so effortlessly, it's hard to imagine a time when Cole wasn't right beside me anytime I want him to be—and sometimes when I don't.

He takes his husbandly duties very seriously and I'm not mad about it.

My baby belly is getting harder and harder to hide. I think I can still pass it off as a food baby, but by the time I graduate it'll be obvious I'm knocked up. The bitches on the cheer squad have been giving me shit about gaining weight for weeks.

Despite all of that, this morning I'm feeling good.

I'm living for the second trimester right now. My morning (ha!) sickness is gone, I've got energy, I've never been hornier in my entire life, and I'm teetering on the edge of being able to show off my cute belly.

But I'm annoyed that I have to go to school. I worked hard for my diploma, so I'm not about to drop out, but it feels like a waste of time. Pretending to be the ice queen as per usual feels tired. I care less and less what people at school think about me.

Between my photography, being a wife and mother, and getting more involved in Cole's and my father's businesses, what's the point?

I tilt my chin up higher as I march toward the front doors of Emerald Hills Prep, feeling Cole's stare burning into my back. A little shiver runs down my spine knowing he's devouring me with his eyes. I don't think I'll ever get tired of that feeling.

An arm wraps around mine and I almost throw a punch before I realize it's Waverly. "Girl, I'm counting down the days until we're out of here." She sighs dramatically. "How's my little peanut this morning?"

I pretty much told Wave about my pregnancy as soon as I found out, so she's already proclaimed herself Auntie Waverly and is following along with everything as if she's going through it herself. I think she even put an app on her phone.

I don't know what I'd do without her.

I think for a second and then smirk. "Insatiable."

She throws her head back and laughs, not giving a fuck that we're blocking the entrance. "That's my girl."

"Ms. Ashwell!" a booming voice calls, raising above the buzz of everyone chattering the halls.

I frown and look for its source and Waverly tips her head to our left where the new principal's assistant, Matthew, is striding toward us.

"Ugh, good luck. Want me to stick around?" Waverly asks, narrowing her eyes at the man as if she's weighing whether or not he's a threat. I have no doubt if she thought he was, she'd be on the phone texting Cole so fast I wouldn't have a chance of stopping her.

Traitor.

"No, I'm sure there's just another new student or something. I'll meet you in first period, but do you mind grabbing my books out of my locker?"

She nods and slides her arm out of mine. "Sure. Text me if you need me."

As she leaves, the principal's assistant moves into my space. I should probably make small talk, but I don't really care. The Fallon who gave a shit about making a good impression in this place is gone.

"Ms. Ashwell—"

"It's Mrs. Callahan."

His cheeks redden and I can't tell if he's annoyed or embarrassed. "Ms. Callahan, Principal Collins needs to see you right away. If you'll follow me." He turns on his heel and hurries off and I try to keep up.

I have no idea what could be so important that I need to rush there like this, but whatever. Maybe there's a new student waiting to be shown to first period before the bell rings or something.

Ever since I agreed to be the official welcome committee for all the new scholarship students, Principal Collins has had me in his office constantly. Getting summoned there is nothing new, and now I'm just annoyed. I wish I'd said no when he foisted this bullshit on me, but it's so close to graduation now that I don't want to make waves.

"I'll let him know you're here," the assistant says as he

rounds his desk and plops down into his chair behind it. He pushes some buttons on the phone and murmurs into the receiver before nodding a couple of times and hanging up.

He looks up at me. "You can go in."

I really want to curtsey obnoxiously at his uptight behavior, but I hold back. When I swing open the door to Principal Collins' office, I stop in my tracks at the man he's talking to. My brain is screaming at me to turn around and get the hell out of here, but my feet are rooted in place.

Seriously, they're so frozen, it's like they've sprouted roots that've dug into the cracks in the expensive stone flooring.

"Fallon, Princess. Come in and close the door behind you," Anton says, rising out of the chair in front of the desk and moving to my side. He puts his arm around my waist and pulls me against him and it's that action that finally snaps me out of my stupor. I stomp on his foot and elbow him in the ribs so he lets go, gasping for air as he glowers down at me.

"Don't call me that." I turn to Principal Collins who's watching us with a look of pure boredom on his face. "What the hell is going on?" It's obvious I don't want to go with Anton, so why the hell is the principal letting this happen?

"Language, Ms. *Ashwell*," he snaps. I grit my teeth at his obvious dig at my name. "Your husband wanted to take you out of school for the day as a surprise and came in to clear it with me first. As you're ahead in all your classes and likely to be our valedictorian, I've, of course, approved and notified your teachers."

I'm gaping at him, totally at a loss for words. What the actual fuck is happening right now? Isn't the school principal supposed to want you to stay in school? And there's no way he doesn't know who Cole is and what he looks like.

"He's not my—" I start to say, and Anton slides his hand over my mouth. Normally I'd bite the shit out of his palm, but the knifepoint digging into my back right over my kidney stops me. I may be able to get out of his hold, but I'm not about to attempt it and put my baby at risk.

"Thanks, Collins. We'll get out of your hair." I imagine the smile on Anton's face is slimy as hell, but I can't actually see it because he's still holding my mouth. What kind of idiot is my principal anyway? It's clear Anton is taking me hostage right now... isn't it?

But then he's a criminal like every other man in my life. I imagine he has access to fake IDs and a shady as fuck backstory that was convincing enough to win over a bored educator like Principal Collins. Or maybe my asshole principal let Anton pay him off. Who the fuck knows?

"Fight me and I'll gut you and then go for your husband. I won't stop until everyone you care about is dead," Anton murmurs in my ear as he guides us out of the office.

I've got my phone tucked in the waistband of my skirt—stupid uniforms without pockets—under my jacket, but when his arm brushes against it I know I'm screwed. His footsteps come to a stop, and he reaches under my jacket and plucks it out, tossing it onto the floor and stomping it to pieces before shoving me forward again.

The only hope I've got now is that Waverly notices I don't show for class and her obsessive texting of every little thing baby and me related to my husband pays off for the first time ever. Otherwise, there's a good chance today is the day I die.

CHAPTER 49

FALLON

"Where the hell am I?" I ask as one of Anton's men rips off the blindfold he tied on me the second we got out of the school.

"My new temporary headquarters," Anton says, striding around the room and running his fingertip along the windowsill. "You like it?" He turns to me with a mean grin. "You can thank your husband for the shitty accommodations since he burned the last place to the ground."

"Good. I hope he finds you and does it again," I say, lifting my chin. Rage sweeps over his face as he takes a step forward, but then he regains control and exhales slowly.

Then he smiles at me again, and instinctively I know whatever he's about to say I'm not going to like. "Do you know why you're here?"

"Because your ego can't take the fact you lost to Cole?" I smile sweetly.

He laughs and it's too loud, booming off the high ceilings of the run-down warehouse we appear to be in. "Oh, Princess. My plans are so much bigger than Cole, your father, or the rest of the Savage Society." He moves to my side, using his finger to tip my chin up and I recoil from his disgusting touch. "And they all start with you."

Heels click somewhere off in the distance and thankfully Anton puts some space between us. I get about thirty seconds of time to breathe and process before my fucking *mother* sidles up to his side. She throws her arm around him—just one because she's got a drink in the other—and kisses him with everything she's got. It's all tongue and lips and gross wet noises that make me gag.

The baby flutters in my belly and *holy shit* I think it just felt it move for the first time.

"Erika? What the hell are you doing here?"

She pulls away from Anton and swipes her finger under her lips to fix the smudged lipstick. "You have something we want."

"Sure, and I want you to fuck off and let Dad go, but we don't always get what we want, do we?"

"Maybe we can come to an agreement," she says, leaning into Anton as he wraps his arm around her waist.

I look past her to him. "You know she's just using you. She'll suck you dry and crush the husk of whatever's left under her heel. You'll never be enough for her."

Anton cracks a smile like he doesn't believe me but whatever. At least I tried.

My mother's eyes darken but I'm intrigued. I want to know what it is they think I have and why they want it. Plus, if I can actually get her to agree to divorce my dad, it'll be my greatest accomplishment and that's saying something. She's got her claws in deep.

"What's it going to take for you to leave Dad for good? Give him a divorce and let him move on with someone who deserves him?" I'm already tired of this conversation and it just started. She smirks before tipping back what's left of her drink and setting the martini glass down. It's ten a.m. and I doubt this is her first.

"Your trust fund," she says, running her fingers through her bleached blonde hair and not even bothering to look at me. She pulls a small mirror out of fuck knows where and frowns at her reflection before snapping it shut.

Laughter slips past my lips. "My trust fund."

She shrugs, finally turning her attention my way. Yay. "Sign it over to me and I disappear."

Why do I think it won't be that simple? "What's to keep you or your pathetic boy toy here from coming back and harassing Dad for more?"

Her eyes sparkle with malice. "You'll have to take my word for it."

I scoff. "Yeah, that's not going to happen. I'm not just going to hand over millions of dollars to you without a contract."

"Then I guess you don't want me gone that bad, do you, sweetheart?" I cringe as she uses the same name for me that Dad does. She slides away from Anton and over to a makeshift bar in the corner, starting to mix another drink. When I say makeshift bar, I mean a folding table with a jug of vodka and a couple of mixers still in the plastic bags from the grocery store on it.

My body burns hot as rage unfurls inside of me. It's not something I typically let happen considering when I do, the consequences are usually deadly.

"You'll sign a contract, or you'll get nothing. You don't step foot in Emerald Hills. You don't contact Dad, or me. You don't contact Cole or any of the guys in the Savage Six. You stay out of our lives completely." I bite my lip, trying to think of any loophole she might be able to exploit, but that's what lawyers are for. "*If* you sign, I'll give you my trust fund and you give Dad a divorce and stay the fuck away."

She laughs lightly while she mixes her screwdriver. Anton watches her like she's a goddess and if he only prays hard enough at her altar, he'll get everything he's ever dreamed of. "I'll think about it."

Fingers curled into fists, I force them to stay by my sides so I don't launch myself at her. "Why would you want to stick around here? It's obvious you hate us and your life. This is your chance, your ticket to freedom. Go fuck whoever you want, not that you don't already."

"That's not—" Anton starts but I talk over him.

"Spend until you can't spend anymore. I don't care, but you need to leave."

She makes a show of pouring the orange juice into the glass and stirring it with her finger. I guess this is her breakfast. "See, when you want me gone so badly, it only makes me want to stay more. Besides, your dad needs me."

"To what? Bring STDs to his bed? Fuck assholes like Anton behind his back?" Now it's my turn to laugh. "To make him look bad? To tarnish every bit of respect we both work so hard to earn?" I move closer. "Do you know the boys at school call you a whore? Pay the right amount and Erika Ashwell will fuck you. You're nothing but a hooker in an expensive dress drowning herself in top shelf liquor. A used up old bitch who sells herself to *teenage boys* because the adults have gotten sick of your diseased cunt."

Even Anton chokes. Bet he didn't know what Romeo dug up on Carter Van Buren's phone when he went for his deep dive. I know I wish I didn't.

I have never in my entire life spoken to my mother like this, but she pissed me off and now I can't seem to stop. We're both shaking with fury, and her long, red claws are digging into her palm. "Isn't it time to find a new hunting ground? Are there so few adult men here you haven't fucked yet that you've had to resort to jailbait?" I step closer. "Let me put it to you this way. You take the money and get the *fuck* out of my town, leave Dad alone and let him move on, and I won't turn in the video I have of you spreading your legs for a couple of high school sophomores. Somehow, I don't think you'd survive jail. Orange isn't really your color."

The one good thing Isaac and Carter did for me was give me what I needed to blackmail my mother.

Although the thought brings me joy, I'd rather have her gone than locked up close by where she can still reach out to people who might help her. I'll still hold on to the video in case she decides to pop her skanky head back up in the future, though. I can't move on and be happy with Cole knowing my mother could ruin everything my father's built with a snap of her fingers. This has to be done.

She sucks in a breath before downing her entire glass. She slams it back onto the table. "Fine, you ungrateful little cunt. I'll sign and disappear but you're giving me that video."

"Sure, I'll give it to you when you sign," I agree, knowing she's not smart enough to consider I've got it backed up to the Cloud. That video is my insurance policy and I worked hard to get it. I'm not just going to hand it over. I'm taking a page from Cole's playbook. Say whatever I need to so the deal gets done.

She nods. "Send the contract to my lawyer."

"Give me a phone and I'll get it done this afternoon." I don't wait to hear whether she tries to beg anything else out of me because I'm not in a giving mood. I've just given away my entire safety net, but I don't care. Having her gone will be worth every single cent, but Anton's not done yet.

He steps forward, glaring at me with hatred shining bright in his eyes. "That was what my love wants from you but satisfying me is going to take something entirely different."

CHAPTER 50

COLE

The barstool scrapes across the dirty wood floor as I take the seat across from Anton. He's wearing a smug grin because he thinks he's won. He thinks he holds all the cards.

He's dead wrong.

I gesture to the bartender who scurries across the room to drop a glass of amber liquid in front of me. I don't give a fuck what it is, but when I sip it, it tastes like paint thinner. Cheap liquor is the best I can hope for in a shithole like this.

"Give me back my wife or die." I waste no time in making my demands known. When it comes to Fallon, my tolerance for bullshit is nonexistent. Anton crossed a line today he can never come back from.

"You think you're so powerful you can snap your fingers and get anything you want?" Anton tosses his head back and laughs while I trace my finger around the rim of my glass.

"Yes, I do, and if you were smart, you'd agree." On the outside, I'm relaxed. Cool, calm, and in control as always.

Inside, I'm seething at his audacity. Already he's stolen my wife, put my unborn child in danger, and now he laughs in my face?

Men have died for less, and his lack of respect is a problem I'm going to have to correct. No more free passes. I don't care that we don't have everything we need from him. He's done the unforgivable, and now he's going to spend his last few moments regretting his life choices.

"And why would I do that? From where I'm sitting, I have everything I want, and you have nothing. Money? Who cares? I've got access to more than I could spend in three lifetimes. I've got your wife. What else could you possibly offer me?" The gleam in his eye tells me he's toying with me, making a meal of this because he's enjoying the game. That makes one of us.

He has no idea that he's so out maneuvered, the game has been over for months. The second Waverly's text came in that Fallon didn't show for class, I had her tracked and knew exactly where she was. Still, his comment about money is interesting and I commit it to memory to analyze later.

"The chance to take another breath? To keep living beyond this meeting?" I throw out, lifting my glass and sipping it while keeping my eyes locked on him over the rim. We're on his turf, in a shitty bar on a broken street in Mulberry, but it wouldn't matter if we were in the depths of hell, and he was the fallen angel he claims to be. I'm fully prepared to take him out if negotiations don't go the way I want.

Hell, I'm going to take him out anyway.

He sobers and the jovial mask slips off his face. His true cruelty shows through in the way he sneers while he leans forward, glaring in my direction while the men standing behind him shift and take a step closer. There are only two of them, and I smirk because I think that's all he brought.

A soft thump sounds from somewhere behind me, one I

wouldn't have noticed if I wasn't paying attention. I don't turn, but it's then I feel a prick against the skin of my back—the point of a knife aimed right at my kidney.

The smug as fuck smile that crosses Anton's face is enough to sign his death warrant. He lifts an eyebrow as if to ask how I plan to get out of this.

"Sorry, Boss. No hard feelings." I glance back and make eye contact with Clint, and when he sees his death shining back at him, the grin drops from his face.

The prospect of violence thickens the air as the tension escalates, but I'm more than a match for him and his thugs. They may be big, but size means nothing in the face of training, ruthlessness, and speed.

"No feelings at all when you're bleeding out on the floor, Clint. You fucked up."

Anton claps his hands, drawing my attention back to him. "I believe you were threatening me?"

"No, a threat would mean I give you a chance to make a different choice. I'm telling you what will happen if you don't give her to me, so hear me now. You won't be leaving this room alive if you refuse to return Fallon. This drink," I say, tilting my head towards the nearly empty glass that sits in front of him, "will be your last. Too bad it was cheap as fuck." I let the corner of my mouth lift in another taunting smirk.

He rolls his eyes. "I don't think you're in any position—"

I don't let him finish, slashing the knife sitting in my lap across Clint's stomach where he stands behind me. A wet plopping sound fills the space around us as his intestines and whatever the fuck else falls out onto the floor and he drops beside them. The clatter of metal beside him draws Anton's attention as he tracks the knife that had been pressed to my back.

It would take me less than two seconds to kill him where he

sits. He may have murdered before, but he's not a trained killer like me. I've honed my craft over many years, as a true artist does. I walked into this room alone, leaving Lucas and Beckett outside, and he laughed at me for being so stupid.

But I don't need them. I think I've more than proven that.

"Do you want to tell me what kind of position I'm in now?" I ask, as he lunges for the knife on the floor. I kick it away before he has a chance to grab it.

I glance at my watch just as the two men behind him start to sway on their feet. One reaches for the wall for balance, but it won't help him. Nothing will save them from their fate now.

Anton spins to face them, mouth falling open as his two men drop at his feet, foaming at the mouth and convulsing. It's only a matter of seconds before they're dead.

"What... how..." he splutters, turning back around with a reddening face and eyes wide with fear. His gaze shifts to the knife on the floor again and he dives for it, this time getting it into his hold. It won't matter.

I drain the last of my drink and straighten my cufflinks. "Now, do we have a deal? You return Fallon to me, and I'll make your death quick and relatively painless."

"You killed my men!" he yells in outrage, but his trembling hands give him away. He never saw this coming, and he doesn't know what I've got in store for him should he say no. Though, to be fair, I warned him.

"I'm out of patience. Will you give her to me, or will I take her by force?" I give him five seconds to answer, but his brain is too slow to keep up, to sort through what's happened here, all the ways he could play this. He doesn't know that when he walked into this room, I'd already won.

He was already a dead man.

The sound of my barstool sliding against the wooden floor as

I stand bounces off the walls. I work the button through my suit jacket, slowing my movements to give him a chance to plan, to try and grasp onto some way he can take me out before I kill him. When he says nothing, I click my tongue in disappointment.

I move before he can react, sliding to his side of the table so fast all he can do is stare up at me with wide eyes. He slashes at me with the knife, flailing uselessly, though he does manage to plunge the thing into my side once. Fucker.

"Tell me what you had planned for my wife," I say, kicking his knees out as he falls to the floor.

"Fuck you," he spits, glaring up at me with nothing but defiance.

"If you tell me, I'll kill you quickly."

He searches my eyes and I let him see the hours of torture I've been imagining and planning for months now play out in their depths.

"I was going to use her to…" his words trail off, becoming mumbled so I can't make them out which only pisses me off more. I yank on his hair and he yelps.

"What was that?"

"I was going to use her to get Tristen to hand over the Savage Society. To me," he says as if that wasn't clear.

"How?" My blood boils at the thought of this peasant using my fucking *wife* to take what we've worked so hard to build. As if he could.

"I was going to have fun breaking her in." A sadistic grin curves across his lips. "I'd start with sending videos, but if they didn't work… I had no problem chopping off a few body parts and sending them his way until he agreed. The ones that wouldn't affect the way she fucks." Anton's smile slides off his face, and his shoulders slump, heavy with his confession because he knows what it means.

His death.

I say nothing because there's nothing more to say. He'll never lay another finger on Fallon.

I tighten my grip on his hair, tipping his head back. "Wai—"

I don't let him finish, using the dagger in my hand to slash across his neck. Blood sprays the table, the walls, painting the room a macabre red.

"I'm done waiting," I tell him, as he bleeds out. His fingers reach for his ruined throat, trying to push the skin back together but it's useless and eventually, the gurgling stops, and he falls to the floor. Dead.

I've known where Fallon is since the moment she was taken, but for once I tried to do the right thing. To *negotiate* when I wanted to set the world on fire for daring to take her and our baby from me. To not start a war. To not stop until I spill the blood of everyone involved. To not make an example so no one dares to test me again.

Anton will go to his grave with the secret of who funded him, where the piles of money came from, but Romeo won't rest until he untangles that web and when he does, I'll have my next target.

Adrenaline buzzes in my veins as I step over Anton's body and leave the room. I don't even feel the cut in my side, only the slow drip of hot blood oozing from the wound. It's not fatal, so it's not important.

Right now, I'm going to get my girl and God help anyone who gets in my way.

CHAPTER 51

FALLON

A loud bang outside the door makes me jump and I lift my head, straining my ears to try and hear what might be going on. There was no doubt in my mind Cole would come for me, but I didn't think he'd find me so quickly.

Maybe Anton's men have turned on him. The thought brings the first genuine smile to my face all day. I let my head fall back against the wall when it's silent for seconds. The quiet stretches into minutes, I think, though I have no way to tell.

The door swings open so hard it hits the back wall and my arms wrap around my middle to protect the baby. My pulse takes off like a rocket, and as I stand up my gaze locks on the Hulk-like asshole who's stomping my way.

Seriously, what does Anton feed these guys? I think the ground might even shake under his colossal boots as he lumbers in my direction. My only hope to escape him is speed, so as he gets closer, I try to dart around him.

There's not enough space in here for me to move out of the range of his reach, so he grabs a handful of my hair as I attempt to pass and yanks. My scalp burns and my neck jerks to the side so I'm forced to stop moving and I cry out before I can clamp my lips closed.

Tears sting my eyes and slide down my cheeks from the intense pain, but I won't give up. I twist and lift my knee attempting to shove it right into his balls, but he shifts his hips away at the last second. I don't hesitate to ram my elbow into his gut, but he barely flinches.

He's just so much bigger than I am.

"Hit me again and see what happens, you fucking bitch," he barks, tightening his grip on my scalp. It feels like the hairs are tearing out and white flashes pop in my vision from the pain. He drags me behind him by my hair and I'm not even attempting to fight anymore because I don't want him to hit or kick my stomach.

We're nearly at the door when he freezes and then something hot and wet hits my face as his grip goes slack and his hand falls out of my hair. I nearly collapse to my knees but at the last second strong arms wrap around me and keep me steady.

When I look up, all I see is my husband looking like the God of Death, dressed head to toe in black, skin splattered with flecks of blood, and a darkness in his eyes that calls to my own.

He's bleeding from his side, but I don't think he's even noticed.

"Fallon," he breathes, like I'm the only thing he needs to survive, and we slide to the ground, me in his lap, clinging to each other. I knew he'd find me, but I didn't know if he'd be in time for whatever Anton had planned. He didn't exactly tell me what he wanted from me earlier, just that we'd discuss it after Erika got her contract.

Then he threw me in this room and locked the door.

I breathe him in, my forehead resting on his chest, under his chin, and I let the tears fall. The tension bleeds out of me as trembling from the adrenaline kicks in.

Finally, I sit up. "Anton—"

"Dead."

"What about his men? And my mom? She was here, too. They were together."

The demon lurking inside of Cole shadows his eyes again. "She's not here, but we'll deal with her later. Everyone else is dead, and you're going to the hospital."

I start to shake my head and Cole narrows his eyes. "Don't defy me, little lamb."

It's then that I notice his fingers tremble, too, and maybe he's not as unaffected by this as he seems. There's worry there in his eyes, too, and if it'll help him feel better, I'll go to the hospital.

"Okay, Cole."

He cradles my body like I'm already cracked and on the verge of breaking as he stands and carries me out like it's nothing.

We pass by the carnage as we move out of the warehouse. A beautiful carnage painted in blood. Beckett and Lucas are here, too, both similarly dressed in black and drenched in blood. As the adrenaline subsides, I find my eyelids getting heavier and I rest my head on Cole's shoulder, letting the movement of his footsteps lull me to sleep.

When they eventually flutter open, I'm being laid down on an exam bed and Cole's hovering over me looking the most worried and disheveled I've ever seen him. He's still covered in blood and his hair's a mess, like he's been tugging on the ends.

The room smells sterile, and I know we're in a hospital, but Cole must see the questions in my eyes because he brushes the hair off my forehead and explains. "We're in a private wing. I've called in Dr. McCarthy to do your exam so we don't have to answer any questions, and Beckett and Lucas are outside the door just in case your mother," he spits out the word like it's venomous, "decides to show her face."

Cole intertwines our fingers as he sits beside me on the bed.

"Erika and Anton were working together. She wanted my trust fund, and I wanted her gone so we made a deal."

He stills. "What kind of deal?"

"I transferred every penny in my trust fund to her in exchange for her leaving, giving my dad a divorce and never looking back."

"You shouldn't have given her a cent. We could've dealt with her in other ways." His tone is frosty and soaked in malice, and I shiver because even though he's quite possibly the most dangerous man in any room, I've never felt safer than I do with Cole.

A nurse pushes inside the room then, looking flustered, and she avoids making eye contact with Cole or me. "I need to draw some blood for labs and I'm going to need a urine sample." Finally, she lifts her gaze to mine. "Which would you prefer to do first?"

I've had to pee for hours, so I grab the cup out of her outstretched hand and let Cole help me down off the bed. He doesn't let me go as we walk to the bathroom on the other side of the room and when he starts to follow me inside, I put my foot down. "I think I can manage to pee by myself without getting hurt."

He looks like he wants to argue, but I don't give him the chance, closing the door in his face and doing my thing. Once I'm finished, I leave the sample, wash my hands, and let Cole tuck me back into the bed.

After the nurse has taken my blood, we sit back again in the quiet. Cole's fingers drift up and down my forearm absently like he's lost in thought, and I'm sure today was a lot to process for him. I'm still tired so I let my mind drift, not thinking too hard about anything that happened and instead daydreaming about what our baby's going to look like.

Will he or she have my bright eyes or his dark ones? Will they be quiet and reserved or confident and in control? Or will they be a mix?

There's a knock on the door before Dr. McCarthy steps inside, letting it close behind him. "I didn't think I'd see you two again so soon," he says, but there's a hint of a smile on his face and his eyes twinkle. I get the impression he doesn't mind Cole calling him at all hours to deal with whatever injuries might come up in his... unconventional line of work.

He must pay him well.

"Your labs look great, but I'm going to check you over just to be sure we don't miss anything. Then we'll check the baby. Sound good?"

Cole and I both nod. For once he's not trying to tell the doctor how to do his job and I almost laugh when that thought crosses my mind. My controlling husband. I shake my head.

Dr. McCarthy puts me through his exam and other than a bruised scalp declares me perfectly healthy.

"You need to rest for a few days, though," he says as he moves his hands to my stomach, gently probing the baby.

"She's not getting out of bed for at least a week," Cole says, and I can't tell from his tone if he means for sex or rest. Maybe a bit of both, if I'm lucky.

"Alright, baby feels like it's where it should be. Let's take a peek at an ultrasound, get Cole stitched up, and then you two can get out of here."

He strides across the room and opens the door, wheeling in a machine the nurse left outside. He turns it on and squirts jelly on my stomach and while the device hovers over my bump he turns to us with a grin. "Do you want to know the sex of your little one?"

Cole and I look at each other, our eyes locked together and for just a second, it's like we're one person. His lips twitch and I grin, finally breaking away. "Yes, please."

"Well, let's see if they're going to cooperate." The doctor's eyebrows furrow as he concentrates on the screen, shifting the wand around on my stomach until eventually his face lights up. "The baby's heartbeat is strong and healthy, and I'm getting a clear shot here…"

Cole squeezes my hand almost to the point of pain, and I hold my breath.

"Congratulations, it's a boy."

CHAPTER 52
COLE

One week later...

My drink dangles from between my fingers as I watch Fallon sleep. It's been a week, and even now I hardly rest. I can't take my eyes off her, not without knowing who was behind Anton's rise. Whoever it was, they're still out there and I don't know what it is they want with me and the Savage Six.

I don't trust they won't come after her again.

My phone buzzes in my pocket and I set my drink down on the small table beside me, digging it out.

"What?" I whisper, not wanting to wake her.

"I just got home from The Lodge and my house is cleaned out," Tristen snaps. "The bitch took everything." He laughs in a humorless way. "Except the stack of divorce papers she left behind."

"When Fallon wakes up, we'll come over and figure it out."

Tristen blows out a breath. "Yeah. Okay."

I hang up, sliding back into my chair while I get lost in my thoughts. It's not long after that Fallon stirs. She's so goddamn beautiful that it hurts, especially now that my son grows inside of her. I'll never tire of seeing her like this, with my child in her belly, sleep rumpled in my bed after I've fucked her into unconsciousness.

There is nothing more perfect in this world.

"Hey," she murmurs as she sits up and I move across the room and lower myself to the bed beside her.

"How are you feeling?"

She rolls her eyes. "I'm fine, Cole. I've been fine for the last week. You can stop treating me like I'm about to shatter. I'm not. You're the one who got stabbed."

I scoff. Of course, she's right. I *have* been acting as if she's made of a spider's silk, easily torn apart and impossible to fix once broken. I should've remembered she's made to stand at my side and not easy to break.

"I think I showed you last night I'm fine, and I'm coming around to the idea that you're okay." I let my lips curve into a wicked smirk full of naughty intentions.

"Hmm," she says, climbing into my lap and straddling me. She doesn't fit as well as she used to with her belly between us and my hands move to it automatically. "I might need another demonstration."

"Sorry, little lamb, but your father needs us at his place. I'll make it up to you when we get home."

She pouts, but she's learning not to fight me when it comes to what happens in our home. She's beginning to trust that when I delay her gratification or punish her, it only leads to more pleasure in the end.

"What's going on with my dad?"

"Your mother left him the divorce papers…"

"And?"

"Took everything else."

She scoffs and climbs off my lap. "I knew she'd find a way to exploit the language of the contract." She moves to the closet and strips out of the tank top she was wearing, slipping a dress over her head. "I hate her."

"I could kill her for you. I've been offering to do it for your father for years."

She laughs with a lightness that lifts some of the misery and anxiety I've been wallowing in over the last week. It's so uncharacteristic of me, and I need to snap out of it if I'm going to help the Savage Six figure out what's going on in our town. Who the new players are, the ones still cloaked in shadow.

"I don't think I want her dead."

"You sound unsure."

"That's because I am. Let's just get over to my dad's and see what kind of damage she did. I might change my mind."

It only takes a few minutes to drive to Tristen's, and Fallon opens the door and walks right in like she still lives there.

"Dad?" she calls out and I follow behind her, looking around at how empty the place is. The artwork has been stripped off the walls, the furniture is gone, and I wouldn't be surprised if the viper stole the fixtures from the bathrooms and any food from the refrigerator.

"In here!" Tristen yells, but it's hard to pinpoint where exactly *here* is with the way his voice echoes around the empty house.

Fallon speeds up and we end up in the kitchen where Tristen is leaning over the island staring down at papers scattered all over it. He lifts his head, and I don't think I like the crazed look in his eye.

"You know that thing you've been offering to do for me? I want you to do it," he says, looking me dead in the eye. "The bitch has made me look like a fool for the final time."

"Dad, no. Cole's not going to kill Mom. You need to let her go."

Tristen's bloodshot eyes cut to me. "You told her?"

I wrap my arm around Fallon's waist and tug her back against my chest, feeling my son move underneath her skin. "I made her the same offer I've been making you. She also declined."

"She's gone. Isn't that what we all wanted? Sign the papers, pretend she's dead, and move on with your life, Dad."

He reaches for the drink he abandoned at some point and drains it, probably something from the stash he keeps locked up in his office. "She's a manipulative whore, and I have no doubt she'll come crawling back when she's pawned everything and drained every cent from everyone she can."

"If she comes back, I'll no longer be offering to kill her. I'll be making it happen," I promise.

Fallon moves out of my hold and steps closer to her father, putting her hand gently on his arm. "It's time to move on, Dad. You've been miserable for years, maybe since the day you married her. It's time to let her go and get out there and find somebody to love who deserves you. Why did you even keep her around this long?"

He sighs. "Her father once helped me out of a situation that would've ruined me otherwise. My father's plane had just crashed, and he hadn't updated his will in years. Our family's business, the wealth... everything was set to get divvied up and sent to various charities. It would've devastated my mom and made it impossible for me to stay in Emerald Hills and form the Savage Society with this guy." Tristen tips his head in my direction.

"If it wasn't for Erika's father stepping in and risking his law practice to help me out, I'd have been fucked. When he got sick a year later, he made me promise to take care of his daughter." He lifts his eyes to watch Fallon. "If it wasn't for what he did for me, Cole and I both would've ended up on the streets. I had to give him my word and keep it."

Sometimes I still can't believe he chained himself to that bitch all this time to save us. It's why I'd gladly make her disappear for him.

"She never deserved you, Dad."

Tristen straightens and the hint of a smile touches his lips as he looks down at his daughter. "You've really grown into a remarkable woman, Fallon. I'm so proud of you."

"Keep that in mind in a few months when you become a grandpa at thirty-six," I tell him with a grin.

"Fuck you." He throws up his middle finger.

"How about I order takeout? I'll call Waverly and have a girl's night with her upstairs," she shoots me a look because she knows there's no way in hell I'm letting her out of my sight right now. "And you two can drink and do whatever manly murderous things you do until you're feeling better."

This is the reason I know Fallon is better than I deserve. Why she'll be the perfect mother to our son and the children that come after him. Why I'll never let her go.

She cares. She cares so goddamn much that she'll never break me even though she's the only one who could. And that's something I'll never, ever take for granted.

EPILOGUE

COLE

Two months later...

"You ever think you want more kids?" I turn to Tristen as we lounge near his pool while Fallon floats on her back, her rounded stomach pushing out of the water up towards the sun.

"I thought I did. When I begged Erika to give me Fallon it was a war—not just a battle—and in the end, the only thing she agreed to do was donate her eggs to the cause. I had to do everything else, and I don't mean in the fun knocking her up way." He sips his beer.

"Over the years, I've wondered what it would've been like with someone who was in it with me, you know? The way you and Fallon are. The way *normal* people are." He laughs. "But we're not exactly normal, are we?"

"No, but in this I think we can come close."

"I can't believe you're the asshole making me a grandpa. Remind me why I haven't killed you yet?"

"Because it would hurt Fallon. Besides, you'd miss me if I was gone."

Tristen sighs. "It's true."

The two of us go quiet then, and I reflect on how much has changed in the last six months. I've become a different person… but only with Fallon. I'm not a good man. I'm a *great* man, but there's no part of me that's good. The best parts, I save for my wife and soon, our son. She brings it out in me, and it's in those moments I realize how futile my mission all these years has been.

For so long, what drove me was a need to be better than my own father. To show him up. To have him look up from where he burns in hell and know that I've done things he could never imagine. That no part of me is afraid of him anymore. That he has no control over what I do.

But that's a lie. Because all he's ever had is control. Every decision I've made, every step I've taken was because of him. And that doesn't mean that I'm not happy about where I've ended up, because I am. I truly believe I was always destined for greatness. I was never going to be an average, mediocre man happy with a white picket fence. That's not me. It never was.

I like the blood too much. The rush when you take a life. The maneuvering and strategizing that comes with building an empire. Fallon is my obsession, my life, but my first loves are Red Rum and the Savage Society. The power that I wield with expert precision like the Grim Reaper does his scythe.

I didn't *care* until her. Not about anyone but myself, the Savage Six, and what I was building. I never thought I'd see the day that someone would matter more to me than my ambition, but it came, and it went, and I continued to live. To thrive. I never dared hope I'd be truly happy. I've seen too much, done too much. If there was a god, he would've smited me long ago.

Instead I'm rich in ways I never thought possible, and I'll cling to that happiness—with nails dug in and chains wrapped around it—until I take my final breath.

The patio doors open and Beckett steps into the yard, crossing the grass toward us with slow, measured steps. Everything the man does is measured—the epitome of focused.

"I've got news," Beckett says, moving to sit on the lounge chair beside Tristen. I tear my gaze off my wife and turn in his direction.

"I just came from Emerald Hills Prep." He flashes a feral kind of grin, and I know that look on his face all too well. He's picked up a trail, a hunt. This is what he lives for. "They've offered me a job and I've accepted."

"A job?" Tristen asks, a wrinkle forming between his eyebrows. "Not working with children, I hope."

"You're looking at the new Creative Writing teacher." The manic gleam in his eyes only intensifies and I glance around, wondering if we should be talking about this outside.

Fallon's climbed onto a flotation device of some kind and looks like she's falling asleep. I'm going to have to jump in and stay nearby to ensure she doesn't fall in and drown, so I want to wrap up this conversation. I have to admit, though... I'm intrigued.

"Why the fuck would you take a job teaching? You know you can't just off your students when they fail a test, right?"

"I'm aware, and I won't draw unnecessary attention to the Savage Society or myself, but there's something fucked up going on up at that school. Students are going missing, and no one seems to know anything about it. Plus what Rome found."

A few days ago, Romeo stumbled on an account connecting Anton to Dr. Collins, the principal I'd been meaning to visit since Fallon was taken. He plays a part in this; I just don't know what it is yet. Beckett appears to have picked up on the same thing.

"Now you're some kind of hero?" Tristen asks with a laugh.

Beckett side-eyes him. "I think by now you know me better than that, but I suspect there's something deeper going on, and it may have something to do with Anton and the underbelly of Mulberry we haven't been able to crack yet." He sits back and takes another pull from his beer. "Worst case, I get a new muse for my next book."

"If this is what you want, you know we'll support you," Tristen says, but I'm no longer paying attention, slipping off my chair and moving towards my wife.

I can only stand distance between us for so long before I gravitate toward her. I'm completely gone for her, and I think that's a large part of why Tristen hasn't come for me. He sees what his daughter means to me, the way I look at her.

The way she looks at me.

She'll forever be my greatest obsession.

When I slip into the water and swim up to her, even in her half-asleep state, she reaches for me.

"Cole." She sighs my name in relief, and I know the feeling well.

"I'm taking you home, little lamb. I've got big plans for you tonight, and you're going to need your rest if you have any hope of keeping up."

She slides off her lounger and into my arms in the water, trusting that I'll catch her. She knows as long as there's life in my body, I'll never let her fall.

"Your son kept me up all night rolling around in my stomach and kicking me in the ribs," she murmurs, as she tucks her head in the curve between my shoulder and chin and breathes me in.

"And tonight it'll be my turn to steal your sleep, but I promise you'll enjoy every second."

My lips tip up and I hold her closer, never wanting this moment to end, but wanting so desperately to move to the next one I can hardly stand it. No amount of time will ever be enough with Fallon, but for now I'll settle for this life.

Eventually, she'll give me eternity, too.

SNEAK PEEK OF SWEET DESTRUCTION

Beckett

Drip. Drip. Drip.

The screams died out a while ago. Now my only company is the steady flow of blood splattering onto the concrete floor and flesh separating under my scalpel.

But my work's only just begun.

Skin, muscle, and bone are my medium and the human body my canvas. I've got an array of tools spread out before me, and the crimson staining my gloved fingers has never been more vibrant.

I breathe in deeply, the smell of copper hanging so heavy in the air I can taste it on my tongue. I imagine tiny flecks of blood floating around me, soaking into my skin as I become the monster I was always meant to be.

The one I force deep down inside until it claws at my skin from the inside, refusing to be caged any longer.

Sneak Peek of Sweet Destruction

As I make another cut, my body relaxes. The tension bleeds away like the fluids from the corpse on my table as I sink into my work. These are the moments I relish, the ones I live for.

Another cut and my pulse steadies. Another and the icy chill of the room draws my attention as goosebumps rise on my arms. With every incision, the world comes into focus.

No longer am I numb.

This right here is the height of my existence. This moment. For a few blessed hours, I *feel*.

I feel *everything*.

At least until the high wears off and I'm dead inside again.

A soft knock on the door breaks my concentration. I try to ignore it, but it happens again. And again.

Finally, I drop my scalpel. It clatters on the metal tabletop as I rip the black latex from my hands. There are only five people who know where I am, and all of them know better than to interrupt.

The heavy metal door bangs against the wall as I throw it open. "What?"

Xander stands outside the door, the only one of the Savage Six crazy enough to taunt me mid-kill. He's leaning against the door frame with his hands shoved into the pockets of his black slacks, but his gaze drifts behind me and lights up.

"You're having all the fun without me," he pouts, and then grins. Xander's smiles are always unsettling, like the monster under your bed trying to lure you into the dark. I still can't figure out how he managed to become a priest of all things. One look at him and even I can tell he's not right in the head. "At least let me sit and watch the master at work. I can pray for your eternal soul."

He's not going to leave until I give in, so I relent, stepping aside and gesturing for him to enter The Icebox. Some might refer to it as my lair. It's also my sacred place. The only spot in the world that brings me true joy.

"Stand in the corner and be silent," I tell him. "No praying for a soul that doesn't exist." I pluck a new set of gloves out of the box beside my tools and put them on. "I mean it."

Xander is pure chaos, and that energy has no place in this room. Not now.

I take a moment, closing my eyes and trying to find the high I was riding before he intruded, but it's vanished. I look down at my creation with a frown. He's only half finished, and yet the vision for what he could become is gone. His potential lost. Disappeared in the black hole of my imagination never to be seen again.

I glower over at Xander where he's bouncing on the balls of his feet and vibrating with excitement. He's doing it all silently, but the second he stepped into the room, the energy shifted. "You've ruined it."

"Maybe if you let me help, we can get it back on track." He takes a cautious step forward as if he's approaching an apex predator about to attack. In some respects, that's what I am. Only I don't strike in the heat of the moment. I'm not that careless.

I tilt my head toward the box of gloves, and he eagerly rushes forward, snapping them onto his hands. "Have at it," I tell him, gesturing at the tools carefully laid out on the table.

He stares down at the row, considering each one. He picks up a saw, turning it over, inspecting the razor-sharp teeth, and setting it back down. He opts for a drill instead and gives me his unhinged smile again. "Does this mean you'll put me in your next book?"

The buzz from this kill is already starting to fade as my anger dulls at the edges. "What this means is you've wrecked him, so now you can have your fun. I'll have to find a new canvas for my vision."

If Xander's bothered by what I said, he doesn't show it. He hums happily under his breath as he carves into the carcass like an absolute heathen. He doesn't have any artistic vision and it shows as he drills through flesh into bone. My lip curls up in disgust as I watch him work wondering how this night went so wrong.

My last night of freedom before I put on the mask of respectability I'm going to be wearing for the next nine months or so. It'll be much more difficult to find the time to discover my next muse.

And I've got a publishing deadline.

Irritation crawls up my spine, but then fades into nothingness. My high is nearly gone now, the familiar numbness dampening anything I might feel. Xander is nearly finished now, the body he's working on practically unrecognizable as human.

He sighs as he sets the bloody pliers down, the ones he swapped the drill for a few minutes ago. The sigh is filled with satisfaction as he glances over at me. Tiny splatters of blood cover his face and arms. "I can see why you do this. It's relaxing."

I nod once but say nothing as I start to clean up. Xander moves to leave, and I step in his way. "You helped make the mess, you help clean it up."

He pouts but then switches out his gloves and grabs a piece of the man on my table and tosses it in a black plastic bag. "I can't believe you're going to teach children."

I raise an eyebrow at him as I mix some activated oxygen cleaner with water, moving quickly so it doesn't freeze. "This from the man who people come to for repentance and advice? Who's allowed to hear confessions and mete out salvation?"

He laughs, wild and loud. "Incredible, isn't it?"

"Indeed."

"You know you can't just murder someone's kid if they fail a test, right?" he asks after a long, blissful stretch of silence.

I look up, my features expressionless, my voice devoid of tone. "I'm aware. And they're hardly children. It's in my contract to only teach the seniors."

"That still doesn't mean you can kill them, even if they're eighteen. Someone will notice."

He's right, of course. It's the reason I'm taking this ludicrous job in the first place. Students are going missing at an alarming rate, and I'm the only serial killer in the area. Between Cole's wife's suspicious abduction at the school right under the headmaster's nose, and Anton's mysterious financial benefactor, I don't like how out of control Emerald Hills is becoming.

Either someone is encroaching on my territory or there's something bigger at play.

The Savage Six rule here, and we're being undermined. Thus, my undertaking the impossible—teaching creative writing to the students of Emerald Hills Preparatory Academy.

"I may have a taste for... unusual art, but I'm not self-destructive." Yet, like any killer, I crave appreciation for my work. It's why my kills are always the basis for my bestselling horror novels. My crimes displayed in homes across the world with no one suspecting the words they're reading are real.

Non-fiction disguised as fiction and sold to the masses.

He stares me down as if he doesn't believe me, but finally nods before going back to the task at hand.

I may not be able to hurt the students, but there is something going on at that school and my instincts tell me whatever I find will make the perfect inspiration for my next novel.

Follow me on Amazon for Sweet Destruction updates: www.amazon.com/Heather-Ashley/e/B08663GYC3

OTHER BOOKS BY HEATHER ASHLEY:

The Ruined Rockstars Series

Deviant Rockers

Fallen Star

Dirty Legend

Broken Player

Vicious Icon

Tainted Idol

Wicked God

The Hollywood Guardians Series

Captive

Chased

Hostile

Deceit

The Twisted Soul Magic Series

Crossed Souls

The Savage Society of Emerald Hills Series

Beautiful Carnage

Sweet Destruction

ABOUT THE AUTHOR

Stalk Me:

Website:
www.heatherashleywrites.com

Amazon:
www.amazon.com/Heather-Ashley/e/B08663GYC3

Instagram:
www.instagram.com/heatherashleywrites

TikTok:
www.tiktok.com/@heatherashleyauthor

Facebook:
www.facebook.com/heatherashleywrites

Facebook Group:
www.facebook.com/groups/thewildridecrew

Patreon:
www.patreon.com/heatherashleywrites

Printed in Great Britain
by Amazon